"Popular pastor, speaker, and bestselling author T. D. Jakes mines the emotions of a couple on the cusp of divorce in his latest contemporary novel, NOT EASILY BROKEN . . . Jakes pulls no punches as he explores the ramifications of allowing your love to grow cold, and your heart to grow hard."

—*Bookpage*

"How does a marriage fall apart, and how does one go about saving it? Bestselling author T. D. Jakes puts those questions at the heart of his novel [NOT EASILY BROKEN] . . . [Jakes] captures the rapidity with which relationships can fall apart, along with the rigorous and painful healing process, which requires honest communication, self-denial, and humility. The story is far from a fairy tale and at times too true to life to be readily enjoyable, but readers will find themselves attached to the characters. Jakes's faith appears throughout the story in a gentle way, which should make this book appeal to both Christian and general market readers."

—*Publishers Weekly*

Not Easily Broken

Broken

T. D. JAKES

NEW YORK   BOSTON   NASHVILLE

Unless otherwise noted, Scriptures are taken from the King James Version of the Bible.

Scriptures noted ASV are taken from the American Standard Version of the Bible.

FaithWords
Hachette Book Group USA
237 Park Avenue
New York, NY 10017

Visit our Web site at www.faithwords.com.

Book design by Fearn Cutler de Vicq
Printed in the United States of America

Originally published in hardcover by Hachette Book Group USA

First Trade Edition: October 2007
10 9 8 7 6 5 4 3 2 1

FaithWords is a division of Hachette Book Group USA, Inc.
The FaithWords name and logo is a trademark of Hachette Book Group USA, Inc.

The Library of Congress has cataloged the hardcover edition as follows:
Jakes, T. D.
    Not easily broken / T.D. Jakes.—1st ed.
    p. cm.
    ISBN-13: 978-0-446-57677-2
    ISBN-10: 0-446-57677-8
    1. Marriages—Fiction. I. Title.
    PS3610.A39N68 2006
    813'.54—dc22   2006006558

ISBN 978-0-446-69384-4 (pbk.)

Dedication

I dedicate this book to all who have lived and loved, survived and succeeded. Also to those who have stumbled and failed but still hold dear the ideals of sacred love and principles of hope. It is you who make me know that even broken people can have whole love with God's grace. If you didn't win yesterday, got hurt or hurt someone special . . . don't give up; learn from your mistakes; and always remember that the reason the sun comes up in the morning is to announce that tomorrow is a new day!

Finally and foremost, I dedicate this book to my wife and all that I have learned because of her. She is truly a lover and friend. Today after nearly twenty-five years of marriage we are still together. We have endured pains, sickness, heartaches, the loss of our parents, and the rearing of soon-to-be five teenagers and so much more! She is an incredible woman and our love remains intact. It is not our success that defines us but our tenacious commitment to staying together through tests and trials. This proves that with God's help and mercy, young love can grow old and remain Not Easily Broken!

Acknowledgments

A special thanks to all the couples I have ever counseled during my thirty years of ministry. Little did you know that you were teaching me and training me. I am sure I gained more than I gave. I must thank you for inspiring this book, also. A special thanks to the entire catalog of gifted people who contributed to the development of this project. These tireless worker bees have given honey to my ideas and made them sweeter and richer. I want to thank Thom Lemmons without whose help this novel would not be possible. Thanks to Curtis Wallace whose administration over this project has elevated its potential and power. To the Warner Faith team, including Rolf Zettersten, Lori Quinn, Jana Burson, Gary Terashita, Cara Highsmith, and Jody Waldrup. Thanks to all.

—tdj

Chapter One

*B*y the time Dave Johnson saw the oncoming headlights it was too late to do anything but hold on and pray. He jammed his foot onto the brake pedal and twisted the wheel to the left, but the blur of steel and glass still came straight for the passenger side of his pickup.

It was weird. One part of his mind knew things were happening in split seconds, but everything also seemed to slow down, like an instant replay where the sportscasters try to show whether the receiver's foot was or wasn't inbounds when he caught the ball. Dave heard Clarice screaming as the oncoming car slammed into the side of his Club Cab. Tortured metal squealed and there was a crunch as the safety glass in the passenger window disintegrated. Dave felt the air whoosh from his lungs as his chest slammed into the shoulder harness; the pickup skidded sideways and the tires screamed against the pavement.

Finally, everything stopped moving. Dave's fingers were jerky and uncertain from the adrenaline pouring through his body, but somehow he thumbed the button on his seat belt. He pulled the latch and shoved against his door. To his surprise, it swung open easily, as if nothing had happened. The damage must be completely on the passenger's side.

Clarice!

He leaned toward her. "Baby! You okay? Clarice?" Her eyes were closed and her head lay back on the headrest, her face turned toward him. Dave's heart crowded up under his Adam's apple. He put his hand on her neck, then her chest, feeling for a pulse, for breathing, for anything. "Clarice, honey! Wake up, baby!" There . . . her chest rose and fell. She was breathing. Relief flooded through Dave like cold water rushing over parched ground. She was alive. *But why wouldn't she wake up?*

Dave got out of the truck and ran around to the passenger side. He sucked in a breath. The right side, from the passenger door to halfway across the front quarter panel, was completely caved in. His wife must be pinned inside the vehicle. Someone was grabbing at him, talking to him.

"Oh my Lord, man, I'm so sorry!"

Dave pulled his eyes away from the pickup and looked into the pale, scared face of a kid who might be as old as seventeen. He had his cap turned backward and the ragged, sleeveless T-shirt he was wearing said something about not caring so much about reality. His chin had a few stray reddish-blond hairs sprouting from it, the beginnings of a beard.

"Man, I tried to stop, I swear to God. Was the light red? Oh God, man, are you okay?"

"You got a cell phone?" Dave said.

The kid nodded.

"Call 911."

"Okay, man, but are you okay?"

"Just dial it! My wife's in there and she can't get out."

"Oh, sweet Jesus—"

"Dial the phone!"

The kid's head bobbed up and down. "Yeah, sure, okay." He tugged a palm-sized silver phone out of his pocket, flipped it open, and started punching buttons.

People were coming out of the grocery store located at one corner of the intersection. Somebody was trying to direct traffic around the scene. Another onlooker peered into Clarice's window. Dave turned back to his pickup.

"I saw the whole thing," a man said while coming up behind

Dave. "You had the green light. The kid never even slowed down. Probably high or drunk or something."

"My wife's in there and I think she's pinned," Dave called, running around to the driver's side. In the distance, he heard a siren. He crawled back inside and realized the pickup's engine was still running. He switched it off and leaned over his wife, cupping the crown of her head in his hand.

Shouldn't move her, in case of spinal injuries. She's breathing, thank you, Jesus. Is she in shock? What do you do for somebody in shock? When's the ambulance gon' get here? Is gas leaking out under the truck? Hope somebody makes sure that kid don't run off. Are the paramedics here yet? Is my wife dying?

He stroked her cheek. "Clarice? Boo, I'm here with you. Baby girl, can you wake up?"

Her lips moved and she let out a low moan. Her eyes shifted back and forth beneath closed eyelids.

"Clarice? Baby, can you hear me?"

The moan was louder this time. Her eyelids fluttered, then opened. Dave thought she was looking at him.

"Hey, Reesie. That you?" He tried to smile.

Clarice moaned again, and this time the sound swelled and climbed the scale all the way to a scream.

"David, my leg, my leg! Lord Jesus have mercy, David, I think my leg must be broken!" She clawed at him and shoved uselessly against the mangled door pressing in against her right side.

Dave stared helplessly and tried to gentle her with his hands, his voice. "Shh now, baby girl, we gon' get you out, don't you worry. They almost here, we gon' get you out of there and you'll be fine, you'll see. Easy now, baby."

He might as well have been talking to the wind. Clarice moaned and twisted her body as much as she could. The pain was killing her, she said. "David, do something, get me some help," she pleaded.

Dave hopped out of the truck just as a fire engine pulled up, its air brakes yelping and hissing. Two firefighters jumped out of the cab and a third was already pulling a chemical extinguisher from a rack and eyeing the pavement beneath the two vehicles. As they came toward him, Dave noticed the kid's car, a mid-nineties Bronco. He realized he didn't need to worry about the boy fleeing the scene; the front end of the Bronco looked like somebody had tossed a hand grenade under the hood, then taken a jackhammer to the front grille. Dave had a fleeting sense of grim satisfaction.

"That your wife in there?" the firefighter asked him.

Dave nodded. "I think she's pinned. Her leg's hurting pretty bad," he said, though he probably didn't need to, since Clarice's announcements about her condition had not decreased in volume. It was good to hear her voice, though; it told him she was at least well enough to keep her lungs aired out.

"We'll have to get the can opener," the firefighter said. He turned to his colleagues. "Hey, guys, we need the Jaws." He went over to Clarice's window and started talking to her. Dave noticed she seemed to be listening, nodding every once in a while. *Good.* She couldn't be that badly off if she could understand and respond. But her twisted face said she was still in immense pain.

Dave replayed the moments leading up to the crash. He and Clarice had been arguing—a scene all too common these last few months, it seemed. Dave searched his memory for any clue that his frustration with Clarice might have caused him to pay less attention. If Clarice hadn't been going off on him, would he have noticed the kid speeding up to the red light?

∞

He could tell when he came home that the evening wasn't going to be smooth. The Board of Realtors dinner was that night, and wouldn't you know it, one of his building managers had a shift leader quit right before closing time. Dave had to go over there and calm down the agitated manager, then walk her through the process of setting up a temporary shift roster so the building would be covered. They'd figure out a more permanent solution the next day, he told her. The main thing was that the customer's building was clean and ready for the next day's business.

So he got home an hour late, and when he walked in Clarice had that pinch-lipped look, and the hands-on-her-hips pose told Dave Mama ain't happy. Which was no big surprise, but he was hoping that for once he could get his explanation in without her going all eastside-westside on him. He couldn't.

"Are you telling me some minimum-wage vacuum jockey is going to cause me to be late to my professional dinner? Is that the best reason you can come up with to embarrass me in front of my peers?" Clarice's voice was rising and falling like a preacher coming to the end of a sermon. She had her dress on, the nice silky red one that draped her just right. She was made up, her lipstick all shiny and wet-looking on her full, soft lips. She was looking fine, or would, if her face wore some expression besides the one she was aiming at him now, looking at him like he was some raggedy, no-count kid who'd knocked a baseball through the front window of her plans for the evening. Clarice had one pump on, and she held the other in her hand and wagged it at Dave as she preached; he found it hard to take his eyes off the three-inch spike heel, considering the mood she was in right now.

"I couldn't help it, Boo, I told you. Charmaine's my newest manager and I had to walk her through this one time."

"This one time. This *one* time, did you say?"

Dave caught himself listening for the organist to start the altar call.

"How many times have you had to drop everything to rescue one of your managers?" The way she said the last word, it sounded like it had quote marks around it. "How many *times* have I gotten home, thinking we might have a quiet evening together for once, only to find out somebody didn't show up somewhere, and you had to take it on yourself to cover? I'm so tired of this, David. I work so hard at the agency to be professional. I work so *hard* to present myself to my colleagues and my clients in a way that speaks well of me . . . and my family."

"Clarice, I know you do. You the hardest-working woman I ever saw. All I'm sayin' is—"

"But it discourages me when, at any moment, my husband can disrupt what I'm trying so hard to cultivate. It discourages me that I can't even count on one simple evening to go as I expected."

"Baby, we'll get to the dinner. Just let me shower and change real quick."

She looked at him slantways, clearly skeptical.

They'd walked out of the house fifteen minutes before the dinner was to start, and Dave thought they were going to make it. The drive was silent for the first three or four minutes. Maybe, just this once, Clarice would resist the urge to take up her campaign for him to sell his janitorial business and find work "that amounts to something." But just after he pulled out onto South First, she said, "David, I know you don't want to hear this, but—"

He felt his shoulders droop and a sigh went out of him. He fastened his eyes on the road ahead and let Clarice's lecture tumble past his ears without stopping, like some kind of really annoying elevator music. Why couldn't she just be satisfied with him the way he was? What was wrong with All-Pro Janitorial and Carpet Cleaning? It was a good business, and he'd built it from the ground up, one contract at a time. After years of teaching and coaching, he finally had his dream: self-employment. They had a nice house and two low-mileage cars, and the only reason Clarice was still selling real estate was supposed to be for vacation money. These last couple of years, though, Dave had begun to suspect there was more to it than that.

∞

Dave watched the firefighters positioning the Jaws of Life, a steel contraption with hoses and handles leading off every which way. The blades looked like they could cut through the hull of a battleship, and as Dave looked on, the firefighters positioned them at the seam between the passenger door and front quarter panel of his pickup. He heard the whine of the hydraulics and watched the blades bite into the frame of his truck. The metal growled and popped as the bottom hinge separated like construction paper cut by scissors. One of the men bent to support the door's weight as they moved the Jaws to cut the top hinge.

"Lean away from the door as much as you can, ma'am," one of them said to Clarice as Dave approached.

"Can I help?" he asked.

"Stand back for just a moment, sir, and then we'll get you to help us make sure we get the door off without hurting her."

The Jaws sheared the top hinge and the door's weight settled into the firefighter's hands. Slowly and carefully, checking with Clarice all the while, they peeled away the caved-in door. Dave scanned Clarice's right side and was almost sick to his stomach.

Her leg below the knee was bent as if it contained pipe cleaner instead of bone. Already the swelling and purpling had transformed her shapely calf and ankle into something resembling a huge spoiled sausage. Her red high heel was still on her foot, but the flesh of her ankle had swollen around it so that the edges of the pump were starting to cut into her.

"Oh, baby girl. We got to get you to a hospital."

"That looks like a pretty bad break," a firefighter said. "Anybody heard from the paramedics?" He reached for his walkie-talkie.

Clarice was moaning softly now, like a child worn out from too much crying. "It hurts, David. It hurts so bad."

"I know, Boo. We gon' get you fixed up soon as we can." He held her face and cooed to her, even as he wondered where on God's earth the ambulance could be.

In a minute or two, the ambulance whooped to a stop and the paramedics started unpacking a stretcher. As Dave looked on, they gently and efficiently unfolded Clarice from the ruined pickup and positioned her on the stretcher. They unfolded something that looked like a beach toy and wrapped it around Clarice's leg, fastening it with Velcro. They started pumping air into it with a small electric pump.

"Inflatable splint," one of the paramedics told Dave. "Should keep her leg still and more comfortable until we get her to the hospital."

A policeman tapped Dave on the shoulder. "Sir, I've already talked to several witnesses and the driver of the other vehicle. Everybody seems pretty unanimous that the kid ran a red light. Could I just get a couple of minutes? It'll be that long before the ambulance is ready to transport her. Just need your name, address, phone number, that sort of thing."

Dave talked to the officer, all the time keeping one eye on Clarice and the paramedics surrounding her. They put a neck brace on her. "Just a precaution," they said. They told her that her leg appeared to be broken in several places below the knee, and that she had severe bruising all along her right side and arm. One of them cut the shoe off her foot. Dave remembered the day Clarice had brought the shoes home. "Forty percent off at Talbot's," she told him triumphantly. Dave wondered how long it would be before she'd be able to wear spike heels again.

The paramedics loaded Clarice into the ambulance and Dave excused himself from the police officer. He crawled in beside his wife and took her hand. "How you doing, Reesie?"

She looked at him. "What's going to happen, David? Where we going?"

"To the hospital, baby. We got to get your leg fixed."

But she must have been addled from the pain, because it was like he hadn't said anything. "Where we going, David? Where we going?" She kept saying it, over and over, like she was talking in her sleep.

Dave patted her hand and wished the ambulance would hurry up and get moving.

Chapter Two

*C*larice didn't remember much about the ride to the hospital; in her mind, the half hour or so after the wreck was a pain-fogged blur of fleeting images and sounds. She didn't really know much of anything until she was lying on a hard table in the trauma center and two overweight nurses in blue scrubs were bustling around her, talking to each other in terse phrases.

"We've got to get that dress off you, honey," one of them said. "I'm just going to snip it down the front, okay?"

Clarice wondered for a second what they'd do if she told them it wasn't, but by the time the thought had formed, she felt the pull of the scissors down the bodice of her Ann Taylor dress, felt the cold air of the ER hitting the flesh of her chest, stomach, and thighs.

"Honey, I need to roll you on your left side for a second, okay?" the other one said, then proceeded to lever up Clarice's right shoulder and hip, like a weight lifter doing curls. She felt something sliding beneath her, then the nurse eased her down. "Okay, now the other side."

When Clarice's weight settled on her right leg, she almost passed out. A long, low moan escaped her lips, though she didn't realize at first she was making the sound. For those few seconds, the pain shooting through her damaged leg was the whole universe.

"I'm sorry, honey," a nurse said. "I know that hurt, but we've got to get this gown on you, okay?"

"Ya'll need to find something to say besides 'okay' when you do something like that to people," Clarice said through clenched teeth. "It's not okay."

"I know, honey. I'm sorry. Now we need to get that bra off."

At least they unsnapped it instead of cutting. It was her favorite, from Victoria's Secret. Feeling its lace against her skin always reminded Clarice that she was special, that there was more to her than met the eye.

She started to recall some of the sounds and images from the ambulance ride, from the moments immediately following the collision. Though the impressions were faint, like echoes heard through gauze, she knew the first face she had seen when she regained consciousness was David's; the first voice that called to her was his. He hadn't left her side for a moment until the nurses came along and shooed him out of the room while they prepped her for the attending physician. "Reesie," he'd called her, and "Boo." The worry was as plain on him as a neon sign blinking on a dark street. Clarice started to feel the beginning twinges of guilt. Just before the wreck, she'd been lecturing him, hadn't she? She'd been trying to talk him into selling the janitorial business.

Wait a minute, sister! Who's got the busted leg? Whose best dress just got turned into somebody's windshield rag? Why are you feeling guilty? What did you do wrong, except ride in a pickup that was running late because of something that wasn't your fault?

Clarice heard her mother's voice ringing in her memory: "You got to take care of yourself, girl, you hear me? Ain't a man in this world gonna give you what you want; you got to get it for yourself. You find something you want, you go and get it, and don't wait for anybody else to hand it to you, 'cause you liable to be waiting a long time . . ."

Somebody wrapped a blood pressure cuff around her left upper arm. As the cuff began to tighten, one of the nurses held aside the partition to the cubicle and David came in, the anxiety still pasted all over him.

"Boo? How you doing, girl?" He took her hand and stroked it.

"I'm all right, David. Don't worry. Has the doctor gotten here yet?"

"He's right in the next room." He looked up at the nurse. "How's her blood pressure?"

"Just one thirty-five over seventy-eight. Not bad for somebody who was just in a car wreck." She patted Clarice on the arm. "Just lie still, honey. Doctor'll be here in a minute."

"Like I've got a choice," Clarice said under her breath.

David grinned at her. "There you go. You got some fight left, don't you?"

Clarice pulled a wry face and stared up at the ceiling. "If I was going to fight, I'd have made somebody pay for that dress they just cut off me."

"Oh, baby girl, don't worry about that now. I'll get you another dress; we got to get that leg taken care of before we think about anything else."

She looked at him. "David, do you . . ." She gave her head a little shake and looked away.

"What is it, Reesie? Do I what?"

"Nothing."

"No, really, baby. What?"

She kept her face turned away and let the words come out in a low voice, as emotionless as she could manage. "I was supposed to get the Achievement Award tonight, David, at the dinner."

"The what?"

"I was the outstanding agent for my office this year. I listed and sold more houses than anybody else in the agency, and just about more than anybody in town, too."

A few seconds passed, and she wondered if he was going to say anything.

"Well, baby, that's . . . that's just great. I'm real proud of you."

"I was really counting on this dinner, David. And now I'm missing it."

Another silence. She thought about looking at him, but decided against it. Most likely, she'd be able to read the lack of understanding in his face, and that would just infuriate her, especially now.

"I'm sorry, baby, I really am," he said finally.

Now he'll say "but."

"But . . . don't you think you ought to spend a little time being thankful you got out with nothing but a broken leg?"

Maybe as many as a hundred thoughts flashed through her mind. *Easy for you to say. If you hadn't been late— This isn't about me, David, it's about your complete failure to understand what's important to me . . .* But he was right, of course, wasn't he? In the end, all she could say was "Mmm-hmm." But her answer didn't convince anybody, she was sure.

The doctor came in, a young man with a neatly trimmed beard and blond hair. He smiled at Clarice and David as he picked up the chart the nurses had left on the small stand beside the examining table.

"Well, Mrs., uh, Johnson, it looks like you've got a banged-up leg," he said, taking a stethoscope out of the side pocket of his coat and warming it on his palm. "Take a couple of deep breaths for me," he said, positioning the scope just beneath Clarice's left collarbone. "Again . . . one more time." He moved to the other side and repeated the process, then had David support her shoulders as he placed the scope in a couple of places on either side of her backbone.

He undid the Velcro straps on the inflatable cast and carefully laid it open without moving her leg. He nodded. "Yep, that's a dandy. I'm going to write an order to get you straight over to orthopedics so they can assess this leg. The way it looks, they may have to pin it."

"What does that mean?" David asked.

"They won't know for sure until they get back an X-ray," the doctor said, "but I'm guessing this leg is fractured in several places. It's likely a simple cast won't hold the bone fragments in place for proper healing. If that's true, they'll either insert pins above and below the break and stabilize the bone with external rods, or they'll screw plates into the bone to hold it all together for healing."

David looked at her, and Clarice knew what he wanted to see: need, helplessness, and a longing for reassurance. Instead she shot him back the strongest, most determined face she could muster. "Well, let's get on with it then," she said to the doctor without taking her eyes off her husband. "The sooner, the better."

She saw David's shoulders sag, and even though he gave her a sad little smile and a thumbs-up, Clarice knew she'd just taken something away from him. Why couldn't she let herself need him—even with a broken leg?

"The good news is, there's no broken skin, so infection shouldn't be as great a problem," the doctor said. "But my guess is you're going into surgery before you get out of here. Sorry," he said, giving them a little smile. "Still, you're pretty lucky, Mrs. Johnson. It sure could've been worse."

"Yeah. It's a good thing we were in the pickup, instead of your Accord," David added. Clarice pinched her lips together, even as she gave him a tight little nod of agreement. He knew she didn't like riding in that pickup.

They wrapped the inflatable cast back around her leg and propped her leg up on some pillows. David followed behind as the nurses wheeled Clarice down a succession of hallways and through several swinging doors until they reached the orthopedics area. An orderly with "S. Khan" on his name badge took her orders from one of the nurses and went through a doorway. He came back a few minutes later and wheeled her into a dimly lit room with a metal table in the center of the floor. Hanging above the table like some torture device from a medieval dungeon was the boom and mortar-shaped lens of an X-ray machine. When the orderly and two nurses moved her from the gurney onto the table, Clarice wasn't sure which was worse—the pain in her leg as they moved her, or the shock of the cold metal table against the skin of her back.

The nurses draped a lead blanket over her torso and the orderly positioned the X-ray machine over her right shin. They removed the splint and everyone disappeared behind some kind of barrier. She heard the X-ray machine hum and click. They repeated the process two more times as the orderly took X-rays from both sides of her leg. Then the nurses came back and moved her back onto the gurney.

They wheeled her back into the hallway and David fell in beside them.

"You okay, baby?"

"Yes, David. I'm fine."

By now, the small of her back was aching from lying flat all this time. When they reached the waiting area, David got the orderly to raise the gurney so she could sit up just a little; they propped her leg with pillows again. After about half an hour, a doctor came in holding three glossy black X-ray negatives. He clipped them onto a light box and the orderly dimmed the room's lights.

Despite knowing what she was likely to see, Clarice still couldn't help sucking in her breath when the image came into view. Her right shinbone was in three pieces; the jagged edges of the breaks were visible on the screen, like tiny saw teeth inside her leg. The pieces of bone were angled back and forth, like wrecked cars after a multiple-vehicle accident. And the side views showed the smaller bone of her shin was broken as well.

"Your right tibia is fractured in three places," the doctor said. "Here, about an inch below your knee; here, about four inches farther down; and here, about two inches above your ankle. And your fibula is snapped about halfway down. Fortunately, it's a cleaner break.

"You're really lucky your knee and ankle joints are unharmed. But it's still going to be a long haul, most likely."

"How long?" David asked.

"Well, it all depends on how serious you are about your follow-up therapy," the doctor said. "But I'd guess we're looking at, minimum, four months to let the bones knit thoroughly and then probably eight months to a year to regain full use of the leg."

David looked at her. Clarice felt herself wilting inside. *A year?* She tried to picture herself showing houses from a wheelchair or hobbling around on crutches while her buyers watched. This was going to set her back on her goals . . .

And then she hardened herself. Fine. If the doctor said it would be a year, she'd be back to full speed in six months. If there was an award for fastest healing, she was getting it. When the going got tough, the tough got going, right? Excuses were for somebody else. What was that phrase from her motivational CDs? "Loser's limp." No loser's limp for her—figurative or literal.

"How soon can we get into surgery?" Clarice said in her most businesslike voice. "Seems to me like we're wasting time here."

Even the doctor looked surprised. She saw the look that passed between him and David. "Well, I can get a surgery team prepping right now," he said. "But don't you want a little time to at least talk this over?"

"Doesn't seem to me like there's any choice," Clarice said. "Let's get it on."

The doctor looked at David again, then shrugged. He turned to S. Khan. "Let's get Mrs. Johnson prepped for surgery. I'll write the orders. And find out who's the anesthesiologist on call."

The orderly nodded and started wheeling Clarice away. David laid a hand on her arm. Her husband was looking at her with that sad look of his, halfway between a little boy trying to find his mama and a man whose favorite team is down by two touchdowns with only a minute left to play. "Reesie? You sure about this? You don't want some time to kind of, you know, brace yourself?"

"What is there to think about, David? The sooner we get started, the sooner I can finish." She looked up at S. Khan. "Let's go."

The gurney moved away and, though she expected David to follow her to the room where they'd prep her for surgery, he didn't. Her husband stayed behind and Clarice could see him in her mind's eye standing in the hospital hallway with his arms hanging at his sides, his eyes staring after her until she turned the corner and was gone.

For a second or two she wanted to have S. Khan stop the gurney. She wanted to call him and have him with her until the medical people pushed him out. She wanted someone there to call her "Boo" and tell her everything was going to be fine, just fine—even though she already knew it would be.

But she didn't hesitate. She let S. Khan push the gurney ahead and through the wide, swinging doors. Somebody would send David to her when it was all over. She'd wait until then. There'd be time for David after she'd taken care of what needed to be done.

∞

Dave felt someone move in beside him as he watched Clarice go.

"Your wife seems like a pretty determined lady," the doctor said.

"You got that right. She's the strongest woman I ever met. Nothing gon' get in her way."

The doctor clapped a hand on Dave's shoulder. "Well, don't worry. We'll take good care of her. I've seen worse breaks."

Dave nodded and tried to smile. "Yeah. Thanks."

The doctor left him and one of the nurses pointed him down the hallway to the waiting room. The room was empty and Dave slumped down at the end of one of the green vinyl couches. He sorted through the dozen or so dog-eared magazines piled on the end table beside the couch. He found a *Sports Illustrated* and held onto it a few seconds, before realizing it was over a year old. He tossed it down and leaned his head back against the cushions of the couch, putting his hands over his face.

He pulled in a deep breath and let it out slowly, trying to clear his mind. He glanced at his watch; just two hours had passed since the wreck. It seemed like a week. He thought about all the paperwork they'd get, all the bills that would have to be paid. Somehow, though, none of that mattered so much—or at least it was easy to let go of right now.

The big thing on his mind was Clarice. He knew his wife. She was already fretting about the loss of independence imposed on her by the broken leg. If you wanted Clarice to do something, all you needed to do was let her think you didn't believe she could. Her sales manager had used this technique on her more than once, Dave guessed.

Dave wondered if she knew how much he wished he could just take her in his arms and rock her like a baby. He wondered if Clarice had any sense of his longing to protect her, to guard her like a pearl of great price. When they were first married, he'd been able to find that soft place in her that wanted to feel safe and cared for. That place was getting harder and harder to find, though. Maybe it was gone. Dave tried to imagine living the rest of his life with a woman who didn't need him—and who certainly didn't approve of him as he was. The prospect stretched before him like a long, straight highway into the desert.

They'd gotten married in the church Dave grew up in; he'd attended with his grandmother every time the doors were open. Dave's main regret was that Granny hadn't lived long enough to see him happily married.

The minister who performed their service wasn't the one he remembered from his childhood, but this younger man did something during the ceremony Dave would never forget. He'd draped one end of a gold cord around Dave's shoulders, then draped the other end around Clarice's shoulders before reading some verses from Ecclesiastes:

There is one alone, and there is not a second; yea, he hath neither child nor brother: yet is there no end of all his labour; neither is his eye satisfied with riches; neither saith he, For whom do I labour, and bereave my soul of good? This is also vanity, yea, it is a sore travail.

Two are better than one; because they have a good reward for their labour. For if they fall, the one will lift up his fellow: but woe to him that is alone when he falleth; for he hath not another to help him up.

> Again, if two lie together, then they have heat: but
> how can one be warm alone? And if one prevail against
> him, two shall withstand him; and a threefold cord is
> not [easily] broken.[1]

"Dave and Clarice," he'd said, looking at them, "this cord I've just draped across you represents the cord in this passage. I believe the threefold cord the writer mentions is two people, plus God. Sometimes we hear about a 'love triangle'—we know that means trouble. But I promise you this: A triangle that's made up of the two of you and God is the best thing there is. As long as you both put God first, your marriage will be a threefold cord that nothing can break."

Dave remembered turning around, Clarice's hand in his, at the end of the ceremony. Just before the minister presented them to the audience as Dave and Clarice Johnson, Dave's eyes had fallen on Clarice's mother, sitting in the front row. Her arms were tucked up under her elbows and she was as dry-eyed and somber as a judge. She was looking right at him, Dave remembered, with an expression that said, "I hope you're sure about what you're doing, boy, 'cause I'm sure not."

The other vivid memory Dave had was of dancing with Clarice at the reception, thinking, *My wife. Clarice Johnson. I'm her husband. We're married.* They spun in soft circles with Lionel Richie crooning "Three Times a Lady" in the background.

Why was he thinking about all this now? Shouldn't he be checking with the nurses, or seeing about their insurance, or finding out when he could see his wife? Shouldn't he be more worried about this immediate crisis than all the maybes of the future? Dave prided himself on being a practical man, on not being one to borrow trouble. But when Clarice had looked at him with that no-nonsense face of hers, when she'd let him and everybody else in the room know, in no uncertain terms, that she was in charge here and there was no time for "messing around," Dave suddenly realized Clarice didn't need somebody to take care of her; she needed someone who could stay out of her way.

Clarice's mother. Dave sighed and dug in his pocket for his cell phone. He'd need to let her know, of course. He keyed in her number and stuck the phone to his ear. He listened to the ringing tone and stared at the blind eye of the TV mounted on the wall in the corner of the waiting room.

Chapter Three

~~

Julie Sawyer was tired. She let her Sentra coast into the parking spot in front of the YMCA and shoved the lever into park. She turned off the engine but the key still hung there because there was something wrong with her ignition switch and of course she didn't have time, much less money, to take it to the shop and get it fixed. So the alarm pinged at her while she fussed with the key and finally freed it from the switch.

She got out of the car and walked toward the front doors of the Y. It was spring, the time of year when things were supposed to be coming alive, but Julie didn't feel so alive this evening. The days were getting longer, the signal to her that summer's heat was just around the corner. Around here, summer seemed to last forever. A rain shower during the dead of summer was enough to make you want to throw a party. She made a mental note to try and improve her attitude . . . tomorrow. Right now, she just didn't have the energy to spare.

She leaned against the glass door, entered the building, and went past the reception desk, down the hall toward the pool. She began to hear the faint sounds of splashing and the reverberations of voices bouncing around the tiled chamber that held the indoor pool. She passed through the double doors and the scent of chlorine washed over her in a damp wave.

Bryson was there, as he always was, sitting on the bench with wet hair. He had his street clothes on, as he always did, and grabbed his gym bag as he came toward her.

"Hi, Mom."

"Hey, bud. How was practice?"

"Fine."

"Ready?"

He nodded and passed her, holding the door for her as they went back into the hallway.

"Did Dad call back yet?"

Julie allowed herself a mental sigh. "No, bud, not yet."

"Okay." They walked a few paces. "You let him know about the meet next weekend, right?"

"Yeah, son, I sure did."

"I hope he can come this time."

"Me too, bud." *But, of course, I also hoped he'd come to the last meet, just like I hoped he'd get in touch to congratulate you on swimming your personal best time three weeks ago. Or maybe send you a card in the mail, for crying out loud.*

"What's for supper?"

"Not sure yet, kiddo. We'll have to see what's in the cupboard when we get home."

"Cupboard?"

"Yeah. You know, like Old Mother Hubbard's cupboard?"

"But we don't have a dog."

"And I'm not old. Not yet, anyway."

"Why don't you just say pantry or fridge? You make it sound like we live in a cottage in the woods or something."

"Oh, where's your poetic, whimsical sense, Bryson? Can't I have a cupboard if I want one?"

"I guess. Just don't try to feed me a bone."

"Deal." She grinned at him and ruffled his wet brownish-blond hair. They came outside and headed for the car.

"How was school today?" she asked, as she jiggled the key into the ignition switch.

"Pretty good, I guess."

"Homework?"

"Done, except for a little English and some reading."

"Right after supper, okay?"

He nodded.

They pulled into the driveway at home. This time, the key slid out of the switch easily, to Julie's relief. "Drop your wet stuff on the washing machine, okay?"

"Yes, ma'am."

She went to the fridge and gave the contents a critical scan: The chicken-and-cheese casserole was from Sunday's lunch; it was only Monday—too soon. The pizza from Saturday night was still okay, but not as nourishing as Julie thought they needed. There were still some canned vegetables in the pantry from her last trip to the store and she thought she had most of what she needed for a salad.

She felt it then. Creeping over her, twining through the muscles of her shoulders, arms, and legs, was the weariness of the day. She was on her feet all day, coaching and coaxing and cajoling her patients to do "just one more" leg lift or elbow bend or step up and down from the platform to the floor. All the while she empathized with their pain, their fatigue, their frustration, their discouragement. It was up to her to reassure them and counsel them and sometimes scold them—whatever she had to do to keep them going, making progress. And tomorrow at eight a.m., it would all start over. She looked through the doorway to the slightly worn overstuffed couch sitting in front of the TV in her living room. She sighed and slid the pizza box from the fridge.

As she peeled loose one of the cold, stiff wedges from the pizza box and laid it on a plate, Julie remembered the memo she'd gotten in her mailbox at the clinic, something about a mandatory employees' meeting the next day after closing. She'd been hoping to finally get her hair done tomorrow, but depending on how long the meeting ran, that might have to wait.

She put a paper towel atop the pizza slice, slid the plate into the microwave, and punched the cook button. Julie thought briefly about calling Ted one more time and leaving yet another message on his voice mail, reminding him to make some effort to come to his son's swim meet on Saturday. She hated to see Bryson wounded again by his father's carelessness. *How does he find the strength to keep hoping his dad will actually take an interest?*

She guessed that no matter what, kids want to believe in their fathers . . . even when their fathers stop believing in them. The microwave beeped and she poured her son a glass of milk. "Come eat, Bryson."

Bryson came in and collected his plate and milk, then went to the table and started eating. Julie punched the microwave button again. She turned to watch her son as she waited for her pizza to heat.

Bryson carefully touched the tip of his tongue to the melted cheese atop his pizza. He started to pick up the slice, then thought better of it. He got up and went to the silverware drawer, retrieving a fork. He sat back down and methodically cut a piece from the tip of the wedge, stabbed it with the fork, blew on it a few times, then put it in his mouth.

When had her son become so careful? *Lord knows he has plenty of reason,* she thought. When your home breaks apart, who knows what might happen next? It was best to take it easy, look ahead, and think of all the ways something could go wrong. Bryson was a forty-year-old inside a sixth-grader's body.

The only time Bryson approached life with anything close to recklessness was when he was swimming. The 50- and 100-meter freestyle were his specialty, and the crawl was his weapon of choice. His arms flashed and wheeled, cutting the water with the untiring regularity of propeller blades. He was almost never nervous before a meet, as far as Julie could tell. Instead, there was a kind of quiet confidence about him, as if he knew he was going to do well—it was just a matter of how well. When his coach hauled him out of the water at the finish line, Bryson was usually smiling like someone who'd just won the lottery, even on those rare occasions when he didn't finish first in a race. Julie guessed that for Bryson, swimming was the thing, and recognition was the icing on the cake. When Bryson swam, he was a different kid, and he knew it.

He had far too much class to brag or swagger, but he was one of the best swimmers in his age group at the Y swim club. His coach had told Julie he was considering adding Bryson to the age fourteen-and-up sprint relay team, a group at least two years ahead of Bryson's own age group. Julie had heard the coach say more than once that Bryson could "go all the way," whatever that meant. She hoped it had something to do with college tuition, because on what Julie made, that was the only way her son was likely to get an education without incurring a mountain of debt. Ted sure wasn't likely to be much help.

She pulled her plate from the microwave, got herself a canned soft drink from the fridge, and went over to sit with her son.

"Pizza okay?"

He nodded. "Fine," he said around a mouthful.

Julie took a bite of her pizza and a sip of her drink. She looked at the clock on the microwave: seven-thirty. Could she make it to ten o'clock without falling down from exhaustion? And where were the laundry elves when you needed them?

Bryson was looking at her. She gave him a smile and reached across the table to pat his arm. "Better eat, bud. You've still got homework."

∞

The orthopedist walked into the waiting room. Dave came up off the couch and met him just inside the door. "How is she?"

"Your wife came through the surgery just fine. We did a spinal, so she was awake the whole time. The bones are all put back together and we've got her in a cast just to hold everything still."

"Can I see her?"

"Sure. Just down the hall, then to your right. The recovery room's through the first set of double doors. You'll see it."

"Thanks, Doctor. We really appreciate you taking care of us so quick and all."

"No problem, Mr. Johnson. Glad we could do it. Just make sure she stays off that leg, okay?"

"That'll be harder than the surgery."

The doctor laughed. "Yes, I can see that. One of the nurses will give you my contact information; you need to schedule the first follow-up appointment in about two weeks. At that point, we'll assess how she's doing and go from there. Okay?"

Dave nodded.

"Well, good luck to you both."

Dave shook his hand and headed for the recovery room. He walked in and found Clarice sitting up in a hospital bed with nurses on both sides of her. Her broken leg was propped up on some pillows, and there was a brand-new fiberglass cast encasing her right leg from just below the knee to just above her ankle. One of the nurses was taking her blood pressure while the other one read aloud from a clipboard.

"If your toes start to turn purple or you lose feeling in your toes, elevate your leg immediately. If you feel unusual pain in your leg for longer than a day, elevate your leg and call the doctor's office—oh, hello, Mr. Johnson. I'm glad you're here; you can listen in."

"David, did they give you a bag with some of my things?" Clarice asked. She turned to the nurse with the clipboard. "They took my bra in the ER, and I'd really like to have it back."

"I'll check with them, Mrs. Johnson," the other nurse offered, as she jotted something on another clipboard. "I'll be right back, okay?" she called as she left.

"I was just telling your wife some of the symptoms you need to watch for these next few days," the other nurse began. "I've got a little brochure here that has most of the information. You probably ought to hang onto this awhile until we see how Mrs. Johnson's leg is going to do. It's also got the doctor's office number."

Dave took the pamphlet from the nurse and stuck it in his pocket.

"We also recommend that Mrs. Johnson get started with a physical therapist right away."

"How am I supposed to do therapy?" Clarice wondered aloud. "I can barely wiggle my toes."

"The therapist can begin working with you to maintain mobility and strength in your leg," the nurse said. "With an injury like this, your recovery time will be much faster if you maintain a good therapeutic regimen right from the start."

"Well, do ya'll have someone you can recommend?" Dave said.

"We can give you a list," the nurse continued. "There's an excellent clinic affiliated with this hospital, as well as several other good ones. Most of them file on insurance, if that helps."

"Thanks. We'll take that list," Dave said.

"Mrs. Johnson, we need to keep you here another half hour or so, just for observation. If you're feeling all right, you can go home; I've already got your dismissal orders. I'll be around, so if either of you need anything just let us know, okay?" She walked away.

"If I hear *okay* one more time, I think I'm going to hurt somebody," Clarice mumbled. "David, I need you to go home and get me something to put on besides this hospital gown. They cut my dress off of me in the ER; I guess they were afraid to move me or something."

"Okay. What you want me to bring you?"

"I don't care, just as long as it isn't pants."

"Yeah, that could be a problem, couldn't it? Okay, I'll be right back up here. Anything else you need?"

"To be out of here as soon as humanly possible, so please go get me some clothes."

"I'm gone, baby."

Frantic thoughts chased each other through Dave's head as he walked toward the hospital lobby. *Wonder if Brock can come pick me up? Guess I could call a cab. Got to get her set up with a therapist. Keep her off the leg, but how? Might need to stay home tomorrow and take care of her. What needs to be covered at work? What do I do about Clarice's office? Need to call the insurance people.*

Then Dave heard his grandmother's voice louder than the thoughts in his head: "You better just slow down, boy. You tryin' to solve tomorrow's problems today. The good Lord had something to say about that . . ." Granny could always tell when he was letting things pile up on him, even when he was a kid in junior high. Nothing seemed to rattle her or get her off her stride. She'd kept Dave centered through some difficult passages. Even now, hardly a day went by when he didn't miss her.

Okay, Granny. First things first.

Dave punched Brock Houseman's phone number on his cell phone. The phone buzzed and Dave heard a click as Brock picked up.

"Hello?"

"Brock? Man, this is Dave."

"Hey, what's up?"

"Actually, I'm at the hospital."

"You're kidding! Are you okay?"

"Yeah, Clarice and I are both fine. We got sideswiped by a kid at South First and Delmont. My pickup's probably totaled."

"Oh man, I hate to hear that."

"You think *you* hate it. Anyway, man, I was wondering if you could come give me a ride to the house so I can get Clarice's car. She's ready to go home, but I've got no way to get us there."

"Sure, but wouldn't you rather just have me pick you both up and take you home? Save you a trip."

"Well, that'd be great, Brock, but I can just—"

"Nope, that's it. I'm walking out the door right now."

"Okay then. I really appreciate it, brother."

"Ain't no thing, Dave."

Dave smiled as he pocketed his phone. Brock was a little goofy sometimes, but he was as good a friend as you'd want to have. They'd known each other ever since college and had stayed in touch during the years Dave spent teaching and Brock spent going to law school and beginning a practice. When Dave set up his business, Brock helped him with his incorporation and even advised him on his business plan. A year or two ago Dave had persuaded Brock to come help him with the Little League team he coached in Eastside. Brock hadn't been easy to talk into it, but Dave was certain it was just the thing to get Brock outside his shell. Coaching a team of tough little brothers from the hood would get him out in the real world, which Brock needed desperately after going nine to five in the suit-and-tie jungle where he worked. And it was even better for the kids, most of whom had few enough excuses to trust a white man on anything like a regular basis.

He saw Brock's car pull into the parking lot and was waiting beneath the covered drive-through at the front door. Brock parked and walked up to him.

"I'm sure sorry this happened, Dave."

"I hear you, babe. But everybody's okay, I think, and that's the main thing."

Brock nodded. "Where's Clarice?"

"Up in recovery. Oh, that reminds me . . . can you take me home so I can get her some clothes to put on? They cut her dress off in the ER."

"Sure, man. Let's go."

Driving home, Dave filled Brock in on the accident and its aftermath. "I don't think the kid ever saw us. He sure didn't slow down."

"Need a good lawyer?"

Dave shook his head. "There you go. Not five blocks down the street and you already taking care of business."

"It's a white thing—you probably wouldn't understand."

"Watch out now, homie, before I have to put a smackdown on you somewhere. If you had any class at all, you'd take off work tomorrow and watch Clarice for me."

"You need my help to watch your wife?"

Dave turned toward Brock. "You know Clarice. You want to try and tell her she's got to stay on the couch and rest instead of messing with her real estate?"

Brock gave a low whistle. "No, bro. I leave all that to you."

"Mmm-hmm. That's what I'd be saying if I had the chance."

They pulled into Dave's driveway and he ran toward the front door, fishing in his pocket for his keys, then realized they were probably still dangling from the ignition switch of his wrecked pickup. He headed to the back door and picked up the fake rock that held their extra key in its secret compartment. He went in, grabbed the first dress he saw in Clarice's closet, paused a moment, then gathered up a handful of dresses. He started out, then went back and picked up a pair of flip-flops from the floor on Clarice's side of the bed. He locked the back door and jogged around to the driveway, where Brock waited with his engine idling.

"Okay, let's go," Dave said, getting in and shutting the door.

"How many dresses does she need?" Brock asked.

"How many trips you want to make if I get the wrong one?"

"I feel you." Brock started backing out.

Dave grinned. "You fit'n to feel something else you don't get us back to that hospital pretty quick," Dave said. "Reesie wants a dress. That's all you got to worry about right now, is getting it to her."

"Yes, sir."

"All right then. Now drive."

Chapter Four

*C*larice heard their voices bouncing down the corridor before she could see them. David walked in, and when she saw him she had to smile. He looked like some hawker from the Garment District in New York, with a dress held in either hand and another one hanging from the collar of his shirt.

"Here you go, ma'am, the latest in fashion for the woman who wants to go home from the hospital in style. Which one of these fine rags strikes your fancy?"

Standing behind David and grinning like a possum, Brock Houseman held out two more dresses for her inspection.

"Brock, how'd you get dragged into this fool's business?" she asked.

"I'm just the driver, ma'am. I told him you'd want the turquoise-and-brown, but he told me I didn't know what I was talking about."

Clarice allowed the chuckle building inside to bubble out in laughter as she shook her head at the two men. "Y'all better be glad you can't see yourselves, 'cause you'd be too ashamed to walk out of here."

A nurse walked up and smiled at David and Brock. "Looks like the welcoming committee showed up," she said.

"I swear I never saw these two before," Clarice said, still laughing.

"How about we at least take one of those dresses off their hands so we can get you out of here. Which one?" the nurse replied.

Clarice shrugged and pointed at the dress in David's left hand. "I don't know—that one, I guess."

David flashed Brock a triumphant grin. "Boy, what did I tell you?"

"Lucky guess," Brock said.

"Here's some shoes, Reesie," David said, pulling her flip-flops from the back pocket he'd stuffed them in.

"I won't need but one of those."

"Will you gentlemen excuse us while we get her dressed?" The nurse started pulling a drape around Clarice's bed.

When she was dressed the nurse helped her sit on the side of the bed. It was so much easier to move now that her leg was protected by the cast. The nurse pulled back the drape and asked David if he'd like to come help her transfer to the wheelchair.

"Am I going to have to stay in one of these things?" Clarice asked. David held her arm and eased her onto her healthy leg.

"I don't think so," the nurse replied. "Usually, you can just use crutches, as long as you feel like it. Your husband can pick up a pair for you at just about any surgical supply."

The nurse held the chair and David helped her sit down. "What about a cane?" Clarice wondered aloud.

"I'd go easy on putting too much weight on that leg for a while," the nurse said. "It's all there in the brochure I gave your husband. You'll want to start rebuilding strength, but don't put too much weight on the bones, at least at first."

"Mmm-hmm." *We'll see about that. I can't be hobbling around the office on crutches.*

The nurse showed David how to adjust the leg support so it held her injured leg out in front of her like a battering ram.

"All right, I guess that's about it," the nurse said. "You take care, Mrs. Johnson, and call us if you need anything."

David pushed Clarice out the door and down the hall.

"I want to read that brochure, David," she said when they'd gone a little way. "I want to see for myself what it says about getting up and around."

"Now, Reesie, you heard the nurse. You not going to do yourself any good if you try too much too soon."

"Like I said, I want to read that brochure myself. It doesn't hurt anything to be well-informed."

Clarice could tell from the shape of the silence that David was having other thoughts.

"Too bad your cast is that fiberglass stuff," Brock said lightly. "Hard to sign."

"If she'd leave it on long enough for someone to sign," David muttered.

"David, you might as well stop acting like my mother right now. I'm a grown woman and this isn't the first broken leg in the history of the world. You just get me home and let me start doing my own worrying, all right?"

"Yes'm."

"And stop it with the Stepin Fetchit, too."

"Yes'm."

"David!"

"Sorry, Reesie."

Brock pulled his car beneath the covered entrance and David held Clarice's hand as she levered herself up from the chair and into the front seat of Brock's SUV. She was glad they'd brought Brock's vehicle instead of her Accord; the higher seat was much easier to navigate. David handed her the bag with her bra, then got in back.

When they got home, David helped her out of the car and up the walk to the front door.

"Let me know what you need," Brock said as he leaned out his window. "And call me if you change your mind about having me represent you on this."

David waved him off and unlocked the front door. Clarice turned toward him and started to awkwardly move past, but then she turned and wrapped her arms around his shoulders.

"Hey, baby girl. You all right?"

"Yes, David," she said into his shoulder. "I'm all right. But I just realized . . . I haven't once said thank you for taking care of everything at the hospital."

"Aw, now that ain't no thing," he said, stroking her back softly. "That's what I'm here for, don't you know?" He held her and the warmth of him was sweet to her; she could feel the strength in his chest and arms, and for just a moment she was able to allow herself to sink into him as if she were a child wrapped in a parent's embrace.

A couple of neighborhood kids wheeled past on their bikes. Clarice saw them grinning at each other, smirking behind their hands as they went by. Right then, she didn't care; her husband was holding her and it felt completely right.

But after a few seconds, she realized the moment had evaporated. She pulled away from him. David held her elbow as she maneuvered the crutches over the threshold and into the house.

Was it really only a few hours ago they'd left here on their way to the dinner? As Clarice hopped on one foot toward the couch, she tried to imagine what her day was going to be like tomorrow. David would probably insist on hovering around like a mother hen, but she didn't think she could take a whole day of that. She'd let him stay for the morning, maybe, but then he was going to need to leave her alone for both their sakes. Her mother always said a man had his uses, but taking care of the sick wasn't one of them.

"What you need, baby?" he said, fussing with the pillow he was putting under her leg. "You want something to drink? You hungry? What can I get for you?"

"I'm fine, David, really. Do you have that brochure they gave us at the hospital?"

"Yeah, right here." He fished it out of his pocket and handed it to her. She started reading.

∞

Julie couldn't believe what she was hearing. She looked around at the others at the meeting, and their faces registered the same shock and confusion she was feeling. Cutting down on hours? Trimming therapists' patient loads? The clinic was bursting at the seams! What were they thinking?

"We know these drastic measures may come as a shock to some of our personnel," the manager standing at the podium said. "But we assure you we've taken into account every budgetary possibility and the simple fact is that in the current health care funding environment, we can't continue to operate at present levels of staffing."

"What are we supposed to do?" someone said from the back of the room. "When are these changes you're talking about going into effect?"

"We, ah, anticipate implementation will begin at the first of next month," the suit said.

"Two weeks," Julie said under her breath. "I'm taking a pay cut starting in two weeks?"

She felt despair dragging at her. Things were tight enough as it was, given Ted's haphazard approach to paying child support. She knew therapists who went out on their own and made a lot more money than the clinic paid, but Julie hadn't ever felt she could afford the risk of starting her own business, with all the expenses and liabilities that entailed. She had health insurance here, and a little retirement package, and the security of the clinic had always appealed to her, until now.

"I can go out and get private clients and not have to put up with this crap," said someone in the row behind her. "I've been looking for an excuse to tell this management to take a flying leap, anyway."

Julie heard much more grumbling as everyone left the meeting. People were talking about lawsuits and forming private associations. Julie wondered how many of them had a kid who was outgrowing his shoes and a car that needed repairs. She looked at her watch. She probably had time to get her hair done before picking up Bryson, but now she wondered if she could afford it.

⁓

Dave tried to talk her out of it, but the next Sunday Clarice insisted on going to church. Not only that, but she assured him she wasn't going to sit anywhere but in their regular place, two-thirds of the way down front and on the left. She got up, got dressed, got made up, and tucked her crutches in the back of the Accord before Dave drove them to church.

Pastor Wilkes made an announcement from the pulpit about the accident and all their friends told Dave and Clarice how grateful they were no one was hurt worse. They got offers of casseroles and cold cuts, cakes and cobblers, fried chicken and mashed potatoes. Dave didn't mind the food so much, of course, but as he watched Clarice downplay her injury and generally make light of her difficulties, he couldn't help wishing he'd been more insistent on having her stay at home. She was doing what she always did: presenting her strong face to the world, not letting on that anything was wrong or that she required anyone's help. It made him feel sad, and just a little weak and useless.

He chewed on it all the way through church. On the way home, he decided to say something about it. "Reesie, you got to take it easy this afternoon. I saw how hard you were working back there at church, making sure everybody knew you were just fine. You're not just fine. Boo, you've got a badly broken leg, and you're not doing yourself or me any favors by acting like it's different than it is."

"Oh, not doing you any favors, is it? Well, I'm sorry, David. I just happen to believe it doesn't do me any good to limp around looking like the tail end of a hard-luck story. I believe in making my own way, and I intend to keep on doing that, broken leg or not."

"I'm not saying you shouldn't do all you can, baby. I'm just saying that sometimes you got to let other people help, for a change."

"Why? So you can feel important?"

Her head and neck were swiveling; she looked like a prizefighter trying to land a jab. The discussion was turning nasty and he should have backed away, but he didn't. Still, he managed to keep his voice even. "It's not about me, Clarice. It's about you. You're driving too fast for too long at a time. You gon' crash one of these days, and I don't want to have to be around to see it."

"Well, who's asking you to stick around?"

"Now, Reesie, wait a minute—"

"Don't start backpedaling now, David. You the one opened up this can of worms. Look to me like the brother better recognize."

Clarice really had herself all worked up. He thought long and hard over his next words. Biting back the sarcasm that wanted to creep into his voice, he tried to calm things down.

"Clarice, let's both take a breath here, okay?"

She sat wedged against her door, her arms folded, looking at him like his grandmother used to look at a cockroach.

"I'm not trying to tie you down. I'm not trying to make you anything you don't want to be. I just want to . . . to take care of my woman. I want to help you. I want to protect you. Is that so bad a thing for a man to want?"

Her face softened a little, but she kept her arms tucked in as if she were trying to fend him off.

"I love you, baby girl. I love the way you light up when you've just closed a big sale. I love the excitement in your voice when you nail down a good listing. I love the way a room can change when you walk in—like somebody just found three or four more bulbs to switch on." He couldn't tell if any of this was soaking in or not, but at least she was still listening. "You got to believe me, Reesie. There's nothing I wouldn't do for you." He turned onto their home street and drove three blocks before she said anything else. He wasn't sure whether her silence was good or bad.

"Do you love me enough to let me be who I am, instead of who you want me to be?" she said softly, just as he turned into their driveway.

Her voice wasn't mean or accusing like a few minutes ago. Dave thought she was really asking him a question; straight up, no tricks. The trouble was, he wasn't sure how he could answer. He switched off the engine and looked at her.

"Maybe I'm having trouble understanding who it is you want to be," he said.

Her eyes held his for a few seconds, then she turned away. He got out and came around to help her out of the car, but she had already flung open her door. She was pulling herself out of the seat and onto her crutches. He reached toward her arm to help her, but she batted his hand away. Dave felt the dam breaking inside him.

"Fine, then!" He knew his voice was loud, but he'd lost the ability to care. "Go on with your bad self, since you don't need anybody's help." He slammed the car door and stalked into the house ahead of her, wondering what a man had to do to get through to a woman as bullheaded as Clarice.

∞

Clarice sat on the couch most of the afternoon, staring at the latest copies of her *Realtor* magazine, *House Beautiful,* and *Essence.* Every so often she'd turn a page, just to convince herself and anybody who might be watching that she was actually reading. But really she was thinking, over and over again, about what David had said to her in the car on the way home from church. In fact, she kept hoping she'd see something in one of her magazines that would interest her, that would lure her mind away from buzzing around and around David's words like a bee circling a bloom under glass—trying to reach it but unable to figure out how to land. So far, no distraction she'd tried was working.

The trouble was, a part of what he'd said sounded enticing. Maybe that was what annoyed her most. If she was completely honest with herself, she had to admit that deep down, maybe so deep it was hidden even from her most of the time, she wanted to be cared for and protected. She wanted to be able to rest in the arms of someone who would never let her down, never disappoint her, never take her for granted, never devalue her in any way. But was David that person? For that matter, did such a person even exist?

Just about the first thing she could remember was her mother talking about how you had to depend on yourself. That was the real security, Mama said, the real strength of a person. And Mama had proved her belief by the way she'd lived her life. She worked two and sometimes three jobs to keep her children fed, clothed, and housed, and she expected them to contribute too, as soon as they were big enough. Clarice started bringing home her babysitting money when she was twelve, and her baby brother and sister had their list of household chores that Mama checked every day, and no excuses. Mama had seen to it they all worked hard, and it paid off. They all had the chance to go to college, even if a lot of the cost was covered by grants and loans. Even now, in retirement, Mama had little use for people who wouldn't help themselves. Her phone conversations with Clarice often featured caustic assessments of her aging acquaintances who had, in her words, "decided to sit down on the front porch and wait for the undertaker." Self-reliance was the chief virtue in Mama's book, and she'd been preaching it day and night for as long as Clarice could remember.

When Clarice had met David, though, something happened to her she couldn't quite explain. She was out of school and working in a local bank, and one day a tall, good-looking young man came to her desk to open a new account. His name was Dave Johnson, and he'd just moved to town to take his first job, teaching and coaching at one of the local high schools. When he looked at her, Clarice felt something stirring deep inside her. It was a feeling she'd never experienced—one Mama hadn't covered in any of her lectures.

Now, she'd certainly had her college-girl flings, but none of them had ever gotten within shouting distance of her heart. This was a different kind of thing. Clarice wasn't sure she was falling in love with this Dave Johnson, but she certainly wasn't sure she wasn't. And when she'd finished opening his account and he picked up one of her business cards, she was fairly certain she wanted him to use it.

She loved David's big heart and the dreams he dreamed with it. He told her he wanted to make a difference in the lives of kids. He said that coaching wasn't mostly about winning—not the way he saw it, anyway. It was about helping kids find out how much they could do, and then figuring out ways to do more. It was about showing them their potential, he said. When he talked about it, his face took on a look Clarice had never seen on anyone except maybe a preacher or one of the old ladies at church. The passion in him called out to her, pulled at her like a magnet. And pretty soon they were passing passion back and forth on a regular basis. When David asked her to marry him, it never occurred to Clarice to say anything but yes.

Even in her worst moments, Clarice couldn't remember anything about those first few years but the heady excitement of learning to know another human being—body, soul, and heart. They couldn't get enough of each other. When David started to talk about wanting his own business, Clarice was delighted. He could do more for the community, he said. He could still work with kids in his spare time, and with his own business he could provide jobs and self-respect for people who might not be able to work somewhere else. It was just like coaching, only with adults instead of kids, he said. He was excited, and his excitement was contagious, despite the risks of starting a business.

It was about then that Clarice began to wonder if she was pursuing her own potential in the right way. She had a good job at the bank and she enjoyed the respect of her supervisors and those she oversaw, but she also had the feeling she was capable of more. One day, she was the officer on duty when a local Realtor came in. The tellers were on break, so Clarice offered to take the woman's deposit. She was a good customer, after all; she and Clarice knew each other by name.

When Clarice saw the size of the check the woman was depositing, something clicked in her head. After work that day, she made a phone call to the Realtor. That led to more phone calls and eventually to the woman sponsoring Clarice to study for and obtain her Realtor's license.

And David had backed her all the way. He was all for anybody realizing his or her potential, and he was her biggest cheerleader . . . right up until about five years ago.

It wasn't as if Clarice had never thought about having children; what woman hadn't? But right now just didn't seem the right time. Her career was starting to really take off. She didn't think David had any idea of her earning potential over the next few years. What kind of opportunities they could give a child if he'd just let her wait until the time was right. But she didn't think David saw that.

She flipped a few magazine pages with a quick, slapping motion. No, David had decided her potential had more to do with making a baby than with being an equal partner in the financial future of their home. He could talk that sweet talk, all right, but when it came down to it, he wanted what he wanted, much like any other man. Mama was right about that, anyway: A man was fine and good until he wanted something different than *you*. And then you better look out, girl.

Clarice had no intention of being blindsided. Broken leg or not, she was far from helpless.

Chapter Five

I don't know, Brock. She's got something stuck in her head and I don't know what it'll take to get it out, or if it'll come out at all." Dave took a pull at his Gatorade and shook his head.

Brock checked his rearview mirror, pulled onto the freeway ramp, and headed for Eastside and their Tuesday evening ball practice. "I don't know what to tell you, man," Brock said. "I guess this is one of the reasons I never got married."

"You just never found the right woman," Dave said, "mainly 'cause any time a woman takes a second look at you, you start trying to figure out what's wrong with her."

"Well, can you blame me? Would you go out with me?"

"Naw, man, you not my type. Too tall."

"So . . . did you find the right woman?"

Dave took another swig of Gatorade. "Yeah. Yeah, I did. Clarice is the only woman I ever really wanted, and I got her. Now if I could just figure out what to do with her. She makes me so mad sometimes, I just want to—"

"Aw, Dave, you guys'll work it out. You and Clarice belong together. Believe it. Blue punch buggy, no punch-back," he said, tapping Dave on the shoulder as a blue VW Beetle going the opposite direction passed them.

"Where, man? There wasn't no—aw, there it is. I don't know how you see those things all the time."

"Concentration, my brother. Pure concentration."

Dave picked up his glove from the seat beside him and started popping his fist into the well-oiled palm.

"So, what's the plan for tonight?" Brock said.

"Work the 6-4-3 double play and try to get George to keep his raggedy little tailgate down when he's fielding a ground ball."

"What about the outfield?"

"About three dozen fly balls apiece, with two hands on the glove every time. You heard anything on Carlos's daddy?"

"No, I called my buddy down at the DA's, but he hasn't come up for arraignment yet."

"If that kid's got any heart left, this'll break it."

"Yeah, that's what I'm afraid of. That sorry so-and-so can't even remember how many promises he's made that kid. But he always goes back on them."

"I heard that. Well, we just gotta keep him from thinking too much about it, at least for tonight."

Brock exited in an area where the freeway was lined on both sides with run-down warehouses and even more run-down tenements. They practiced in a park mostly frequented by crackheads and gangbangers, but for some reason the local thugs thought Dave's Little League team was cool. He only had to get physical one time, early on, with a fat-mouth high school scrub who didn't know Dave specialized in pulling the hold card on would-be gangstas. After that, things were usually peaceful—except for the inevitable flare-ups that happened when you got a bunch of tough little homies together in a competitive situation.

The kids were waiting for them where they always did, in a loose group gathered by the rusty chain-link backstop. They pulled up and Dave got out and opened the door to pull the equipment bag out of the backseat.

"Yo, Coach, what happened to the pickup?" somebody asked.

"Somebody tried to drive through it last week," Dave said. "I had to catch a ride with Coach Brock."

"Say, Coach, when can I show you my curveball?"

"About the time I say your arm is grown enough to be throwin' it, Jaylen," Dave said.

"Aw man, Coach, I been workin' on it, man."

"Mmm-hmm, and I been workin' on ways to make you ride the pine for about a month if you keep messing with me."

"Ooh, boy, he told you."

"Ta-DOW!"

"Mmm, I heard me some of that."

"Everybody line up at home for wind sprints," Brock said. This was greeted by a chorus of groans and complaints.

"I know ya'll not fixing to dog it on these sprints," Dave called, "'cause that would mean we run sprints till this time tomorrow. Isn't that right, gentlemen?"

The boys quieted and lined up. Brock carried the second-base bag out to the point of the diamond, pegged it into the ground, stood on it, raised his hand above his head, then dropped it. The boys took off with a sound like a bunch of people shaking the dust out of some old quilts. As usual, Darius, a wiry kid with a natural that was always leaking out from under whatever cap he was wearing, reached second before anybody else, and the slightly tubby Marcus chugged in last, puffing like somebody finishing a half-mile straight uphill. Fortunately for Marcus, he was also the tallest kid on the team, which landed him the first-base spot. He didn't generally need much speed to handle his duties there. They lined up facing home and took off when Brock dropped his arm again.

"Marcus, if you don't beat somebody on one of these sprints, I may have to put a dress on you," Dave said. "Now ya'll turn around again and run to second like you mean something."

By the time they'd run the boys for five minutes, most traces of wisecracking and trash talking had faded into a chorus of panting and wheezing. When even Darius was resting with his hands on his knees between sprints, Dave decided it was time to get started.

"I want the outfielders in center; Coach Brock's going to hit you fly balls. I told him to run anybody who doesn't keep both hands on the glove until the ball's in the pocket. Jaylen, you and Malcolm go over there and start throwing. I want Marcus on first, James on second, George at short, Darius on third. We're going to work on double plays."

For the next half hour Dave alternated between tapping grounders to the infielders and talking to them about turning the shortstop-second-first double play. Just to keep it interesting, he also drilled George on covering second when the ball was hit to the second baseman.

"George, keep your rear down till the ball's in your glove, boy! How many times I got to tell you? You got a way better chance of catching a grounder on the chin when you poking at it like a bug. Stay down on the ball, you hear me?"

He ended by hitting the ball randomly around the infield, calling out the play just before making contact. He had Darius scoop the ball and step on the third base bag for a forced out, then pivot and make the throw to first. He had Marcus come off the bag and field the ball, then turn and throw to James, who was covering first. He had George field a ball hit between second and third, then make the throw to James at second, who turned and completed the play to Marcus at first.

After a while, he whistled in Brock and the outfielders and sent them all to line up at the drinking fountain behind the backstop.

"Water break, then BP," he said. "Malcolm, get a drink and then suit up. You're catching me first today."

Dave watched them as they jockeyed for position around the drinking fountain. For some of the boys, these practices and games were the only time of the week when they were part of something both constructive and bigger than themselves. Eastside didn't have much in the way of facilities even at the high school level, much less the elementary and junior high schools these boys attended. And the academic challenges faced by many of the kids, coupled with the state's no-pass, no-play policy, meant fielding a decent team for any sport could be a real problem.

But Little Leaguers didn't have to worry so mu
Out here, the boys could forget, for a little whi
about the uncertainties of life in the mean streets
about everything except making a clean catch, pic......
runner, keeping their eyes on the ball and listening to what Dave
told them to do. No matter how hardheaded some of these little
brothers were, they all knew Dave and Brock were here because
they cared—about baseball and about them. And that was as good a
place to start as any.

"All right, gentlemen, I want everybody in the infield who was
just there, and Deshawn, Carlos, and Tim in the outfield. We'll ro-
tate in to bat. Malcolm, you got your gear on? Jaylen, you're up first,
my man."

Dave pitched batting practice, and Brock backed up Malcolm
behind the plate. He also acted as umpire.

"Come on, Jaylen! That was right over the fat part of the plate.
What are you waiting for, an invitation?"

"Aw, come on, Coach Brock, man, that ball was high."

"Sure, if you're two feet tall. You gotta take your cuts, man."

When they'd started the team, most of the boys' ideas about
technique were limited to what they'd learned from playing street
ball with a can and a stick. It was good to see them getting more
balanced at the plate, more selective and controlled in their
swings.

Dave threw to the first five batters, then came to the plate to re-
place Malcolm, who was getting out of his catcher's gear to take his
batting practice. Brock took a turn on the mound, and then Dave let
Jaylen throw to several batters.

By the time all the boys had taken a turn at the plate and in the
field, the sun was nearing the tops of the apartment buildings on the
west side of the park. Dave called them all in to home plate and had
them gather the equipment and put it all in the green canvas equipment bag.

"All right, gentlemen, circle up here, circle up. Everybody get a

...d in. Everybody in? All right. We had a good practice today, and I'm proud of each one of you. I want you to go home, do your homework"—he paused to allow the groans to subside—"listen to your folks, and stay out of trouble. I'll see ya'll back out here Thursday afternoon, same time. Anybody know why Jamal wasn't here today?"

"He got in trouble at school. His mama kept him home," somebody said.

"All right, well, I'll find out more about that later. Remember, games start in two weeks, so we got to get down to business out here every time. Ya'll understand what I'm saying? Now, on three, I want a big yell for the Hawks, and then I think Coach Brock got something for ya'll in his trunk. Ready? One, two, three, 'Go, Hawks!' "

The boys screamed "Hawks" at the top of their lungs and then made a mad dash toward Brock's car, hollering like a mob of marauders. Brock opened the trunk and handed out cans of soft drinks and candy bars from an ice-filled chest. For a bunch of streetwise little toughs, these boys carried on like it was Christmas; it was the same scene every time Dave and Brock handed out the end-of-practice treats. It was one sign that told Dave there were real kids inside those hard little shells they wore all the time.

By the time Brock dropped him off at home, Dave was coming down from the emotional high he always got from a good practice. He waved to Brock as his friend backed out of the driveway, then carried the equipment bag into the garage, dropping it just inside. He went in the door that led from the garage to the kitchen.

"Reesie? Where you at, girl?"

He looked in the living room. The television was on, but she wasn't on the couch in front of it. "Reesie?"

He heard the sound of clicking keys coming from the den. Dave walked in and found his wife staring at the computer screen.

"Hey, Shorty. What you doing?"

"Just . . . looking . . . for something . . ."

He came around and tried to look at the screen, but she quickly tapped two keys and the Web site she'd been browsing disappeared. She started pushing herself away from the workstation, reaching for her crutches.

"What was it, Reesie?"

"Nothing, David. Really. Did you get something to eat?"

He looked at her for a few seconds. What was she trying to hide from him?

"No, I just now walked in. You want something? Fix you a sandwich?"

"I'm not hungry. Sitting around all day doesn't give you much of an appetite."

He didn't miss the hint of irritation in her words. "Well, I'm going to go grab something, okay? Sure you don't want anything?"

She shook her head and swung past him into the living room. He watched her navigate to the couch, then hop on one foot as she positioned herself to sit. She settled into the cushions, her back to him, and aimed a remote at the screen.

Dave went into the kitchen and scanned the contents of the refrigerator. "I did some calling today, Reesie, while I was at work. Got in touch with some of those physical therapy people the hospital told us about. Asked about when you needed to start, what you needed to do, that kind of thing."

He waited to see if she'd respond to his lead, but all he heard was the muted chatter of the television.

He got out some bread and meat, then reached for lettuce and tomatoes. As he squeezed mayo out onto one of his bread slices, he looked over his shoulder at Clarice. She was sitting on the couch and staring at the television, but her face hinted that her mind was somewhere else.

He thought about what he'd heard from the various physical therapists he'd talked to. Of course, none of them would give him many specifics without having a chance to see Clarice and learn more about her condition. But one thing was sure: recovering from a fracture of the type she'd received wasn't something anybody was taking lightly. Clarice could talk all she wanted about getting up and around in no time, but the professionals were saying months, not weeks. Still, the way she looked right now, it wasn't the time to tell her that.

He put the finishing touches on his sandwich and poured some tea into a glass. Dave thought about eating on the couch next to his wife, but he decided to sit at the kitchen counter instead. He was tired; he didn't need the burden of her silence to go with his supper.

∞

Julie looked at the telephone log sheet. The name of one of the call-ins was familiar to her for some reason. Johnson . . . Dave Johnson . . . she couldn't place it, but she knew the name from somewhere, that was for sure. The caller had requested information about therapy for a broken leg sustained in an automobile accident.

Johnson! Dave and Clarice Johnson from church; that's it. Julie remembered when the accident was announced and the pastor had asked them to pray for Clarice's speedy healing. The Johnsons sat closer to the front than she, and it was a big church, so it wasn't really any wonder she'd never run into them before. They were a nice-looking couple, Julie remembered. Clarice in particular always looked like she'd just stepped off the pages of *Vogue;* she wore the most interesting hats Julie had ever seen. They had a lot of friends at church, Julie guessed; they seemed to be the sort of folks who met people easily.

On a whim, Julie decided to follow up. Hey, if this place was cutting back on hours, it couldn't hurt to bring in more business, right? She looked at the number listed in the log and started dialing.

On the second ring, somebody answered. "All-Pro Janitorial. May I help you?"

"Hi, um, this is Julie Sawyer at All-Saints' Hospital physical therapy clinic. I was trying to reach a Mr. Dave Johnson? He called here earlier this week."

"Hang on." The music on hold was from a local oldies station; Julie had listened to most of a song by a group she thought was Earth, Wind & Fire when a man picked up the line. "This is Dave."

"Oh, hi, Dave. This is Julie Sawyer with All-Saints' physical therapy clinic. You called here a couple of days ago, right?"

"Yeah, that's me."

"Well, I just wanted to follow up with you and find out how Mrs. Johnson's doing and maybe see if there's anything we can do to help."

"Sure."

"First of all, let me ask a question. Don't you and Mrs. Johnson attend Lifeway Bible Church?"

"Yes, as a matter of fact, we do. How'd you know?"

"Actually, I go there, too, with my son. We've been coming for about a year now."

"Is that right? Well, that's kind of coincidental, isn't it?"

"Yeah, I guess so. I was pretty sure I remembered your names from when Pastor Wilkes said something during morning worship."

"Yeah, G.A. likes to embarrass me whenever he gets the chance." He gave a little chuckle.

"Well, anyway, as I said, I noticed you called and I just wanted to follow up. Is Mrs. Johnson working with anybody on her physical therapy?"

"No, not yet. But I think she's anxious to get started."

"Great. Is there any chance you'd consider coming in and letting me take a look, talk to you both for a bit, and give you some idea of what we'd recommend?"

"Ah . . . sure, I don't see why not. Let me talk to Clarice. When do you have an opening?"

They agreed on a time at the beginning of the next week and Julie penciled it in on her schedule. He exchanged a few more pleasantries, saying they'd be looking for her in church next Sunday.

When she hung up, she was smiling. It was nice to feel good about her work for a change. Who knew? Maybe she and Bryson would make a couple new friends.

Chapter Six

Clarice could tell David was in a happy mood as soon as she heard him walk in the door from the garage. She watched as he tossed his keys onto the kitchen counter. He was humming to himself and did a little boogaloo move, dancing to whatever song was in his head.

"Hey, baby girl," he said, walking toward her. "Give your man a little cupcake, what you think?" He leaned down and she gave him the most obligatory kiss she thought she could get by with. His face registered disappointment for an instant, but then he got all jiggy again.

"I got some good news for you, girl," he said. "We got us an appointment with a physical therapist next Tuesday. How you like that?"

She tried to show some enthusiasm, she really did. "Who is it?"

"Turns out she goes to church with us. Name is Julie Sawyer. She works in the clinic at the hospital."

"Really? How'd you get in touch with her?"

"I called there a couple of days ago to get some information, and she called today to follow up. She sounded cool, so I went ahead and made an appointment. That okay with you?"

"Well, yes . . . sure, I guess so."

"What's wrong, baby?"

How could she tell him? How could she admit to someone else that she was fighting depression? Since she'd gotten home from the accident and the reality of her injury had started to soak in—every time she rolled over in bed, every time she wanted to move from one place to another, every time she went to the bathroom, for goodness' sake—Clarice had been fighting to keep her head above water.

She forced a smile that felt more like a grimace. "Sorry, David. I'm just having a kind of down day."

"Well, that's all fit'n to change, sistuh. We gon' get you in there next Tuesday and they gon' get you back on the road to lookin' good in the hood, you know what I'm sayin'?" He scooted in beside her and put a hand on the back of her neck. "Now, how about a little of something that's good for both of us?" He leaned in for a kiss.

She turned her head and started reaching for her crutches. "David, please. I don't feel that way right now."

"What's wrong, baby? I thought you'd be happy. You wanting to get out of that cast, right? I thought I was helping."

She pulled herself to her feet. "You were. Are. I do want to get better and I appreciate what you did, I really do. I just—" She started moving toward the bedroom.

"You just what? Come on, Reesie. You got to talk to me, Shorty."

"I don't know. I can't right now, David. I'm sorry. I just need to lie down for a while."

She went into their bedroom and fell headlong onto the bed. She wished she could cry, or scream, or . . . something. Anything would be preferable to the gray, empty *nothing* she felt inside. It was scaring her, but she couldn't admit that to David. She could barely admit it to herself. Maybe he was right. Maybe seeing a therapist and doing something would give her a track to run on. Maybe feeling she had some ability to get her life back would pull her out of this weird emotional swamp she was stranded in. She probably ought to be grateful to David, in all honesty. She probably ought to give him what he was wanting. He was probably sulking on the couch right now, staring at the wall and wondering why his wife could barely stand to be in the same room with him. She wished it weren't that way; she wished she felt like getting skin-to-skin with him right now, right there in the living room on the couch. But she didn't. In fact, she couldn't. The thought was as hateful to her as crawling on broken glass. And that just made her feel even more guilty and helpless.

Why was her life slipping out of her control? All sorts of people got broken legs—sometimes people were laid up in bed for months. And they got better, didn't they? What was wrong with her? Why couldn't she snap out of this nasty funk that was sucking the life out of her?

She could hear David moving around in the kitchen. Glasses clinked and the silverware rattled in the drawer. He was getting himself something to eat. He'd eat by himself again tonight, as he had for quite a few nights in a row.

She ought to get up and go in there. She ought to try to talk to him, to show some interest in what he had to say. But her body refused to obey her intentions. The fog closed in on her and weighed her down.

∞

Bryson crouched on the starting block, tensing for the signal. Julie sat in the stands with her fists gripped in her lap, her eyes glued on the lean white body of her son as he readied himself.

It was a tri-city meet and this was Bryson's first time to swim on the boys' fourteen-and-under 200-meter relay. Bryson had the first leg, a position not as critical as the anchor but strategically important for setting the pace. Compared to the rest of the kids on the blocks and waiting at either end of the pool, he looked so small. He was three years younger than most of the kids in this race, and those three years made a huge difference at this time of a boy's life.

But if he was nervous, he didn't show it. In the car on the way to the meet, he'd been reading the newest Harry Potter book. He'd eaten his usual pre-meet breakfast: orange juice, cereal and milk, and three strips of bacon. She'd had to practically roll him onto the floor to get him awake. He was fine. She, on the other hand, was a nervous wreck.

The horn hooted and the racers arrowed into the water. Bryson came up first, arms churning. By the time they reached twenty-five meters, he was actually opening up a lead. He touched the side, as nearly as she could gauge, a little more than an arm's length before his nearest rival. The boy on the second leg made a clean start and maintained the lead Bryson had given him. The third-leg racer gave up a little; it was all going to come down to the anchor legs, and there were three teams within a body's length of each other. The anchors flashed into the water and the crowd was on its feet. The finish was going to be incredibly close. At the end, Bryson's team won by a few hundredths of a second—less than the length of a forearm. Julie was screaming and hugging people she didn't even know.

At the end of the pool, Bryson's teammates were surrounding him, clapping him on the shoulders and hugging him. Julie felt her eyes stinging with tears; the acceptance, not to mention enthusiastic appreciation, of these older boys would be like the rarest wine to her son. Now they were all hugging and high-fiving each other.

And then she remembered. Ted wasn't here. She saw Bryson's face turn toward her. He raised his fist in the air and pumped it in victory. Then she saw his eyes roving the crowd, looking for another face he wasn't going to find. After a few seconds he turned his attention back to his teammates and their coach, who had now joined them for some backslapping and handshaking.

Bryson kept his medal on the whole way home. He couldn't stop smiling.

"So, what were you thinking during the race?"

He stared out the window for a few seconds. "Well, when I'm in the water, I don't really think. I just am. You know?"

"In the zone, they call it."

"Yeah. Like that. I guess instinct kind of takes over."

"Makes sense to me. What about when your leg was done and the other guys were in the water?"

"It was weird. Once I was finished and out of the water, I was . . ." he looked at her, "I was nervous. I mean, with butterflies in my stomach and everything."

She glanced at him. "What's so weird about that?"

"I've never felt that way before. I've never been in a team event before, see? Every other time, when I get out of the water I know what the results are right then. But today . . ."

"You had to wait and depend on someone else."

"Yeah, I guess that's it. I'm not used to that."

"Well, I hate to tell you this, kiddo, but a lot of life is going to involve those two things."

He nodded his head and stared out his window for a while.

"I'm going to have to work on it then," he said finally.

"Yeah. We all do, one time or another." *Some of us more successfully than others, Bryson.*

That night she made sure he had his favorite supper: homemade mashed potatoes (boiled and mashed in her very own kitchen) with brown gravy (from a packet, of course) and extra-crispy fried chicken (from the Colonel). They sat in the living room on the floor in front of the television and watched a Disney movie about a bunch of misfit kids who form a hockey team and conquer the world. It was about the four hundredth time Bryson watched it, but it had been one of his favorites since he was old enough to walk. The videotape was getting worn and the movie was hardly visible in some places through the static, but Bryson knew every line and scene. One of these days she was going to have to break down and buy him a DVD player so they could get the movie with a little longer life span. And to be honest, Julie loved the scene where the unlikely team defeats the heavily favored bad guys as much as her son did. Who didn't love it when the underdog came out ahead?

When the movie ended, she sent him to the showers. "Church tomorrow, bud. Get cleaned up and get some sleep."

He went down the hall, and in a few minutes Julie heard the water start. For some reason, though, she couldn't quite make herself get up and take the greasy paper plates and used glasses back to the kitchen. The VCR whirred to the end of its rewind cycle and clicked off, and still she sat and stared at the blank blue screen of her television.

Today, for just a few minutes, she'd been able to forget about all the less-than-optimal facts in her life and simply rejoice in her son's success. It was a good moment, and she was grateful she'd been able to recognize and enjoy it. Sure, the junk came crowding back in soon enough, but somehow, having those few minutes of clarity made the junk easier to manage. *Sometimes,* she thought, *you just need reminders that good exists. You need a reason to hope things won't always be difficult.* Today, Bryson had given her that reminder. Sitting there in front of her blank TV with greasy paper plates in her hands, Julie said a silent little prayer of thanks.

∞

Dave woke up and looked at the clock. *Time to get going.* He sat up on the edge of the bed and rubbed his face and the top of his head to get a little circulation started.

He'd awakened with "Three Times a Lady" playing in his head. When he turned and realized Clarice was already out of bed and somewhere else in the house, he felt the return of the sadness that had been his constant companion since his clumsy attempt at love-making three days before.

He got up and went into the bathroom. Some hot water in the face would do him good; maybe it would rinse away some of these hangdog blues. After drying off he threw on a bathrobe and went into the kitchen. Clarice was sitting at the counter, her crutches leaning on the bar stool next to her, sipping coffee and staring out across the living room.

"You feel like going today?" he said.

She nodded her head.

"I don't mind going by myself, if you'd rather not," he said.

She gave him a quick look, then her eyes moved away again. "No, I want to go to church, David. I'll be ready in a few minutes."

"Okay, that's fine." He doctored his coffee with sweetener and milk, then carried his mug back to the bathroom.

It was like talking to somebody who wasn't really there. And the worst part of it was that he felt more and more as if he weren't really there, as if he were just saying lines somebody else had written. When had he started feeling this way with her?

While he was shaving, he heard her moving around in the bedroom, scooting hangers back and forth in her closet. This, at least, was normal: Clarice's morning ritual had always involved what appeared to Dave to be a large amount of unnecessary agonizing over which outfit to wear. Clarice always looked good; why did she think she had to fret so much over it? Even on her crutches, she'd be the one people would pick out of a crowd. She had that kind of presence. He guessed that was part of what made her a good real estate agent: Her appearance and manner inspired confidence. You looked at her and figured she had to know what she was talking about.

Dave padded across the bedroom toward his closet. Clarice was sitting on the corner of the bed, trying to reach the toenails of her right foot with a pair of clippers. But the cast was throwing off her balance and she couldn't quite manage it.

"You need some help, baby?"

He said it without thinking and almost immediately regretted it. *Why'd I say anything?* It was one more setup, one more opportunity for rejection, one more chance for her to remind him that she'd rather have just about anything before she'd want any help from him.

She looked at him, and he braced himself for the inevitable. But then he looked more closely at her face, and he realized something was there besides the blank stare she'd been wearing for most of the last week. There was indecision, uncertainty, and maybe a little fear.

What did she have to be afraid of? Didn't she know he'd walk barefoot across broken glass to do whatever he could for her?

"Yes, David," she said finally. "Would you mind?"

"Of course not, Reesie. Here, let me see."

He kneeled down and cradled her foot in his hand. He clipped the ragged, chipped toenails she hadn't been able to reach. "There you go, baby girl. Is that all right?"

He looked at her and saw the faintest glimmer of a look he hadn't gotten from her in longer than he could remember: appreciation. Right then, it was like showing a water fountain to a man who'd been digging ditches in the hot sun all day.

"Thank you, David."

He nodded and handed her the clippers. Then he went to his closet. For once, he didn't try to say or do too much.

Maybe there is still something there, Dave thought. Maybe Clarice would start to see that he really cared for her, really wanted to make her life better. He knew the part of him that wanted the best for her was still alive, still trying to hang on.

They drove to church in Clarice's car. Dave remembered again that he was supposed to call the insurance people about a replacement for his pickup. It was pretty inconvenient in his line of work not to have plenty of hauling space.

"Hopefully, here in a few days you'll have your car back," he said. "You'll be back blowing and going before you know it."

She gave him a little nod and tried to smile.

Dave parked in their usual spot in the church parking lot and came around to help Clarice out of the car. As usual, ten or twelve people stopped them to talk on the way to the sanctuary. By the time they got into their accustomed pew, the choir had already started the opening anthem.

When the service was over, as Dave was helping Clarice onto her crutches, someone tapped his shoulder. He turned and saw a woman of medium height with shoulder-length brownish-blonde hair. She stuck out her hand.

"Dave Johnson? I'm Julie Sawyer, from the physical therapy clinic. I talked to you on the phone?"

"Oh yes, hello!" He shook her hand and introduced her to Clarice.

"So, you guys still going to be able to make it on Tuesday?"

Dave looked at Clarice and she nodded. "Yes, Julie, we're planning to be there. I sure hope you can give me some good news."

"Well, we'll do the best we can. The important thing is to get started and I'm sure—" she turned around to see a young boy who was clearly her son holding out a stack of papers.

"Mom, can you hold this stuff for me? They gave it to us in Bible class."

"Bryson, can you say hello to Mr. and Mrs. Johnson?"

"Hi." Bryson nodded and waved.

"Hello there, Bryson," Dave said, grabbing the boy's hand and giving it a firm shake. "What are you, about twelve?"

"Eleven." He smiled and waved at Clarice.

"I'm pretty proud of this guy," Julie said, laying a hand on Bryson's shoulder. "His swim relay team won a gold at the tri-city meet yesterday."

"Is that a fact? Well, congratulations, Bryson."

Bryson grinned and ducked his head. "So, Mom, can you take that stuff?"

"I guess."

He handed her the sheaf of papers and vanished into the crowd.

"Good-looking boy," Dave said.

"Yes, he takes after his mother," Clarice said.

"Thanks. Well, I guess I'll see you guys on Tuesday. Just wanted to say hi."

"She seems nice," Clarice said, as they watched her walk away.

"Yeah. I think we're going to like her."

Chapter Seven

*T*he physical therapy clinic for All-Saints' was in a low brown building on the east side of the hospital complex. Dave parked as close as he could to the front door, then went around and helped Clarice out of the car. The parking lot sloped up slightly toward the building, so they had to take it kind of easy. Clarice was still not as steady on her crutches as she needed to be. Dave hoped that with a few sessions here she wouldn't need to get too much more familiar with them.

The front door slid open as they approached and they came into a lobby painted in relaxing cool pastel tones. A skylight provided natural illumination and the variety of potted plants, large and small, provided a garden feel. *So far, so good,* he thought.

They went to the front desk where an attendant waited. "We're here to see Julie Sawyer," Dave said. "We've got an appointment."

The young man flipped some pages on a clipboard. "Dave and Clarice Johnson?"

"Yeah, that's us."

"Through these doors on the right, third door on your right."

"Thanks."

The third door on their right, however, opened to a large room that appeared to be separated into about ten or fifteen cubicles by six-feet-tall cloth-paneled partitions.

"How we supposed to find her in this?" Dave wondered aloud. There were no information desks and no signs, nothing to give any sort of visual cue about how Julie Sawyer—or anyone else, for that matter—was to be located.

"I guess we'll have to ask somebody," Clarice said. She moved toward the nearest partition and stuck her head in the opening. "Excuse me, we're trying to find Julie Sawyer."

Dave heard the click of a phone handset and the sound of a button being pushed. "Julie?" a man's voice said. "Folks up front for you." The handset clattered back into its nest.

"Sorry to bother you," Clarice said in a low voice when she rejoined Dave, rolling her eyes toward the cubicle she'd just left. Dave shrugged.

In a few seconds Julie came around the corner, holding out her hand. "Hello, guys," she said. "Sorry, things are a little disorganized right now." She shook Dave's hand, then Clarice's. "I meant to be waiting for you up front, but I got caught on a call with a patient. Come on back, okay?"

They followed her past several of the tiny office spaces until she turned and gestured them through the doorway of one. The space was about eight feet by eight feet, barely big enough to hold the workstation and two chairs that were its only furnishings.

"Welcome to my spacious office," Julie said with an apologetic grin. "As you can see, we don't like our therapists feeling too comfortable at their desks. I guess it's a passive-aggressive management strategy to keep us out in the working area."

"It'd be effective if I worked here," Dave said.

As Clarice settled herself into a chair, Julie went to her desk and took out a file folder and pen.

"Okay, let's get some preliminaries out of the way." She took their names, addresses, and phone numbers at home, work, and for their mobile phones. She asked for the name of their family physician and also the orthopedist who treated Clarice in the hospital. She noted both Dave's and Clarice's insurance carriers and also the date, time, and place of the accident.

"I can probably get a lot of the clinical stuff from the orthopedist," she said then, "but I'd like for you guys to tell me whatever you can about the accident. It helps me understand a little more about how I can be helpful in your recovery process."

Dave told her everything he could remember.

"I was out when the collision happened," Clarice said, "but the first thing I remember was my leg hurting."

Julie nodded and took notes as Clarice related her experiences immediately following the collision. "Well, it's great the orthopedist on call that night got to you so quickly. Just gives you a little bit more of a jump on healing, you know? Okay, Clarice, how about talking to me about what it's been like for you these last few days, hauling that cast around and all."

Clarice gave her a strange look. "I thought you were a physical therapist, not a counselor."

Julie gave a little chuckle. "You'd be surprised how much cross-over there is. I guess I don't think of myself as just working with arms and legs; I work with people. To me, your mental and emotional attitude is as important as your physical performance. Not only that, but your state of mind has a tremendous impact on the way you approach your therapy and the way I approach helping you with it. Make sense?"

Dave realized he was nodding. This lady was impressive; she sounded almost like he did when he was working with his baseball team. Attitude and performance: you couldn't separate them.

He looked at Clarice. She'd pulled inside. He wondered why. What was so hard about answering Julie's question? Now she was looking at him like someone trying to do long division in her head.

"Hey, ya'll want me to step outside for a minute?" he said.

Clarice gave him a look that he could have sworn was gratitude. He realized Julie had caught it too: She was peering back and forth between him and Clarice. Her face carried an expression like someone who'd just found a pair of socks in the china cabinet.

"I'll take a walk," he said. He stood up and went out feeling a little bit like he'd just been kicked out of his own birthday party.

What was Clarice's problem? Why was it so hard for her to just say what was inside?

He went back to the hallway and walked to the nearest drinking fountain. Then he went back out to the main lobby and sat on one of the couches for a few minutes. When he judged the time had been long enough, he headed back to Julie's cubicle.

The two women were both looking at the floor when he came in.

"Ya'll get it all figured out?" he said, trying for a lighthearted tone.

Clarice gave a tight little nod.

"Yes, I think we've got plenty to work with," Julie said, looking at Clarice like she was afraid she might get contradicted. "Now, Mrs. Johnson—"

"Call me Clarice, please."

"Okay. Clarice, even if you're just sitting around at home, there are some things you can be doing that will get you ready for what we're going to be working on and even help you further down the road. First, I want you to work on wiggling your toes."

"That shouldn't be too hard."

"No, I mean *really* working them. Try to expand the range you can move each toe on your right foot. That'll keep the muscles and ligaments working and make it easier when we've got you ready to start walking. You'd be surprised how much muscles will atrophy when they're isolated and inactive like your calf muscles are right now. So I want you doing lots of work with those toes, all right?"

Clarice nodded.

"The next thing I want you to do is some leg lifts, both sideways and frontwards. We don't want your thigh muscles to get lazy just because you can't put weight on that leg yet, okay?"

"Sounds like PE class all over again," Dave said.

Julie grinned at him. "Not far off, actually. But we've got to make sure we do all we can to have Clarice's right leg ready for weight as soon as the doctor says the bone's ready. By the way, when's your next follow-up with him?"

"Later this week sometime," Clarice said, looking at Dave. "Thursday, maybe?" Dave nodded.

"Okay, great. Be sure and let me know what he says about weight-bearing for this leg."

"Okay."

"One other thing. Your left leg and hip are having to pretty much work double-duty right now. The last thing we want is to mess up the left side while the right side's healing. Take it easy as much as you can. Rest. Relax. It'll help you in the long run."

Dave saw from the way Clarice was sitting and the way she wouldn't look at anyone that this wasn't advice she was crazy about.

"Listen to her, Reesie," he said. "She knows what she's talking about."

Clarice nodded, but she still wouldn't look up.

Julie leaned forward and laid a hand on Clarice's arm. "I know it's hard for you right now, Clarice. You're used to doing what you want, when you want to do it. You probably feel at least a little helpless and isolated, don't you?"

Clarice gave Dave a guilty glance and nodded.

"That's totally normal," Julie said. "But remember what we talked about: you still get to choose how to react."

Dave was becoming more impressed with Julie by the moment. She was saying exactly what his wife needed to hear, whether Clarice realized it or not. Clarice's back was stiff and her face looked like she would've gotten up and walked out had she been able to do it without having to climb onto her crutches.

Doesn't she realize Julie is trying to help her?

"Well, that's about all we need to do for today," Julie said, standing. "Be sure and let me know what the doctor says at this next appointment, and we'll take it from there." She turned to Dave and held out a hand. "Dave, it's good to see you again. I'm glad you got in touch the other day."

"Me too, Julie, me too. I think you're just what the doctor ordered."

"Well, thanks. I'll do my best." He thought there was a little rose-shaded color rising in her cheeks.

She turned to Clarice, who was on her crutches now. "Clarice, I'm looking forward to working with you."

"Yes, Julie, it'll be great," Clarice said. Her voice was brittle with politeness and the smile she had on didn't reach past her lips. "Thanks for meeting with us." She swung past Dave and waited in the doorway, her back to Dave and Julie.

Dave looked at the therapist, and an expression of silent understanding passed between them. She shrugged and he gave her a sad little smile, and that was all they needed.

"Now, Dave, I'm counting on you to keep Clarice honest on her exercises," Julie said. Dave had a feeling it was more for Clarice's benefit than his, though.

"Oh, you can count on it. I used to be a high school coach, you know."

"Cool! You ever think of going into physical therapy?" They both laughed, but Clarice didn't.

When they got back to the car, Dave said, "Well? What did you think?"

"She'll be fine," Clarice said, looking away. "She seems nice, and she sounds knowledgeable."

I'll take that for now, Dave thought.

They drove home with neither one saying much. Dave helped Clarice into the house.

"I need to head on back to the office," he said.

"All right. See you later, I guess."

She offered him her cheek. He gave her a chaste peck.

He was about a block away from the house when his cell phone rang. He didn't recognize the number. "Hello?"

"Dave? This is Julie Sawyer."

"Oh! Hi, Julie."

"Excuse me for calling, but I just wanted to talk with you a little bit about Clarice's therapy."

"Yeah?"

"Yes. It's going to be really important for you to support her, you know."

"Well, sure. I've always tried to—"

"Yes, I know. I'm sorry, I didn't phrase that very well. I could tell in a second that you're very devoted to her."

"You could?"

"Oh sure. A woman knows."

There was something in her words that pleased him.

"Anyway, Dave, without saying anything specific about the conversation I had with Clarice, I just need to let you know that for folks like her, these early stages can be really tough. I'd guess Clarice is a pretty independent woman, right?"

"Oh yeah."

She laughed. "Yeah, I thought so. Just try not to take it too personally if she's kind of withdrawn. I'd imagine she's a little depressed."

Clarice? Depressed? "You think so?"

"Sure. For active people, an injury like this can be a real shocker. But the good news is that my job is to help her get back to her normal routine as quickly and safely as possible. And I want you to be as comfortable as possible with the process, because I can tell how much she means to you."

"Thanks. And I want to tell you how impressed I was with everything you said while we were in your office. I can tell you really care about the people you work with."

"I appreciate that. And yes, I do. So if there's anything I can do to make this experience better for you and Clarice, just give me a call, okay?"

"You got it, Julie."

"Great. Okay, I'll be in touch."

"I'll look forward to that."

He punched the end button and wondered why he'd said that last thing he did, and if he meant anything by it he shouldn't have.

When he got to the office, he started to put his cell phone in his pocket. He looked at the screen and realized Julie's work number was still showing. Hers was the last call he'd received. He looked at the screen for a few seconds. Figuring he'd probably need the number again sometime during the course of Clarice's treatment, he thumbed the sequence that saved the number in his phone's memory.

∞

Clarice heard David close the front door and then start the engine of her Accord. He'd be back at the office in about ten minutes or so, back into the details of his day and his staff and his customers and his business.

And she'd be here, watching the hours pass and wondering if she was ever going to feel normal again.

She decided to call in to her office. Surely that would be better than just moping around, waiting for time to pass. She picked up the phone and dialed the number.

"Hastings Properties and Real Estate; Clarice Johnson's office. How may I help you?"

"Hi, Michelle, it's Clarice."

"Well, hello there, girlfriend! You back on your feet? Or should I say 'foot'?"

"I'm trying, Michelle. How are you doing?"

"'Bout it, 'bout it. It's been kind of a madhouse around here today, but we hangin'. Girl, when you gonna get yourself back up to work? I'm missing my sister time. I'm liable to start losing it up in here, if I don't see your beautiful black face pretty soon."

"I know, Michelle, it's been hard. Hopefully David'll hear something from the insurance company pretty soon on his pickup and we won't be a one-car house anymore."

"Yes, and how is that fine man of yours? You making him bring you breakfast in bed? Or anything else?"

Clarice winced as Michelle's suggestive giggle came over the line. Michelle was a street-tough girl who'd pulled herself up by her own bootstraps. She'd come to the office a year or so ago from a job at Judson Enterprises with glowing recommendations from both her supervisor and Mrs. Judson herself, who was not exactly known for handing out accolades. Michelle was smart and a quick study; she was soon promoted from receptionist to the sales assistant pool. When Clarice started establishing herself as a top producer for the office, she'd requested Michelle as her personal sales assistant. She thought they made a superb team. Michelle had recently reconciled with her estranged husband, and sometimes she still carried on like a newlywed. Clarice hadn't minded it so much before, but at this moment Michelle's enthusiasm for the conjugal bed grated on her like fingernails on a chalkboard. She tried to keep the irritation out of her voice.

"Michelle, now girl, you know we've been married too long for all that."

"Well, maybe so, but you never know, girl; a little of the right kind of exercise might help you get well that much quicker. It sho' helps my attitude, I know that."

Got to change the subject! "Michelle, have we heard anything from the Townsends yet?"

Michelle turned on a dime; now she was all business. "I followed up with them yesterday, per your request. They're considering a counteroffer. I told them the buyers had contingencies, but they seemed okay with that. They're still interested, but they would entertain other offers at this point."

"Good. Well, we don't have anybody else to bring to the table right now, so let's just make sure we keep in touch with them and see if the buyers are serious. Their agent seemed to think they were. What about Reid?"

"Mrs. Reid's trying to bring her husband around. He still thinks they can sell the property themselves and save the commission, but she's ready to move to the same town as her grandbabies and is trying to make him see the light. I sent her a note yesterday. She asked about you, by the way—wanted to know if you were doing okay."

"How sweet. Tell her I'm fine and see if there's anything we can do to help Mr. Reid get off the dime."

"Got it."

"Did the Farber lady ever show up?"

"She was in this morning, as a matter of fact, asking for you. They just got to town last week and are still settling in. I told her about the accident and she said that was fine, they'd just set up an appointment sometime in the next week or so. I tried to nail her down, but she seemed like she was in a hurry. I think they're still interested, though."

"I hope so. I'm planning to come in for a while, maybe toward the end of this week. I'll let you know so maybe you can set it up for me to show her some houses. I don't know for sure how I'm going to be able to navigate, though, with these stupid crutches."

"From what I heard, your leg was busted up pretty good."

"Yeah, afraid so. But I saw a physical therapist today, so I'm hoping I can start getting back to normal soon."

"Well, sister girl, you don't worry about a thing on this end. I've got your back."

"I know you do, Michelle, and you don't know how much I appreciate that."

To her horror, Clarice felt her throat closing with a sudden onrush of emotion. She clamped her jaws together and prayed Michelle hadn't noticed, but no such luck.

"Clarice? Honey, you all right?"

"I'm fine, Michelle, I'm just . . . a little stressed, I guess, with everything that's happened."

"Well, sure you are, sure you are. But don't you worry, my sister. I've been praying over you every day, ever since I heard about the wreck, and the Lord's going to take care of you, don't you worry. Not only that, I've got Miz Ida praying for you, too."

Clarice had heard many "Miz Ida" stories from Michelle. She

was an elderly woman from Michelle's old neighborhood who had been not only like a grandmother but as much of a mother as Michelle had while growing up. To hear Michelle tell it, Miz Ida and Jesus sat on the front porch together every single day. "She's got a wisdom that doesn't come from her own head," Michelle often said. Clarice felt she could certainly stand to have the prayers of such a person.

"Thanks, Michelle. I'll be okay. I just need to get everything back on track and I'll be fine."

"There you go. You just focus on getting that leg better, and let Michelle take care of the details, all right?"

"Sounds good. Okay, I'll probably check back in a day or two. But call me if you can set up something with the Farbers, all right?"

"You got it, sister."

Clarice hung up. Talking to Michelle had actually helped her a little bit. She felt slightly reconnected to the office and her business, and it was reassuring to know Michelle was bringing her efficiency to bear on keeping Clarice's clients informed and serviced. Clarice guessed she could probably get back up to speed at work without too much trouble.

But her personal life . . . the way she sometimes felt inside—all jumbled up and fragile, as if anything could hurt her—was another story. Clarice wasn't sure she could keep it together long enough to get back to work. There were moments when it took all her concentration just to keep from running out the front door in a panic. If getting onto her crutches wasn't so much trouble, she might have done it.

She could just imagine what Mama would say: "Girl, you better get yourself together. A broken leg ain't the end of the world. Why don't you think about what you need to do instead of getting yourself all lathered up over something you don't even know what it is?"

The fact was that Clarice didn't have an answer to her mama's question. She didn't understand what she was afraid of. The source of her dread and anxiety was a mystery to her. All she knew was that she had no defense against an enemy that seemed to live inside her own mind; she carried it with her wherever she went. There was no escape. And that was maybe the most frightening thing of all.

Her cell phone rang. Clarice looked down at the screen; it was Mama.

Chapter Eight

*W*ondering if her mother had somehow sensed her thoughts from afar, Clarice pressed the button to answer the call.

"Mama?"

"Clarice, how you doing today, honey?"

She sounded all anxious and concerned, like you'd expect a mother to be, but Clarice thought carefully about her answer anyway. After all, it was Mama.

"Not too bad, Mama."

"You sure about that?"

How did she know? I'd have sworn I kept it out of my voice.

"Yeah, Mama, I'm—"

"I think maybe I better come down there and see for myself."

"Mama, really, David is taking good—"

"Yeah, I know about David. A man's got his uses—"

"—but taking care of the sick isn't one of them. Really, Mama, we're doing just fine."

"Well, you don't sound right to me. I'm going to have Freddy drop me off there next Friday."

Her phone beeped, ending the call. Clarice stared at the screen for maybe ten full seconds. Then she sighed and let her head fall back on the cushions. Sharing her house with David and Mama. *What a cozy little triangle this will be . . .*

Julie looked at her weekly planner and shook her head in disgust. She had five empty slots that she couldn't fill because doing so would put her over the maximum hours the clinic had imposed on all the therapists. It was crazy; because of some bean-counter's fretting over insurance companies and what they were willing to pay for policyholders' therapy, she was supposed to limit the number of people she was seeing. Not only did it not make sense for the people who needed her help, it didn't make sense for Julie's bank account, either.

Ted was late with the child support check this month, again. It had gotten so that Julie almost looked on Ted's payments as a surprise bonus. Meanwhile, Bryson's swim coach wanted to take the team to a meet out-of-state, and even with the fund-raising the Y and the kids were doing, each parent was being asked to pony up around two hundred and fifty dollars. Julie didn't know where that was going to come from, especially since it was due in two weeks' time—exactly halfway between her already-decreased paychecks from the clinic.

She stared at her planner and fumed . . . and thought. She started remembering what some of the other therapists had threatened as they left the employee meeting and wondered if she could see a few patients on her own time, outside the clinic's hours. She wasn't sure, but she thought as long as the patients had a doctor's order and Julie had a valid license to practice therapy in the state, she ought to be able to take on some outside work. She might need to do a little research on the reimbursement question, but the professional association had resources to help with that; she just needed a little time to go online and get the facts.

She looked at her contact list and started thinking about whom she might call. Her pencil paused at Dave and Clarice Johnson. What about them? Given Clarice's emotional state, Julie thought she might welcome the chance to work on her recovery in the privacy of her own home instead of taking on an unfamiliar regimen in front of a roomful of strangers. Slowly she drew a circle around the Johnsons' names as she thought. A few seconds later she picked up the phone.

∞

"Clarice, I got a call today from Julie down at the clinic. She had an idea I thought you'd want to hear."

Clarice was sitting at the computer desk, her fingertips poised above the keyboard. Dave stayed in the doorway; he decided not to try to see whatever it was she was working on. The way her state of mind had been lately, she might club him over the head with one of her crutches.

"What's that?" she asked.

"She said that if it was agreeable to us—to you—that she'd be willing to come to the house and get you going on your therapy. She said you might appreciate the privacy, especially at first, and she had some open time in her schedule. She said all we needed to do was let her know what the doctor said, and she could get you started as early as next week, depending on how the doctor rates your leg. Well? What do you think?"

Dave had immediately liked the idea, but he knew better than to let Clarice know that, so he tried to downplay his own opinion of the plan. He watched her as her eyes flickered back and forth, considering.

"That might be nice," she said finally. "I've been trying to re-member to do the things she said that day, but I don't know how much more she'll want to start with . . ." She looked up at him, and Dave saw the closest thing to enthusiasm he'd seen in his wife's face since before the accident. "Yes, David, I think that sounds good. What did you tell her?"

"I told her I was gonna have to talk to you. But if you want, I'll call her tomorrow and get it set up."

"No, why don't you let me call her? Actually, I never really thanked her properly for all the time she took with us at her office. I need to mend that. Let me do it, okay?"

He studied her face, looking for signs that Clarice was putting up some kind of smokescreen to keep from having to actually take action, but he didn't see that. He nodded and smiled at her. "Okay, baby. You got it."

And then she smiled at him. "Thanks, David. Thanks for everything."

"Ain't no thing, baby girl. Goes with the territory. You want something to eat?"

∞

The next day was Thursday. At her appointment, the orthopedist looked at Clarice's X-rays and nodded.

"Mrs. Johnson, your bones are knitting nicely. I did a pretty fine job of getting them reset, if I do say so myself. I might just put these X-rays on a billboard with the ones we took the night you came in . . . sort of a before-and-after kind of thing. What do you think about that?"

Clarice gave him a cautious smile. "Sounds good to me—if that means my leg's getting better."

"Well, it is," the doctor said. "Not that you're ready to go out dancing, but I think these bones are okay for partial weight-bearing."

"What does that mean?" David said.

"Among other things, it means you can start light physical therapy."

Clarice saw David's grin and realized she was wearing one, too.

"It also means I can take this fiberglass job off and give you a pneumatic walking cast. Not exactly the height of fashion, but considerably more portable than what you've got now. And you can take it off to bathe. Unless, of course, you'd rather keep what you've got . . ."

"No, I don't think so," Clarice said quickly.

"Hallelujah!" David said. "You hear that, Reesie?"

"Sounds like I need to call Julie again," Clarice said.

Clarice agreed to have Julie come over the following Tuesday afternoon at three o'clock for a one-hour session. "Wear something comfortable, something you can move in," Julie suggested. "We won't
need much in the way of equipment—nothing I can't haul in my
trunk. I'll see you then."

Clarice hung up, realizing that for the first time in a good while,
she was looking forward to something.

Then she remembered. Tomorrow was Friday, and Mama was
coming.

∞

Dave heard the sound of tires rolling up the driveway and looked
at Clarice. She gave him a little shrug and tried to smile. He
pushed himself out of his chair and walked to the front door like
a man going to the gallows. He went outside just in time to see
Clarice's mother hauling a suitcase out of the trunk of her son's
car.

"Here, Mrs. Clark, let me get that for you."

"Never mind that, I been carrying my own suitcase for nearly
seventy years and I can still do it for myself. Freddy, you'll be back
to pick me up next Friday?"

"Yes, Mama."

"All right. Drive carefully."

She walked past Dave, grunting with the weight of her suitcase,
and stepped through the front door. Dave watched her go, shaking
his head.

"Just as cuddly as ever," Freddy said, giving him a sad smile.

"I feel you. How's it going, Freddy?"

Clarice's brother shrugged. "Doin' awright, I guess. How's
Clarice?"

"Getting there. She sees her physical therapist early next week."

"Hope Mama likes her," Freddy said, grinning.

"Well, if she don't, ain't nobody gon' have to wonder how she feels," Dave said.

"I heard that. Catch you later, man. I gotta get on back."

"Take it easy. I'd say thanks for bringing her down, but—"

Freddy waved him off, laughing.

∞

On Tuesday, Julie rang the doorbell right on cue. Clarice was waiting for her.

"Hi, Clarice. Ready to get this show on the road?" She had a foam pad rolled up and tucked under one arm.

"Sure. Come on in." Clarice moved herself away from the door and Julie walked into the living room.

"Wow, Clarice. This is a beautiful house. Oh . . . hello." Julie was looking toward the couch. Mama sat with her arms crossed over her chest.

"Thank you. We've worked hard at it. Julie, this is my mother, Mary Clark."

Julie stuck out her hand. After the briefest hesitation, Mama took her hand. "Glad to know you."

"Yes, ma'am. You came down to help your daughter for a few days?"

"I came to make sure she's able to help herself."

Julie absorbed this with only the barest waver of her smile. "Well . . . it's nice to meet you." She turned toward Clarice, looking relieved to have that particular bit of socializing taken care of.

"Okay, so the first thing I want to do is see you get up and down off the couch," Julie said.

"Really?"

"Sure. You've got to start where you are and go from there, right?"

"I guess."

"So just crutch over to the couch there and sit down beside your mom, then get back up again." Julie tossed the rolled-up mat onto the floor behind the couch and watched as Clarice lowered herself onto the couch, sat for a few seconds, then got herself back up on her crutches.

"Not bad, not bad. The doctor said your leg was partial weight-bearing, right?"

"Right."

"Okay. So this time, I want you to do the same thing, only with one crutch instead of two."

"You sure about that?"

"Absolutely. I'm going to spot you, so you don't have to worry about falling or anything. But one immediate goal I have is getting you where you can use a cane instead of those clunky crutches. And with that snazzy new walking cast, you ought to be able to do it. We just need to work on your confidence a little bit."

For the next fifteen minutes, Julie helped Clarice get up and down from the couch using only one crutch. Next, she had her walk across the living room to the kitchen. Finally, she had her go all the way to the bathroom, open the shower door, and step inside.

"See how well you did that? Now, for a while, when you're taking a shower you might want to sit in a plastic or aluminum lawn chair, just until you're feeling good about your balance again."

"Okay."

"But we're going to start working on that, too, pretty soon."

Clarice was getting tired just listening to the plans Julie had for her. But she felt good, too; she was finally doing something about her situation. This was more familiar territory.

Next, Julie had Clarice go back to the living room. The therapist spread out the foam mat and asked Clarice to lie down on the mat on her back with both legs stretched out straight.

"Okay, I want you to bend the knee on your good leg. Then I want you to slowly raise your right leg—keep it fully extended—up to the level of your knee. Got it?"

"I think so. These are those leg lifts you warned me about, right?"

"You got it. And now you're going to wish you'd been working on them before I got here." They both laughed. Clarice was feeling as if a cold, dark crust were breaking loose inside her, letting the air get to her lungs for the first time in weeks.

"Okay, now hold it right there at the top for one . . . two . . . three . . . counts. And now let it back down. Slowly, though."

"This cast is heavy!"

"Oh, gosh, I totally forgot. You can take the cast off while we do this."

"I can?"

"Sure. The cast is to hold the bones when you're walking or putting slight weight on them. They're knitted, just not securely. But for stuff like this, you can take the cast off, just like when you're bathing. Just one more reason to look forward to our little visits."

"I heard that." Clarice sat up and started ripping back the Velcro straps that secured the cast. She slid the bootlike device off, then carefully peeled away the athletic sock that protected her skin from chafing.

"Looks like you lost some muscle mass while you were in the hard cast," Julie said.

"I know. I look deformed with these scars and all."

"No, you look like someone who had a broken leg."

Clarice really liked Julie; her encouraging manner and expertise were doing wonders for Clarice's confidence.

"Okay, lie back down and let's do a few more reps. And since you don't have that walking cast on anymore, your form should be perfect."

"You sure you weren't Jane Fonda in another life?"

"Where I come from, the stuff she did was for sissies."

Julie took her through several repetitions of the straight-leg lift. Then they moved to what Julie called hip abductions. She had Clarice lie on her back with both legs extended and then move her broken leg in a scissor motion to the side to try and extend the range of her hip joint. For the weeks following the accident, she explained, Clarice's right hip joint hadn't had anything more strenuous to do than just hang there, holding her motionless leg. Sure enough, when Clarice did the exercise, it felt like her hip had been in cold storage for about a year.

"When you're a little stronger," Julie said, "I'll have you do that lying on your left side, scissoring your right leg up into the air. But let's build a little more flexibility and strength first."

"Amen, sister."

Next, Julie took her to the kitchen counter and had her hold onto it as she raised her right knee like someone in a marching band. She did that several times and then, at Julie's direction, Clarice kicked her leg straight out behind her, then to the side.

"Okay, that's enough, Clarice. You do ten reps daily of everything I showed you today and it ought to keep you busy until the next time we get together."

"I heard that. I think I was wrong about you. You weren't Jane Fonda; you were Idi Amin."

"Whatever it takes to get you back on both feet. And I plan to recruit Dave as my assistant, just to make sure you don't slack off when I'm not around."

At hearing her husband's name, Clarice felt a little of the wind leave her sails. "Oh, he'll keep me honest; don't worry about that."

"He really cares about you, Clarice. You're lucky to have him."

There was a sniff from the couch.

Clarice looked at Julie. "I guess you're right. But what about you? I don't see a ring on your finger, Julie."

Julie gave her a sad smile and a shrug. "Kinda lost my interest in wearing it after he moved out," she said.

"I'm sorry. That must have been hard."

"Yeah, I don't recommend it."

A few seconds of silence slogged past in cement shoes.

"Well, I'd better get going. I'm supposed to pick up my son from school and take him to a swim club on the other side of town. His coach has arranged for a former Olympic trainer to work with them today."

"Fantastic. He seems like a good boy."

"Light of my life," Julie said. "I don't know how I'd live without him."

Clarice smiled, hoping the jab of chagrin she felt wasn't showing in her face. Julie helped Clarice get back into her walking cast, then gathered up her mat.

"Good-bye, Mrs. Clark. It was nice to meet you." Mama gave her a limp wave; Clarice suppressed the urge to roll her eyes.

She and Julie agreed on a time to meet the following week as Clarice was walking her to the door. She watched as Julie went to her car and got in. But the car didn't start. Clarice watched as Julie fiddled with the ignition. After a few minutes, she shook her head and got back out of the car.

"I've been having trouble with my ignition switch," she said. "Looks like it finally jammed completely. I can't start my car."

Just then, David pulled into the driveway.

"Hi, Julie," he said as he got out. "How's the patient?"

"The one who lives here is great," Julie said, "but the one I'm driving is terminal. My car won't start. I think the ignition switch is jammed."

"David, she has to go get her son from school," Clarice said. "Can you take her and drop her off? Maybe we can get somebody to come look at her car in the meantime."

"Oh, that's too much trouble," Julie protested.

"No, you go on," Clarice said. "David?"

"Well . . . sure. Come on, Julie. What school does Bryson go to?"

Julie looked at Clarice, then David. "Are you sure?"

David walked around and opened the passenger door of the Accord. "One hundred percent sure. Let's go."

Clarice went back inside and closed the door. Mama was staring at her, and Clarice knew something was coming. She just didn't know what.

"He took her home?"

"Yes, ma'am. Her car won't start."

"Mmm-hmm. That's what she said."

"Mama! What are you hinting at?"

"Nothing." Mama picked up the magazine she'd been looking at and stuck it in front of her face like a shield.

Chapter Nine

I really appreciate this," Julie said, as they were driving away from Dave's house.

"And I really appreciate what you're doing for Clarice, so let's just call it even."

They drove for a while in silence. "So, how'd she do today? Really?" Dave asked finally.

"Better than I expected, actually," Julie said. "Her attitude seems a lot more positive. More so when we finished than when we started, as a matter of fact."

"Yeah, I could see it in her face, even in just the short time I was there. You were good for her. Just what she needed."

"I'm glad you think so. I meant what I said before. I really do think it's great the way you look after her."

Dave shrugged. "I don't know. Clarice is pretty independent-minded. Sometimes it seems like I get in her way more than I help."

He could feel her eyes on him. "Maybe you do and maybe you don't," Julie said in a few seconds, "but I'm here to tell you that a man who really cares is not such a common article as some people seem to think. Clarice is lucky to have you."

Something started blooming in Dave's chest then, a spot of warmth that started small and grew, spreading a comfortable glow all through his insides.

"Thanks. That was a nice thing for you to say."

"Just call 'em as I see 'em," she said, looking out the windshield. She pointed. "Left here."

"Bryson goes to Thomas Middle School?"

Julie nodded.

"Yeah, when I was coaching, we used to get some of our best athletes from Thomas."

"What did you coach?"

"Football, of course. No getting around that in this part of the country. But I really loved coaching baseball. I still coach a little, as a matter of fact. Just volunteer, though . . . Little League."

"No kidding? I always thought Bryson would get involved in Little League someday, but we just never got around to it, I guess. He has his swimming, of course."

"Well, hey, we should get him out on the diamond sometime. The kids over in Eastside are a little rough around the edges, but Bryson might enjoy it."

"Eastside? Why would you coach over there? Oh, gosh. Sorry if that sounded bad."

"Naw, that's what everybody says when they find out what I'm doing. Shoot, even my lawyer friend said it—right before I talked him into being my assistant. I'll tell you, Julie, the way I see it, most folks talk about how bad the cities are getting, but they don't get around to doing anything about it. And the reason they don't, I think, is because they think they can't. They think what the cities need is more police or more government money or more jail time or higher fences or . . . I don't know. But what they ought to be doing is figuring out what they *can* do, then doing it someplace where it can make a difference.

"Now, me, I'm a coach at heart. Always have been, always will be. So I figure what I can do is take some kids who were born competitive—good Lord, you have to be competitive just to stay alive over in Eastside—and give them something to compete about that's constructive instead of destructive. I don't know if our little team'll keep them out of the gangs and off crack, but it's bound to be better than if they weren't playing ball. At least, that's how I see it."

She was looking at him with a strange expression, something between a smile and disbelief. "That's wonderful, Dave. Really wonderful. I'm very impressed."

He shrugged and waved her off. "What about you, Julie? What are you interested in—besides your son's swimming career, of course."

She gave him a sort of confused smile and stared off into the distance for a few seconds. "You know, that's a good question. I got married and had a baby, and for a while I was a stay-at-home mom, which pretty much took up twenty-five hours a day. Then Ted left and I had to go back to work. That plus taxiing Bryson back and forth seems to soak up most of the average week. So I guess I don't really know what I'm interested in, to tell you the truth."

"Ted was your husband?"

"Was. Yeah."

"I'm sorry."

"Me too."

"But there must have been something, back in the day, you know? When Julie was a little girl, what did she dream of doing someday?"

He drove a block and a half before she answered.

"I always wanted to learn how to fly," she said in a voice so quiet he could barely hear.

He thought about that for a minute. "Well . . . I bet you get the chance someday."

"Thank you. I hope you're right."

The space in the front seat was different now. It felt to Dave as if something had crossed the empty air between them, like a thin line carried across a canyon by a bowshot. Sometimes that was how you started a bridge. What was starting here?

Bryson was waiting by the flagpole in front of the school, but he wasn't expecting the Accord. Julie had to get out of the car and wave to attract his attention. He hustled over and crawled into the back-seat.

"Car wouldn't start," Julie told him. "Lucky for us Mr. Johnson was willing to give us a ride, or you'd be pretty late for swim practice."

"Thanks, Mr. Johnson," Bryson said.

"Mr. Johnson's my dad," Dave said, "and he lives in Tennessee. How about you just call me 'Coach'?"

"Sure . . . Coach."

"Now, how do we get to this swim club?"

Cruising down the freeway, Dave listened as Bryson filled his mom in on the school day. It tickled him to hear Bryson complaining about his teachers and gossiping about who was "going out" with whom.

"Say, Bryson. When you said Cal and Becky were 'going out,' what exactly does that mean? Where they going?"

"Well, they're not really going anywhere, they're just . . . going out."

"If they not going anywhere, how can they be going out?"

"See, going out is like . . . they *like* each other."

"Oh, I see. You like Cal, too?"

"Well, sure . . . I mean, he's a friend of mine, I guess, but, umm . . . he and Becky are going out, see, and—"

"But where they going?"

Julie was grinning at him, then at her son, clearly enjoying listening to him trying to explain to a rank outsider the intricate customs governing middle-school romance.

"If you can make sense of this, Dave, you're way more hip than me," she said.

"Aw, I'm just trying to give Bryson a hard time."

Bryson rolled his eyes and grinned.

They got to the swim club; Julie and Bryson got out. Bryson came to Dave's window and stuck out his hand. "Thanks again, Coach. Sorry my mom's car broke down."

"You know what, Bryson? I'm glad it did, 'cause I really enjoyed talking to you."

"Me too." He shouldered his backpack and jogged toward the entry to the pool. Julie was still standing beside the car, watching her son go. She turned to Dave.

"Dave, really, thanks so much. And thanks for talking to Bryson. He thrives on male attention. His dad doesn't give him much of that."

"Well, that's too bad, 'cause I can tell a great kid when I see one. You gonna need a ride home from here? And what about in the morning?"

"Oh, I can probably get one of the other moms to take me home from here. In the morning we'll figure it out. What should I do about my car being in your driveway?"

"You should let me worry about it."

She gave him a confused look. "Well . . . if you say so."

"I do. You got your cell phone?"

She nodded.

"All right. I'll take care of your car and call you to let you know what I did. And I can come by and get you and Bryson situated in the morning, no problem."

She offered him a grateful smile. "I don't know what to say."

Dave shrugged. "Don't say nothin'. Now you better get on in there and watch your boy make you proud."

As he drove away from the swim club, Dave noticed a tiny voice at the back of his skull asking if he was sure about his motives in being so nice to Julie and her son. He told the voice to mind its own business, that he was just doing what any slightly helpful person would do under the same circumstances. But the voice didn't buy that. Instead, it asked him if he would've pulled out all the stops like this if Julie, say, weighed about two hundred and ten pounds, or if Bryson had a smart mouth, or if Clarice had been sitting in the front seat listening to everything he and Julie had talked about.

When Julie was a little girl, what did she dream of doing someday?

The voice wanted to know if that was the kind of question you asked somebody when all you were trying to do was be helpful.

Dave decided to ignore the voice for a while.

When he got home, he called the garage where he took the vehicles for his business. He told Frank, the owner, that he needed a favor and got him to send a guy over with a replacement ignition key cylinder for Julie's car. Frank groused about it a little, but Dave reminded him how much business he gave the garage and Frank let up, as Dave knew he would. They'd done this dance before. Then he called Brock to see if his friend could follow him to Julie's house in his car so he could deliver her vehicle tonight. Brock was just leaving the office and suggested that Dave call him when he was ready to go.

Clarice was standing at the kitchen counter doing some kind of leg exercise when he came in. "You get them where they needed to be?" she asked when he hung up from talking to Brock.

Dave nodded. "I'll have Brock bring me back. She needs her car in the morning."

Clarice agreed. "David . . . you were right about her. She was really helpful to me. For more than just my leg, too."

There was a loud sniff from the couch. They both looked in Mama's direction, then back at each other. Dave rolled his eyes and Clarice gave him a little grin and a shrug.

"I'm glad to hear it, baby girl," he said. "You been pretty down for a while now. It's good to see you doing your exercises and working on getting better."

Clarice looked as if she were going to say something else, but then she shook her head.

"What?"

"Nothing," she said. "I'll tell you later." She tucked a crutch under her right arm and went toward the bedroom. "I'm going to change," she said over her shoulder.

Dave warmed some leftover lasagna in the microwave. He put servings on three small plates and set two of them on the kitchen counter. The third one he carried toward the couch.

"Mrs. Clark? You want some lasagna?"

"I guess so," she said, giving the lasagna a look like she thought it might contain some kind of insect.

Dave was walking back toward the kitchen when, on a whim, he went to the wine rack and pulled out a bottle of Chilean merlot. He uncorked it and poured a glass for himself and one for Clarice. "How about some dinner?" he said when she came back to the living room a few minutes later.

"All right."

Not much enthusiasm, but at least she didn't tell me to eat in the garage.

They ate sitting in the armchairs on either side of the couch, watching a fairly stale rerun of *Fresh Prince of Bel-Air*. About the time Dave had finished his lasagna, the doorbell rang. It was the mechanic from Frank's place; he'd finished replacing the ignition cylinder in Julie's car. Dave gave him his credit card information and told him to have Frank run it through and send him a receipt. He also handed the guy a twenty. "Get some burgers on the way home, man. And thanks for coming over and taking care of this." The guy stuck the bill in his pocket and left.

He closed the door and went back to the couch to pick up his plate and empty wine glass. Clarice was looking at him curiously.

"What?"

"That was a nice thing you just did, paying for her car."

"Why? You think I shouldn't have?"

"No, I just said it was nice."

Clarice's mother was staring at both of them like somebody listening to people speaking in a foreign language.

"Yeah, but you said it with something else hiding in the back of your face," Dave said.

"I don't know what you're talking about, David. Can't I give you a compliment?" She moved her eyes pointedly toward her mother, then back to him.

She's trying to give me props in front of her mom. Dave wasn't sure why Clarice thought that was going to change anything between him and her mother, but he guessed he ought to be grateful she was making the attempt.

"Sure, baby, whatever. Thanks."

She turned back toward *Fresh Prince*. She carefully pried a piece of lasagna away from the portion still remaining on her plate, speared it very precisely with her fork, put it in her mouth, and began chewing. Dave picked up his plate and glass and went to the kitchen. He felt Mrs. Clark's eyes following him every step of the way.

Maybe Clarice was right, or maybe he was just feeling guilty because of what that voice in his head had said back at the swim club. There wasn't anything wrong with paying for something when somebody had helped your family the way Julie had. Was there?

He called Brock and asked him to come on over. Then he called Julie. She answered on the first ring. He could hear the sound of kids' voices and splashing in the background.

"Y'all haven't left yet?"

"Oh, hi, Dave. Actually, we were just walking out when you called."

"Okay, you want me to bring your car to your house? It's all ready for you."

"Dave . . . that is so nice, but I can't let you pay for—"

"Uh-uh, now. Don't even go there. All I need to know is where to bring your car. My buddy's going to follow me over there and bring me home. You remember the guy I told you about? The lawyer? So, where do we need to go?"

She gave him her address and he said it back to her. "All right then. See you there."

Brock knocked on the door a few minutes later.

"Reesie, I'll be right back, okay?" said Dave. She waved at him without looking. But her mother was staring at him hard enough for both of them.

Nothing wrong with what I'm doing. If I was planning an affair, would I be talking with her in front of my wife . . . and her mother, for crying out loud? 'Course not. Just helping somebody out, that's all it is. Ain't nothing to it.

He told Brock the address as he was opening Julie's car door. He nearly broke his kneecap on the steering wheel before he remembered she was shorter than he was. When he had the seat adjusted so he could fit behind the wheel, he inserted the key the mechanic had given him. The switch turned smoothly and the car started right up.

Julie lived in a pretty nice part of town. Her house was a nice, fairly new brick home with a low, rambling modern-ranch look. Dave guessed the house was one of the few useful things her ex had left her. He hoped the guy was sending child support; the payments on this place couldn't be chicken feed.

He pulled into the driveway almost at the same time Julie and Bryson were getting out of another vehicle that had just pulled alongside the curb in front of the house.

"Hi, Coach," Bryson said, waving. Dave pointed at him and gave him a thumbs-up.

Brock came over. "Bryson, I want you to meet Mr. Brock Houseman, brilliant attorney and so-so baseball coach. Brock, this is my man Bryson. His mom is Clarice's physical therapist."

Bryson stuck out his hand and Brock shook it. "Hey, Bryson, glad to meet you."

"Glad to meet you, Mr. Houseman."

Julie walked up as the other car was pulling away from the curb. She turned to wave at the woman who was driving, then turned back to Dave and Brock.

"Well, hello again," she said. "You're really being way too nice to me."

"I don't think so. Julie, I want you to meet Brock Houseman, that lawyer buddy I was telling you about."

"Thanks a lot, Dave. I was going to tell her I was a piano player in a bordello," Brock said.

"Oh, I wouldn't worry about it," Julie said, shaking Brock's hand. "My ex is a lawyer, so you never had a chance to begin with."

Brock threw up his hands. "No respect. Not a single grain."

"Mom."

"Sorry, Bryson. I promised him I'd lay off the lawyer jokes," she explained.

"Hey, we tell 'em all the time," Brock said. "Like, there were these three lawyers in a lifeboat—"

"Okay, okay, down, boy," Dave said. "Here's your new key, Julie. And I really want you to think about what I said about letting this guy come play some ball." He grabbed Bryson's shoulder. "What about it, homie? You ever think about taking up baseball? I know it's not as challenging as swimming, but . . ."

Bryson gave him a doubtful look. "I don't know, Coach. I've played a little, but not on a team or anything. And I don't have a glove."

"Hey, wait a second," Brock said, trotting toward his car. He came back with a creased, well-worn fielder's glove. "Try this one on." He handed it to Bryson.

"Hey, isn't that my extra glove?" Dave asked.

"Yeah. You loaned it to one of the kids and I found it lying by the water fountain after practice last week. I forgot to tell you."

"Well, I'll be."

Bryson slid the glove onto his hand. He wiggled it. "I guess it's okay . . ."

"No, let me show you," Dave said, slipping the glove off Bryson and wriggling his fingers into it. "It's a little tight for my big ol' hand, but here. What you gotta do is pop it with your fist." He balled up his right hand and smacked it into the palm of the glove, where the leather was dark and shiny from frequent use. "Like that, see? Just pop that fist in there and that'll seat the glove on your hand real good." He handed the glove back to Bryson. "Go ahead and give it a try."

Bryson put on the glove and gave it a couple of experimental slugs.

"Yeah, there you go. Pop it in there real good. You'll get the feel of it."

"Well, I hate to break this up, but it's time for A-Rod here to get started on his homework," Julie said, ruffling Bryson's hair. "Hand over the glove."

"No, let him keep it," Dave said. "It's just an extra I've got for when one of the kids forgets his stuff. He can bring it with him when he comes out to the park."

Bryson looked up at his mom. She looked at Dave. "I'd object, but so far I haven't won a single one of these exchanges."

"No, Dave can be pretty bullheaded sometimes," Brock said. "I'd just humor him if I were you. And that's coming from a lawyer."

She grinned at Brock, and Dave was surprised to feel something a little like jealousy starting up inside him. *Naw, that ain't nothing. Besides, Brock's too goofy for her; anybody can see that.*

"I guess it's okay," Julie said. Bryson grinned and took off for the house before his mom could change her mind.

They said their good-byes as Dave and Brock headed for the car. Then Julie called to Dave, and he looked back.

"Thanks so much, Dave. For everything."

He smiled at her for a few seconds, then turned. When he got in the car, Brock was giving him a funny look.

"What?"

Brock shook his head. "Nothing, man. Never mind."

Chapter Ten

*I*t felt so good to sit behind her desk at the office. If she'd had
to stay at home one more week staring at the walls and the TV,
Clarice thought she might have lost what was left of her mind. Of
course, it also helped when Friday came around and Freddy showed
up to take Mama back home.

She'd finally talked David into driving one of the company pickups
until the insurance company made a settlement on his pickup. She'd
worked out a way of driving left-footed since the walking brace didn't
have the flexibility to let her operate the gas pedal with her right foot.
She'd taken it easy and stayed off the busy streets on the way here, but
it was worth all the trouble to be back in the office. Clarice felt the
earth right itself; she felt competent and in control. Here at the office,
everything in her world sorted itself into the proper categories.

She looked up and saw Michelle escorting her prospective buyers from the reception area. Clarice looked over the Farbers. They
appeared to be plain, non-adventurous people. The husband had
pale hair almost the same color as his skin; he wore it in a bad comb-
over. Mrs. Farber had a worn, creased look, like somebody who'd
been driving into the sun all afternoon. But Michelle was chatting
them up like they were Tom Cruise and Sandra Bullock. Clarice
hoped she wasn't telling them about her sex life. The image got
caught in her mind, though, and she was glad no one suspected the
source of her wide grin when they walked into her office.

"Clarice, this is Phil and Barb Farber." Clarice was pretty sure she was the only one who heard the giggle threatening to break out in Michelle's voice as she said their names. "Folks, this is Clarice Johnson."

Clarice shook their hands—limp and clammy though they were—and gestured them into the upholstered armchairs in front of her desk. "Can Michelle get you folks something to drink? No? Well, all right, then, let's just go over a few things before we go look at some properties, shall we? Thanks, Michelle."

For the next fifteen minutes, Clarice profiled the Farbers. She already knew from their call-in why they were moving to town and roughly what price range they had in mind. But that was the easy stuff, the basic facts that meant these people would buy from anybody. That kind of information was little more than a commodity. Before she started showing them homes, Clarice wanted to know the kinds of things that got them excited, the little details that would thrill them and transform these wary house shoppers into motivated, eager homebuyers. Though from the look of them, excitement wasn't a major feature of life with the Farbers.

"Well, I think that about covers it for now," Clarice said, jotting a few final notes on her folder. *Lord, have mercy. Getting anything useful out of these folks is harder than pulling teeth with tweezers. Oh well. I've seen worse . . . I just can't remember when.*

"Would you like to look at some properties now?" she asked. "My assistant, Michelle, is going to drive us around because I'm still recovering from a little accident a few weeks ago."

"Oh, I had to wear a walking cast a few years back," Phil said. "The doctor said I'd be out of it in six weeks, but I ended up wearing it four months."

Thank you, Mr. Sunshine.

"My goodness! Well, I'll be glad to get this off, but this is such an improvement over the fiberglass one—"

"Yeah, the insurance paid about half what it was supposed to," Barb said. "We had to borrow money to pay off Phil's medical bills."

"That's too bad."

They were still sitting in the armchairs; they hadn't budged since Clarice mentioned looking at houses. She grabbed her crutch and started the process of getting herself up and moving, hoping Phil and Barb would take the hint.

They watched her like two big blond toads sitting on mushrooms. She started moving from behind her desk and their eyes followed her. She kept thinking about Tweedledum and Tweedledee, but she doubted these two had the gumption to work up any sort of tussle.

"Well? Are you folks about ready to go?" She gave them a smile that was about a hundred and eighty degrees from what she was feeling.

Phil squished up out of his chair and then held Barb's elbow as she got up. The gesture, which Clarice would have never expected of him, struck her as sweet . . . all the more so because it suggested personality and caring—something she'd had no clue to expect with the Farbers.

Michelle was standing by the door to escort them outside. Michelle had reserved one of the agency's minivans for this tour; getting them all in and out of Clarice's Accord would be too much to handle, especially for Clarice. And the minivan seemed like an even better idea now that she'd seen the Farbers.

Clarice could hardly wait for the orthopedist to clear her to start using a cane. She might look like one of the little old ladies at church, but at least a cane wouldn't be so hard to maneuver. It was giving Clarice a headache in the relatively close quarters of the office. She was always having to swivel her head around to make sure she wasn't about to knock something over, whack somebody, or trip herself. Fortunately, Michelle was making the obligatory small talk with the Farbers so Clarice could concentrate on navigating the hallway and the lobby. And Phil—sweet Phil!—held the door for them as they went out to the parking lot.

"Michelle, let's start over in Tanglewood, all right?" Clarice said when they were all in the minivan. "Barb, there's a really nice 3-3-2 over there I think you'll love." Barb shrugged as Michelle started the vehicle.

While they drove, Clarice gave them the standard patter about schools, hospitals, museums, and other community services and amenities. She could do this bit with about half her attention. With the other half, she was still thinking about Phil holding Barb's elbow as she dislodged herself from the armchair in the office.

Looking at them now sitting beside each other in the second seat of the minivan, Clarice realized that Phil and Barb, nondescript and impassive though they might be, really liked each other. He sat with his arm casually draped along the seat back behind her, and she leaned into him slightly. These two unremarkable people had something Clarice and David didn't: they had each other. Clarice could easily imagine that Phil and Barb would always be there for each other. There might not be many surprises or thrills along the road, but these two were traveling it together.

Clarice felt the sadness coming back, oozing out from wherever it had been hiding inside her. She and David had so many advantages: good health, rewarding jobs, a nice home, good friends . . . and even, she liked to think, a reasonable amount of good looks. When the two of them got dressed up and went out someplace nice, people noticed them entering a room.

So why wasn't it working?

They reached the address of the house in Tanglewood and Clarice asked Michelle to go get the key from the lockbox and open the house. She moved up the sidewalk with the Farbers and started giving them the pep talk: lots of built-ins; the previous owners had remodeled the den and screened-in back porch, creating a combination family-entertainment-sun room; new appliances in the kitchen; ceiling fans throughout the house. Next Clarice told them about the new intercom system. Phil and Barb looked at each other and smiled.

Paydirt! Barb is all about talking to somebody on the other side of the house without having to walk over there.

Clarice's hunches about people nearly always paid off.

∞

They saw Julie and Bryson at church the next Sunday. They were walking up the aisle after the service when Dave heard somebody yelling "Coach! Coach!" He turned around and saw Bryson hurrying toward him, with Julie following in his wake.

"Hey, Coach, remember what you said about me coming to practice with you sometime?"

"Sure."

"Well . . . Mom says it's okay if you say it's okay. So is it okay?"

Dave looked at Julie. She gave him a little shrug.

"All right, then. We've got a practice next Tuesday after school. Can you make it?"

"Yeah, I think so. We had a meet this weekend, so practices'll be light this week."

"Cool. Where you want me to pick you up?"

"I'll just bring him with me to your house, if it's not too much trouble," Julie said. "Clarice and I have a session that day, so he'll be there waiting for you. About four?"

"Yeah, we start at four thirty, so four would be good. All right then." Dave stuck out his hand. "Come on, my man, don't leave me hangin'."

Bryson slapped his palm.

"I'll have to show you the rest of the shake later," Dave said, grinning. Julie gave him a little wave as he turned back toward Clarice.

"He's a baseball player?" Clarice said as they walked on.

"I don't know. But he wants to come out and try, so I guess we'll find out. Nice kid, no matter what."

"Mmm-hmm."

Dave got out of the truck and reached into the bed to pull out the green canvas bag of bats, balls, catcher's gear, and extra gloves. He slung the bag over his shoulder and started walking toward the rusty chain-link backstop where the boys and Brock waited in a loose half-circle. He heard the passenger door shut behind him and looked back for Bryson.

The boy was moving forward, but barely. His eyes fastened on the faces staring back at him. He was walking like someone trying to cross a field full of snakes.

"Come on, Bryson, they not gon' bite you," Dave said with a grin. "And if they do, I'll put my foot alongside somebody's skinny black butt."

Bryson gave him a halfhearted smile and walked a little faster. They got to the backstop and Dave set down the bag with a grunt. "Ya'll, this is my man Bryson." He laid a hand on Bryson's shoulder. "Bryson thinks he might be interested in playing a little ball. Anybody got a problem with that? Good. Bryson, you already know Coach Houseman. Why don't ya'll go around and tell Bryson your names?"

"Jaylen." "Deshawn." "Malcolm." "George."

As the boys mouthed their names at Bryson, one after the other, Dave saw it—the look—the dead-eyed, empty-faced expression these kids gave anybody they didn't know. Especially somebody white. The first time Dave had been able to coax Brock into coming out and helping him with the team, the kids had given Brock the look. It made sense when you thought about it, of course. In the kinds of places some of these kids lived, what sort of second chance did they have if they guessed wrong about somebody? Caution and distance were safest, usually. That was one thing that kept Dave coming back. If these boys ever got a chance to make something of themselves in or out of the hood, it would help to know at least one black male role model who cared enough to keep showing up when he said he would. It would also help them to know it was okay to do something for somebody who couldn't necessarily do anything for them in return. Trust was a tough sell to these boys, but how could you ever be human without it?

"Awright. Deshawn, take left field and let's put Carlos in center." He turned to Bryson. "Bryson, you want to take a turn in right?"

Bryson hesitated for a second, then gave him a quick nod. He slipped Dave's glove on his left hand and gave the pocket a pop with his fist, just like Dave had shown him. Then he turned and started following Deshawn toward left.

"No, boy, you in right," one of the kids said, grabbing at Bryson's shoulder and pointing to right field. "Right field, boy. Right."

Bryson mumbled something and started jogging in the correct direction. Dave tried to keep the wince he felt from showing on his face. "Okay, then. Jaylen, take Malcolm over there and start warming up your arm. And don't let me catch you trying that raggedy curveball you keep telling me about. Just keep it slow and easy. The rest of you start playing some catch while I warm up the fielders. Tim, you catch for me." Tim usually played right field, but giving him the job of catching incoming balls might keep him from resenting Bryson—for a little while, at least.

Dave started tapping some easy grounders to the infielders. "Okay, Darius, take it to first, okay?" Darius scooped the two-hopper and hummed it into the glove of the waiting Marcus, hitting him right in the letters. Darius had game, no doubt about it. If he could stay out of trouble and in school, he could make some high school coach sit up straight someday. By the time Marcus flicked the ball to Tim, Dave was already reaching for a ball to hit to George, the shortstop.

He went around the infield and was pleased that only two throws made Marcus jump off the bag, and one of them was catchable. He pointed the bat at Deshawn, who was waiting out in left with his hands propped on his bent knees. He popped a little blooper that made Deshawn get on his horse and race in toward shallow left to take the ball in the air. He made the catch, though, and flipped the ball to short as if the catch were strictly routine. Dave grinned; Deshawn had a bad tendency to take little mental vacations out in the field. Might as well wake him up early in the practice. "Yeah, Deshawn, baby, that's what I'm talkin' about," he called. Deshawn flashed him a grin and hustled back to his position. Dave fungoed one out to center and Carlos barely had to move. He made the catch—with both hands, Dave was glad to see—and tossed the ball in to second.

Dave turned toward Bryson. "Okay, Bryson, here you go." He took a little off of it so the ball would bounce in front of Bryson; he wanted to ease him in. Bryson stutter-stepped back and forward for a couple of seconds, then ran for the rolling ball like he had a hell-hound on his trail. He grabbed the ball and flung it somewhere in the direction of the infield, sailing it high between first and second base. Marcus would've had to be twelve feet tall to have any chance of cutting off the wild throw.

"That's whack," Tim said, shaking his head as Bryson's throw bounced across the third baseline and Brock jogged over to retrieve it. "Yo, where you find that kid, Coach? Cheerleader camp?"

"Don't be all up in my Kool-Aid, dawg," Dave said in a low voice. "I'm still the coach, you know what I'm sayin'? Good hustle, Bryson," he called. "Try to hit the first baseman next time, awright?"

"Aw, man, don't tell him that, Coach," Marcus said from first. "He fit'n to tag me on the dome next time."

"For real," somebody said, laughing.

"Hey, George," Brock said, tossing the stray ball at Tim. "How about me telling Bryson how you threw the ball into the stands behind third base last week during a game? I'll bet that lady still has a bruise on her arm."

George scowled as the other boys snickered.

"Ooh, boy, he tagged you straight up, man."

"I know that's right."

The guys settled down as Dave took them through the warm-up; he kept them moving enough so they didn't have breath to waste on talking more smack. And Bryson's throws got better, though Dave never felt safe hitting him a real fly ball; a concussion didn't seem like a good souvenir from his first organized baseball practice. Dave rotated the other players on and off the field until everyone had gotten a chance to spend some time fielding grounders or fly balls. After about thirty minutes, he called them in for a batting drill. While Malcolm donned the catcher's gear and Brock organized the hitting order, Dave took Bryson aside.

"Now, you don't have to bat if you don't want to, Bryson. These guys been hitting since late March. You want to just watch, it's okay with me. Nobody gon' say nothin'."

"No, I want to try, Coach. I don't care if I strike out, I still want to try."

Dave was falling in love with this kid. "Okay, little bro. You stand up there when it's your turn, and I'll give you something to swing at."

Dave gathered up as many loose balls as he could carry, grabbed a glove, and went to the mound. Except for the first four batters, the other boys scattered to positions in the field.

Jaylen was up first and, as usual, he was clowning around in the batter's box, shaking his booty at the other boys and generally acting like a fool. Dave sent the first pitch just a little inside and high. Jaylen took the dirt and came up sputtering.

"Say, Coach, you tryin' to dust me off or what?"

"Oh, sorry, my man. Guess I turned loose of that one a little too quick, huh? Good thing you were watching, though."

He flicked the next one over the fat part of the plate and Jaylen got good wood on it, sending it between short and second; a solid hit in anybody's ballpark. He threw nine more pitches to Jaylen and the boy tagged three of them, fouled two off, and fanned four.

"All right, Mr. Jaylen, grab a glove and go take over for Marcus. Marcus, come on in and get ready to take your cuts."

He threw to George, then Darius. Next up was Bryson.

Chapter Eleven

*D*ave could see the other boys watching Bryson, sizing him up as he walked toward the plate. A few of them were hiding their smirks behind their hands, thinking Dave didn't see.

"Bend those knees, Bryson, awright?" he said. Dave was hoping hard that Bryson would connect with at least a few of the pitches. A kid with a heart that big didn't need to fail in front of these Eastside kids; they were merciless. And if Dave protected Bryson too much, it would only make things worse. "Keep both eyes on the ball and swing level, okay?" Bryson nodded.

Dave sent an easy one toward the plate; Bryson stepped almost out of the batter's box with his left foot and flailed wildly. *This could get ugly,* Dave thought. He wished he'd been able to talk Bryson out of taking BP.

"You stepping in the bucket, my man," he said. "Step into the pitch, not away from it."

Bryson nodded again. His jaw was clenched and he was staring at Dave like he meant business. Dave could still hear the muted giggles coming from the other players.

He gave Bryson another pitch. Bryson stayed in the box with it, but his swing was late and high. "Little behind and over the top that time." Bryson nodded again.

Dave's hope that the third time would be the charm was foiled when Bryson got way around on the pitch and swung so early and so hard that he nearly lost his balance. By now, Dave could easily hear the laughing of the other boys. Brock was behind the plate, though, talking low and steady to Bryson, trying to help.

Dave brought the next pitch in about belt level. Bryson swung and, wonder of wonders, connected. He caught it a little in toward his hands and the ball was easily fielded by the second baseman, but at least he'd gotten the bat on it. Dave could tell Bryson's hands were stinging from contacting the ball so low on the bat, but he just put down the bat, rubbed his palm on his pants, and then got ready for the next pitch.

He managed to foul off the next two pitches, both to the right of first base. "Swinging a little bit late, Bryson," Dave heard Brock say. "Try to get a little more of a jump on it."

Dave made sure the next pitch was medium-speed. He was afraid Bryson would overcompensate and swing way too early, but maybe the boy's instinctual, athletic sense of timing finally kicked in. Bryson made a nice level swing and nailed the pitch right in the sweet spot, sending the ball on an arc into deep left-center for what would've been a stand-up double in anybody's park.

"Yeah, baby, that's what I'm talking about!" Dave called.

Bryson grinned. "It didn't sting."

"One of the best feelings in the world, isn't it?" Dave said.

Bryson made contact with the next three pitches, fouling one off and hitting grounders on the other two. "Okay, Bryson, grab a glove and take Tim's spot in right. Who's next? We need a batter."

He pitched to three more hitters. By then his arm was tired. He swapped places with Brock and went behind the plate. When everybody had batted around, they lined the boys up for some closing wind sprints. Bryson's conditioning showed up when he finished at the front of the pack every time without panting and wheezing like the other boys.

Then it was time to go. Dave gathered the boys for his little closing pep talk, then released them for the raid on Brock's ice chest. Bryson stayed back and helped him gather up the bats, catcher's gear, gloves, and balls.

"Well, Bryson, what'd you think?" Dave asked, after they were loaded up and headed back to Bryson's house.

"I'm not as good at baseball as I am at swimming."

"Course not. How could you be? But you made good contact with that one pitch, and your throws from the outfield improved as you went on."

"Thanks, Coach. And thanks for letting me give it a try."

"Can't ask a man to do more than try."

They rode a while in silence.

"Coach, I've got a meet coming up."

"You do?"

"Yeah, and I was wondering . . . I don't guess you'd want to come watch, would you?"

"You kidding? I'll be there, my man. Just tell me where and when."

"Really? That's great!"

The excitement in Bryson's voice made Dave want to weep—or punch out the lights of the father who didn't know what an amazing kid he had.

"Absolutely, Bryson. I wouldn't miss it for anything."

When they got to the house, Bryson ran inside. Dave could hear him yelling. "Mom! Mom! Coach is coming to my next meet!" He smiled as he backed out of the driveway.

He was about halfway home when his cell phone rang.

"Dave, it's Julie."

"Hey there."

"Dave, I can't tell you how grateful I am for what you've done for my son."

He could hear the emotion in her voice. "Hey, he's a great kid. I want to come see him tear it up at that meet."

"Yeah, I know. You don't know what this means to him."

"I think I have some idea."

"Or to me."

He paused long over his answer. "I think I have some idea," he said finally.

"Well . . . okay. The meet's next Saturday morning at the State Street Y, starting at nine o'clock." After a few seconds she said, "I'll save you a seat."

"That sounds good to me."

She ended the call. Dave switched on his favorite hip-hop station and cranked the volume.

The next Saturday, Dave and Julie were in the bleachers at the Y when Bryson came out of the dressing room to take his place for the eleven- and twelve-year-old boys' 50-meter freestyle. He looked up in the stands toward the spot where Julie had told him they'd be and waved. Dave and Julie waved back. Bryson went toward his starting block as the event was called.

"He looks good," Dave said.

"Yeah. I've never seen him this nervous before a meet, though. On the way here, he kept talking about wanting to do well. He never does that."

"What's that about?"

She looked at him. "You really don't know?"

"What? Because I'm here? He doesn't need to do anything to impress me."

"Maybe not, but he doesn't know that."

"Now, Julie—"

"No, I didn't mean it that way. You've become incredibly important to him in a very short time. He talks about you constantly. Today he wants to swim the best he's ever done—because he wants you to be proud of him."

Dave swallowed and looked away.

The boys were all up on their blocks and poised. The starter's horn blew and they were in the water.

"He got a little bit of a slow start," Julie said, a worried look on her face.

"Come on, Bryson!" Dave yelled. "Go, man!"

Bryson was up and swimming, but two other boys were actually fighting him for the lead.

"How many laps in this race?" Dave said.

"Just one length. It's a sprint," Julie said.

"Come on, Bryson! Come on, baby, you can do it!"

They were at about thirty meters and it looked like Bryson was starting to pull away, but then another boy put on a burst of speed and moved past him by half a length. Dave was on his feet, pumping his fists in the air and hollering for Bryson to go, go, go, go, go! Bryson pulled even with the other boy with maybe five meters to go and it was neck-and-neck from there to the wall. The touch was too close to call, but somehow Bryson managed to edge his opponent by a couple hundredths of a second. When his name came over the PA as the winner, Dave jumped up and down. Without thinking, he grabbed Julie and hugged her.

"Did you see that? Did you *see* that? That other boy took him on and Bryson just put it right back in his eye, I'm telling you!"

She smiled at him. "Calm down, Coach. That was just the first heat."

"Say what?"

"That was a qualifying heat. There'll be two more, and the top finishers will compete in the final."

"Oh, Lord have mercy. You mean I got to sit through this again?"

"'Fraid so, Coach."

"I can't take this. Swimming is too intense for me."

"Just wait until the relays."

After his relatively shaky beginning, Bryson seemed to settle down. He won his final for the 50-free by a handy margin, beating the other swimmers—including the boy who had challenged him so closely in the first heat—by a full body length.

"Man, that boy can swim," Dave said, shaking his head when the race was over.

"Yeah, that was the normal Bryson you saw that time," Julie said. "When he's on, most kids in his age group can't stay with him."

"I heard that. When do the relays come up?"

"Well, he's swimming with an older team, so they'll probably be after lunch sometime."

"You want to go grab something? Can Bryson come with us?"

"Yeah, that'd be good. He won't need to eat much, though, and what he does eat will need to be high-carb."

"Do I hear somebody saying pasta?"

She grinned. "Let's go ask his coach when he needs to be back here."

The three of them went to a nearby mom-and-pop Italian place Dave knew about. In fact, he felt a little twinge when they walked in. He'd brought Clarice here on their first date. But right now, for reasons he didn't want to admit to himself, he didn't want to think about that.

Julie ordered fettucine Alfredo and Bryson wanted spaghetti and meatballs. Dave asked for his favorite, lasagna. The waitress brought iced tea for Dave and Julie and water for Bryson.

"Man, Bryson, you just dominated that final," Dave said. "You owned that pool."

Bryson grinned and ducked his head. "Thanks, Coach."

"Seriously, man, you are gifted. You could get a scholarship somewhere. Go to the Olympics."

"That's what his swim coach says," Julie said, as she tore a packet of sweetener and poured it in her tea. "I wouldn't mind a scholarship to, say, UCLA or USC. That way I could go visit my kid in Southern California."

Dave nodded. "Yeah, that could happen. Or Pepperdine. I hear they got a pretty nice layout."

"Hey, guys, I'm only in sixth grade," Bryson said. "Don't book your tickets yet, okay?"

They laughed.

"So, tell me about this relay team you're on," Dave said.

Bryson told him about how the coach asked him to think about swimming with some older kids "to stretch his competitive muscles." They'd won the last three meets they'd competed in. Bryson was swimming the leadoff leg, but his coach was thinking about giving him the anchor.

"Anchor leg? No kidding? I don't know much about swimming, but I ran track in college and the anchor leg was where it all came down to the ground, you know what I'm saying?"

Bryson nodded. "Coach thinks I can handle it."

"Well, from what I've seen so far, I'd say your coach was right. You are one awesome brother in the water, my man."

With her chin propped in her hand, Julie watched them talking. Bryson was almost visibly blooming under Dave's approval and encouragement; the sight made her throat tighten with gratitude.

Dave Johnson was one of the kindest, most decent men she'd ever met. It was clear to her that he genuinely cared for Bryson, as she was sure he did for all the boys on his Little League team.

". . . Mom? Can I?"

Julie snapped back to the present. "Sorry, bud. What did you say?"

"I said, can I get a smoothie? They have them here, Coach says."

"If you don't think he'll get too full for his next race," Dave said.

"Well, sport, they haven't even brought your spaghetti and meatballs yet, so . . ."

"Mom. The race isn't until two o'clock. It's barely twelve-thirty."

"Okay, sure. Just don't drown, okay?"

"Yeah, right," Bryson said.

Driving back to the Y, Dave switched on the oldies station. The music faded in and it was Lionel Ritchie and the Commodores doing "Three Times a Lady." Almost without thinking, he switched off the radio.

"What's wrong?" Julie said. "I like that song."

"I just remembered I need to make a call real quick." Dave fished out his cell phone and pushed the speed dial code for his office, which, he knew, was vacant on Saturday. He let it ring through until the voice mail picked up, then ended the call.

"Nobody there," he said. "Say, reach up over your visor and pick out a CD, all right?"

They got back to the Y a little after one o'clock and Bryson left them to go get back into his swimsuit. Dave and Julie walked toward the stands and he could feel her knuckles tapping against his as they went. He had to fight the urge to take her hand. *Way over the line, homeboy, way over the line.*

But he didn't let go of the thought—not quite. He kept it in his pocket and took it out every so often to look at it again.

They watched several girls' events while waiting for the boys' 4 × 50 relay. Finally, at a quarter after two, Bryson and three older boys came out of the dressing rooms, along with the other teams competing in the event. Bryson was talking and laughing with the older boys in a way that told Dave they regarded him as an equal.

Dave tried to imagine one of the kids on his ball team—Jaylen, for example—showing up at one of Bryson's swim practices. How would he feel? Would he even be willing to get in the water? There were some differences, of course: Bryson had been training since he was a little guy, and swimming was a slightly rarer skill than throwing a ball or swinging a bat. And yet, Bryson had come out to the diamond and taken his cuts along with everyone else, even though he didn't know anyone there except Dave and Brock. He'd been willing to try. Bryson had more guts than most adults Dave knew, he decided.

The officials whistled them to their places and Bryson stepped onto the block. He was swinging his arms and shaking out his hands, getting loose for the race. He glanced up in the stands at his mom and Dave, gave them a quick thumbs-up, then refocused his attention on his lane, the other end of the pool, and on what he needed to do.

Bryson's team had one of the center lanes. The boys on either side of him were taller and more developed through the chest and shoulders. To Dave, Bryson looked thin, pale, and overmatched. *But he doesn't look worried.*

"He's loose this time," Julie said, echoing Dave's thoughts. "I bet he gets a good start."

The boys went to their marks and the horn blew. The leadoff legs went into the water, submerging briefly before coming to the top. Bryson's arms arced into the water with clean, even motions; his head swiveled smoothly with each stroke. As Dave watched, he pulled steadily ahead of the older boys. By the time he touched and his teammate launched himself toward the other end of the pool, Bryson had given his team perhaps a full-meter lead.

The second leg didn't fare so well. As far as Dave could tell, Bryson's teammate was swimming well enough, but a kid in the lane at the edge of the pool farthest from where they sat swam a heroic lap, taking away the lead Bryson had established and edging his team in front by half a meter or so. The third leg for Bryson's team didn't lose any ground, but he didn't gain much, either. As the racers neared the end of the pool and the anchor legs got ready to go, Julie was looking worried.

"Our anchor swimmer hasn't done too well the last couple of times out," she said. "It used to be that they pretty much kept whatever lead Bryson gave them and just counted on the other three legs to maintain, but we're behind today."

The noise built as the anchor legs went into the water. The team on the far side still held a slight lead over everyone else, but now at least two other teams besides Bryson's were within striking distance. Eight swimmers sprinted for the home end of the pool, lashing the water furiously as each tried to pull himself past the others. The crowd noise rose to an indistinguishable roar; they were all on their feet. Dave felt himself straining toward the finish, as if his effort might somehow aid his swimmer's progress. With ten meters to go, it looked like a three-way dead heat. A couple of strokes later, the team in lane eight appeared to have a hand's-breadth edge. With five meters left, Bryson's teammate might have just pulled ahead. Three meters, two, one . . .

The finish was so close that instead of cheers, a hush fell as everyone stared at the electronic clock for each lane, trying to read the seconds, the tenths, the hundredths. And then, at almost the same instant, they comprehended the data: lane eight had won by a scant two hundredths of a second. Bryson's team had finished runner-up. The partisans for the team in lane eight erupted in yells and whistles. Dave felt like a balloon with all the air squeezed out.

He watched as Bryson and his third-leg partner made the long walk to the other end of the pool to shake hands with their teammates and to congratulate the winning team. The boys looked disappointed, but not crushed. *They gave their best,* Dave thought. They stood a good chance of winning their next time out. Or the one after that.

"Well, it was a good race," Julie said. "I wish you could've seen his team win, but at least you saw Bryson swim well."

"Yeah, he's got no reason to hang his head. He did the job; the other team just did its job a little better today, is all."

"Well, that's it for us today," Julie said. "We might as well get him and head home."

"Whatever you say."

When Bryson came out of the dressing room, he gave his mom a little smile and a shrug.

"You swam a great race, Bryson," Dave said.

"Thanks, Coach. Just wasn't quite good enough, I guess."

"Hey, you gave your team a lead," Julie said. "The rest was up to somebody else."

"I guess. Hey, Mom, can we get milk shakes on the way home?"

"He's pretty torn up," she said.

"I can see that," Dave said, chuckling.

When he pulled into his driveway, Dave sat for a couple of minutes with his engine idling. He looked at Clarice's car sitting in the driveway next to him and wondered if she was going to ask him about the meet. He thought about what he might tell her and realized that if he had his way, he wouldn't tell her anything. He felt protective and proprietary about Bryson and Julie, about the time he'd spent with them. He didn't want to share the words, the feelings, the experience of it with Clarice. The pride that had surged through him when Bryson won his preliminary heat, then his individual event—that was Dave's own; it belonged to him. What would Clarice know about it? How could she understand the way it made him feel to know this kid cared enough about what Dave thought that it would actually make him nervous about his performance?

Could Clarice even comprehend something so far outside the boundaries of her career and aspirations? Was there anything in her that could still care about something just because it was important to Dave? He didn't know. And as he switched off the engine and opened his door, he wasn't sure he cared.

Dave hadn't realized how tense he was until the well-trained fingers started digging into the muscles and tendons of his shoulders. He winced with the delicious discomfort of the massage, feeling the twang as each keyed-up nerve released its grip.

He was a little self-conscious about lying on a table with nothing but a towel covering him, but she'd assured him there was nothing to worry about. She was a professional and this was the way it was done. Still, he was glad he was on his stomach. The feeling of her palms gliding over his skin was starting to make him think about things that probably weren't included on the list of services.

Oh, man . . . she was working up and down either side of his spine now, alternating between little circling probes with her thumbs and hard kneading motions with the heels of her hands. She sure knew what she was doing. Dave couldn't remember when he'd been this relaxed.

"That feel good?" she asked him. Dave thought he heard a smooth, gliding sound in her voice . . . an inviting, husky tone. He felt himself starting to respond down there and felt a little embarrassed. Get a grip, man! Relaxed is one thing, but . . .

And then her hands moved lower . . . into the small of his back, then inching toward his buttocks. She sent one hand down his out-stretched upper arm. He could feel the touch of her clothing against his back as she leaned over him. He could see her hand, so white against the dark brown of his shoulder, gently squeezing and releasing, squeez-ing and releasing. Her lips were close to his ear; he could feel her breath.

"Why don't you roll over, and I'll give you the rest of the treatment?" she said.

His heart was going like a trip hammer. His flesh was fully awake now, pressing almost painfully against the table beneath him.

"What . . . what are you talking about?" he said, unable to keep the tremor of desire out of his voice.

"Don't you know?" Julie said, sliding her hand beneath the towel, lifting it from him. She eased a hand beneath his hips and gently turned his body toward her, and Dave suddenly realized he wasn't going to stop himself, not this time . . .

Chapter Twelve

*H*is eyes snapped open; he was staring at the ceiling of his bedroom. He swiveled his head to the left. Clarice was breathing slowly, her shoulders rising and falling as she slept with her back to him.

Dave's heart was still racing from the arousal of the dream. Where had that come from? Sure, it was only a dream, and he had no control over what his subconscious did while he was asleep, but there was still something a little weird about having such images in his mind while his wife was asleep next to him. It was uncomfortable . . . in a sort of nice, guilty way.

He got out of bed and went to the bathroom. Maybe a hot shower would help him get his mind back on track. Come to think of it, maybe what he really needed was a cold shower.

Clarice was elated; the orthopedist had upgraded her right leg to "weight-bearing as tolerated," which meant she could get a cane and bump these goofy crutches. It also meant she could begin putting more weight on the leg and maybe start walking a little bit without the cast. Julie advised her to keep the cast on when she went to work or ran errands, however. That made sense to Clarice; outside the relatively controlled environment of her home, she wanted to protect her healing leg from the unexpected. At home, though, she wanted to concentrate on returning all the joints and ligaments of her injured leg to the fullest possible range of motion. Her toes, she'd noticed in particular, still felt a little weak and chancy. Julie had told her she needed to rebuild their strength for when it was time to start walking without the support of a cane or crutch.

Clarice was certainly getting stronger under Julie's supervision, no question about that. And gradually she was resuming more and more of her former routine. She was going to the office at least four days each week now and staying for a minimum of five hours each time. She'd closed two sales this month—one being the Farbers, who bought the house in Tanglewood with the new intercom system. She also had five promising listings. She was well on her way to resuming her star performance in the office.

Things were getting back on track in her world . . . except for David. The rift between them seemed to be growing, and Clarice didn't know what to do about it. Actually, when she was honest with herself, she did know what she might do about it; she just didn't feel capable of doing it.

Sometimes, as she watched TV on the couch and David rustled around in the kitchen or sat in his recliner and leafed through a magazine, she thought about saying something to him. She thought about stepping onto the shaky ground of her own uncertainties, of opening herself up to him for a discussion of what might be happening to their marriage and what might be done about it.

But the trouble with starting such a conversation, she knew, was that you never knew where it was going to end. If things got too honest, she was actually afraid of what she might say. Clarice knew that once certain bridges were crossed—or burned—the way back was hard, if you could get there at all.

And so, night after night, she stared at the TV and listened to him rummaging in the kitchen or flipping the pages of his magazines. The wall of silence and uncertainty just grew higher in her mind.

One day she came home from the office and saw David's pickup in the driveway. They'd finally settled with the insurance company, and David had gotten a Club Cab nearly identical to the one he'd lost. It was a little odd for him to be home this early, but not unheard of; if the shifts were running smoothly and the managers were all fully staffed, there might not be anything that needed his attention at the end of the day. As she levered herself out of her car and steadied herself on her cane, she thought little of it. She went in through the garage and tossed her keys on the counter. David's voice was coming from the bedroom.

"What?" she asked, assuming he was saying something to her. But then he laughed and said something else too low to distinguish.

"What, David?" she said, moving toward the bedroom. Just as she reached the doorway, she heard him say, "Okay, then. Yeah. All right, I'll talk to you later."

She looked inside and he was sitting on the bed, his cell phone in his hand. He looked at her. "Yeah? What?"

"Who was on the phone?"

"Nobody."

His face was impassive, as if a stranger on the street had walked up and asked him the time of day.

"Oh. Well, I heard you talking when I walked in and I just . . . wondered."

He looked at her and gave her a shrug. She didn't know how to respond, so she didn't. But something was odd about the way he was acting.

The rest of that evening, when she knew he wasn't looking, Clarice studied her husband. In most ways, nothing was different; he still walked the same, sounded the same as he moved through the house, watched the same TV shows, and read the sports pages just like always. He went to bed at his usual time. The silhouette of his presence was almost the same in her awareness as it had always been.

But only almost; something was different. It wasn't so much anything he said or did, but was more like the absence of something. At first she blamed it on the chasm of noncommunication growing between them, but as she studied on it some more, she knew that wasn't it—or at least not all of it. Even when David was withdrawn from her, angry at her, she could still feel him, in some way she couldn't even explain to herself, reaching toward her, gauging her, measuring the distance between them. It was like he had some kind of interpersonal radar constantly sweeping the terrain between them, waiting for an opening.

Now it was as if the radar was switched off. Not only had he pulled away from her—he didn't care. Or at least that was how it was starting to look to Clarice.

Behind her, she heard the bedroom door close. She picked up the remote and thumbed the volume down to a quieter level. She channel surfed for a half hour or so through the late-night talk shows and infomercials and reruns of shows from two or three seasons ago. After a while, she punched the power button and tossed the remote onto the couch beside her.

She'd actually shut David out, it seemed. She did a quick internal scan to see how she felt about that. In the depths of her depression immediately following the accident, when David had been so constant in his wish to help, to get her going again, she hadn't been able to feel anything like gratitude—only frustration with herself, guilt for her inability to respond, and, she hated to admit, a sort of helpless aggravation with him for not being able to get it. A little later, when, with Julie's help, she started to feel as if she were moving back into some measure of control, she still hadn't found the strength or desire or whatever else she would've needed to reach across the growing abyss toward her husband. Now, with the rift between them all but complete, he'd finally quit trying.

Was it possible their marriage could really come apart?

Was she willing to do anything to prevent that?

Clarice sat up until well past midnight turning this question over in her mind. She constructed scenarios and envisioned futures, attempting to try on this odd new life she'd suddenly realized as a possibility.

What would her mother say? Mama had been dumped by two different men. Even so, Clarice never remembered seeing her mother cry. But the few times Clarice could recall asking about her daddy or the man who had sired her brother and sister, Mama closed up tighter than a clamshell. After a while, Clarice learned not to ask anymore. The experience that gave her mother an iron determination to make her own way and teach her children to do the same also left her hard and wary, like an old, sullen catfish that'd had too many hooks in its mouth.

Is that what's happening to me? Am I trying to insulate myself from going through the same thing that happened to my mother—even before I have to?

Still lying on the couch, she finally drifted off to sleep.

When she woke up, the thick, buttered sunlight of morning was leaking through the seams in the blinds.

And David was already gone.

∞

Julie's cell phone rattled in her purse. She felt a bright ripple of anticipation as she dug it out and looked at the screen.

"Hello?"

"Hey, Julie."

"Hi, Dave."

"How's it going this morning?"

"Oh . . . fine, I guess."

"You guess?"

"Yeah. Good, I mean. I'm good. How are you?"

"You busy today?"

"Pretty much, yeah. I've got patients all the way up until noon. You?"

"Oh, just paperwork. You know what they say: The job ain't finished till the paperwork's done."

"They say that? Really?"

She heard his chuckle, low and warm. It spread a glow throughout her body.

"Well, I just wanted to see how you were doing this morning," he said. "I'll talk to you later, okay?"

"Okay, Dave. Take it easy."

"You, too. Bye, now."

"Bye."

She touched the end button, feeling sad and happy in equal amounts and at the same time. She stared at her desk and shook her head, a sardonic look on her face.

What is going on here? As if you didn't know. But . . . he's married. Yeah, and so were you once. He's a good man. A good man who's unhappy at home. But he's not *your* good man, is he?

His voice, rich and sweet as cocoa . . . the look on Bryson's face when he saw Dave sitting beside her in the stands.

Her cell phone was ringing again.

"Hello?"

"Okay, so I didn't really just call to see how you were doing."

"No?"

"No. I called to see if you had plans for lunch."

An alarm started somewhere inside her head, but as she sat there and concentrated on the image in her mind—Dave's face, engaged and interested, his eyes looking into hers from across the table—the siren got softer and softer until finally it faded into the distance.

"No, not really."

"Yeah? Well, that's cool. What do you like to eat?"

"Umm, it doesn't really matter. How about—"

"—Pasta," they both said at the same instant. They laughed.

"Great minds," he said.

"That's what they say. So . . . Gino's?"

"The place where we ate the day of the meet, right?"

"That's it."

"I'll see you there. Around 12:15 or so?"

"It'll be crowded, but okay."

She ended the call, but this time she only felt happy.

At least, that was what she decided to tell herself.

∞

Dave pulled into the parking lot. Julie was right; he'd be lucky to find a parking spot. He cruised around back and took the last remaining place, which happened to be in a spot of shade, he noted with satisfaction. Good karma, maybe.

He went inside, appreciating the blast of air-conditioning that met him when he pulled open the glass door. He looked around and saw Julie waving at him from a table in the corner.

Gino's had once been some sort of fast-food chain; the squared-off architecture and plate-glass windows running down the front and one side gave Dave the distinct impression of burgers, fries, shakes, and various ice cream desserts served up by ticket number from the counter that now housed warming trays filled with sauces, pastas, and pizza by the slice. The guys who ran the place looked and sounded vaguely Mediterranean, maybe eastern European. But the food was delicious and reasonably priced.

And Gino's was on the opposite side of town from Clarice's office.

Dave scooted into the chair across the table from Julie.

"Hey."

"Hey yourself," she said.

"Been waiting long?"

She shook her head. "Like I said, it's crowded."

Dave glanced around and nodded. One of the Mediterranean guys was standing beside him, holding a pad. "You guys ready to order?"

"I'll have the cannelloni special," Julie said. "Iced tea to drink."

"Same," Dave said. The guy scribbled a couple of seconds, nodded, and left.

"When's Bryson's next meet?" Dave said. "I want to be there."

She smiled at him. "You don't have to do that, Dave."

"I know. That's not why I'm doing it."

She dug a daily planner out of her purse. "Let's see, it looks like Saturday—oh."

"What?"

"It's a road trip." She told him the name of the club that was hosting the meet; it was in a city about three hours away. She said they'd probably leave after school on Friday and find a cheap hotel near the swim club.

"Do you know what time he swims on Saturday?"

"No, that won't be posted until after his next practice, tomorrow evening. But Dave, that's a lot of trouble—"

"Chill, sister," he said, holding up a hand. "If I want to drive over on Saturday and watch my man Bryson, you don't need to make a thing out of it, you know what I'm sayin'?"

She looked at him and shook her head, giving him a sideways smile. "All right. Fine. It'll mean the world to him if you can make it."

"Awright, then, that's settled."

The waiter brought their drinks and set a basket of bread on the table. The basket was one of those red oval plastic jobs that looked like it was used to holding a Burger Buster Basket with fries and ketchup. Dave pinched off some bread and offered the basket to Julie. She pulled out a piece for herself and took a bite, chewing as she gave him a thoughtful look.

"What?"

"Nothing. Just you." She looked at him a few seconds longer. "I'm wondering if I should tell you something."

"Well, it sounds like you already started. Why not finish?"

She shook her head and rolled her eyes. "You're just a bottom-line kind of guy, aren't you, Coach?"

He shrugged and waited.

"It's just that I'm not used to anyone taking an interest in Bryson. Or . . ."

"Or you?"

She gave him a startled, deer-in-the-headlights look. After a few seconds, she nodded. "I guess so."

"Well, Miss Julie, I . . ." *Careful, boy. Careful, careful, careful . . .*

A plastic plate loaded with cannelloni and swimming in marinara sauce chunked onto the table in front of him. Another one landed in front of Julie, then the waiter was gone.

Dave stared at his food for a few seconds, suddenly grateful for the interruption. When he looked up, her eyes were digging into him like a drill boring through soft pine. Then she nodded.

"Never mind," she said. "You don't have to say it."

They started eating their pasta. Dave asked about Bryson's school, what kind of music he liked, if he was into the ladies yet, who his friends were. He was trying to keep the conversation light and neutral, but there was a part of his mind that realized all the questions about Julie's son were only proxies for the questions he wanted to be asking about her. For example: How could any man in his right mind walk out on a woman as beautiful, talented, and caring as Julie? And why wasn't she with someone already? Someone who could see what was so plain to Dave—that here was a woman worth cherishing.

He kept these questions out of his mouth, though, and kept stuffing in pasta and bread. But every so often, despite his efforts to guard himself, he thought he must have let something leak out of his eyes, shown something in the way he looked at her. Because every so often, he caught her looking at him the same way.

And then an image flashed across his mind from the dream that woke him a few nights before. Dave tried to stuff it back where it came from, but his mind got away from him and followed its own lead. He saw their bodies entwined together on the table, her pale flesh pressed against his dark flesh. He imagined the look on her face when he kissed her . . .

Come on, man! Where you going? This isn't about that—is it?

They were finishing up their second glasses of tea when someone grabbed Dave's shoulder.

"Hey, Dave, Julie. What are you guys doing here?"

Dave looked up. It was Brock.

Chapter Thirteen

❧

His friend's eyes moved back and forth, from his face to Julie's. "I was sitting over in the back there. I didn't even see you guys come in."

"Well, hey, Brock, whassup?" Dave said, doing his best imitation of a man who was glad to see someone. "I didn't know you ever came to this place."

"Well, my office is just down the street," Brock said. "I come here all the time. But I never saw you here before."

"Hey, Coach Brock," Julie said. "Who's ahead today, the good guys or the bad guys?"

"Hard to tell, Julie, hard to tell. Depends on whom you're representing, I guess."

"Integrity for sale," she said, shaking her head.

"Ouch. I really wish you hadn't found out I was a lawyer until a little later on in our relationship."

She shrugged and grinned. "I call 'em as I see 'em."

Dave felt a little surge of jealousy. *Those words are for me, not him.*

"I'll bet you do. Well, gotta run, guys," he said, clamping a hand on Dave's shoulder and giving it a brotherly squeeze. "No rest for the innocent."

"So what's your excuse?" Julie said.

Brock pointed at her and shook his head. "Shame on you. I'm going to have to change my opinion of you." He gave them a final grin and wave. Dave thought his eyes lingered on them for an extra instant, then he turned toward the cash register and started reaching for his wallet.

Dave turned back to Julie. "Well. I didn't expect to see him in here today."

"Who did you expect?"

He moved his fork around on his plate for a few seconds. "You, I guess."

"Okay then. Mission accomplished."

He gave her a guilty grin from under his eyebrows. "Yeah."

"I gotta get back to work," she said, reaching for her purse. He put a hand on her arm.

"No, I got this."

"No, definitely not," she said. Her voice had an edge to it, one that told him he needed to sit back and pay attention. "I'll pay for my own this time."

"Sure. Well, then . . . thanks for meeting me on such short notice."

She softened slightly. "Thanks for calling. I think."

He gave her another twisted grin. "Yeah. I think, too."

Michelle came into Clarice's office without knocking. She closed the door, then sat herself down in one of Clarice's armchairs and aimed a flat, no-nonsense look at her boss.

"What?" Clarice said, after enough seconds had passed that she assumed she was going to have to provide the opening.

"Something going on with you, sister girl, and Michelle's here to find out what it is."

"What are you talking about?"

"Girl, you better chalk that English teacher voice with me. This is Michelle, and no matter how hard you tryin' to act like it's all good in the hood, the sister ain't buying. I can tell when somebody's got a weight on her soul, and you carrying about a hundred extra pounds, best I can figure."

Clarice stared at her assistant for several seconds, but Michelle never budged. Clarice blinked first and sighed. That was one thing Michelle's hard raising had done for her: the girl was intimidated by just about nothing.

"Oh, Michelle, I don't know. I thought if I could just get over this broken leg and get back to work, I'd be fine, but—"

"But you're not."

"No."

"Only thing I know of that'll make a woman look and sound the way you do right now is a man. Either she's worrying about the man she's got, or she's worrying about the man she doesn't have, or she's worrying about one of those men finding out about the other one."

If anybody but Michelle had been sitting across from her, Clarice wouldn't have been able to stand it.

"Well, as the lawyers say," Michelle said, "I take it by your silence that you agree. So that just leaves figuring out which one of the three is you. I sure hope you're not seeing somebody on the side, 'cause girlfriend, I been down that road, all the way down it, and there ain't no answers anywhere along the way."

"No, of course I'm not cheating on David."

"You thinking about it?"

"No!"

Michelle cocked her face sideways. "You sure? 'Cause there's more than one way to cheat. There's the way I did it, and then there's also keeping yourself away from your husband, and just not giving yourself to anybody else."

Clarice held herself still, but she was squirming inside.

"You're the star in this office, Clarice, and no doubt about it. I'm proud to work for you. I'd like to be more like you in a lot of ways. But, honey"—she leaned forward, laying her arms on Clarice's desk in what looked almost like a child reaching, or a gesture of supplication—"I hope I don't ever sacrifice my husband's heart for any career. I don't care if I'm making more money than Shaq and Beyoncé put together. I nearly lost him once. Girl, I don't ever want to get close to doing it again."

Clarice held Michelle's eyes as long as she could, but in a few seconds she had to look away. "Michelle, it's . . . I don't know. What you say is right, of course, but . . . things have changed."

"Changed how?"

"I'm different after the wreck. For those first weeks, I was almost completely dependent on David. It scared me. I became very depressed. And then, when I started getting better, I couldn't talk to him about it. And now . . ."

Michelle waited. Clarice knew she wouldn't budge until she'd heard everything there was to hear.

"Now David's different."

"Meaning what?" There was a new sharpness in Michelle's tone, a heightened level of alert.

"He's . . . I think he's stopped caring. I think maybe it wouldn't matter, even if I told him I wanted to work things out." She looked at Michelle. "I think he's ready to leave."

"He said that to you?"

"No, he hasn't said anything. Really, he hasn't spoken to me in days. We're just living in the same space, trying to not bump into each other."

"Clarice, honey . . . you think he's seeing somebody else?"

Despite herself, Clarice emitted a harsh little laugh. "David? No!" Then she gave Michelle a worried look. "I mean, he's not the type . . . is he?"

Michelle gave her a serious look. "Man'll do a lot of things you wouldn't think about if the wrong situation comes along."

"But . . . he goes to church! He was the one who insisted we attend together. He wouldn't do something like that. I think you're on the wrong track, Michelle."

"Well, for your sake I hope that's right. But even if you're not, Clarice, you got to make up your mind what *you* want."

"I know, and so far, I can't."

"Well, sister girl, here's what we'll do. I'll leave you alone and let you gather your thoughts. I'll pray, and I'll get Miz Ida praying, too. And somehow, amongst you, me, Miz Ida, and the Lord, this gonna get solved."

Michelle got up and came around the desk toward Clarice. She leaned over and wrapped her boss in a good tight hug.

"All right. Get yourself together. I'll always be around if you need me."

"Thanks, Michelle. Really."

"You're welcome. Really."

"I don't know why you can't see what's going on right under your nose," Mama said. "That man is playing you for a fool and you're either too afraid or too stupid to admit it to yourself!"

Clarice rolled her eyes and wished again that she'd resisted the urge to call her mother after work. Mama always had all the answers—for everybody else.

"Yes, well I guess you'd know, wouldn't you, Mama? About being left and all." Clarice almost immediately regretted saying it. Mama's silence crackled over the phone line like a noiseless slap.

"Yeah, I think I do know a little more about it than you do," Mama said, the bitterness in her voice making her words heavy and slow. "But I tell you what, you do whatever you think you got to do. You a grown woman, so I guess you don't have to listen to me if you don't want to."

"Mama, I—"

But Mama was already gone.

∞

Dave grunted as he hoisted the equipment bag into the back of his pickup. He took one more look around the ball field, then opened his door and scooted behind the wheel.

"Pretty good practice today," Brock said from the passenger seat.

"Yeah, not bad. Why'd you say your car was in the shop?"

"Air conditioner."

Dave nodded. "Right. Getting to be the time of year when you got to have one of those."

"Yep. The heat'll get you."

Dave started the pickup and backed out of the parking lot.

"I thought you were a little rough on Jaylen, though," Brock said. "He's been working hard on that curve. You ought to at least let him try it out a little in practice."

"That kid's too young to be throwing a curve. He'll damage his arm."

"He's throwing it the right way, Dave. I don't think it'll hurt his arm."

"You been letting him throw it?"

"I caught him a little bit today while you were working with the outfielders. I think he can handle it."

Dave chewed on this for a while. For some reason, Brock was getting on his nerves. In fact, pretty much everybody was getting on his nerves.

"Well, I still think he's too young."

Brock just looked out his window. A few seconds later he said, "So when did you and Julie start eating lunch together?"

"Say, man, who died and made you my mama?"

"Easy, bro. I just asked, that's all."

Now Brock was looking at him. Dave could imagine the questions crowding into his friend's face. Why did it have to be anybody else's business if two adults decided to eat lunch together in a crowded restaurant in the bright light of day? It wasn't like he and Julie were sneaking around somewhere. What difference should it make to Brock if he ate lunch with Julie?

"We were talking about Clarice's therapy. That's all there was to it."

"Oh."

Brock was still looking at him. Dave felt like he was on some kind of witness stand.

"That's it? Just 'oh'? You got something to say to me, Brock, you might as well just lay it out, man, you know what I'm saying?"

For a long time Brock didn't say anything. He looked at Dave for a while, then stared out the windshield. Dave merged onto the freeway.

"Julie's a nice-looking woman," Brock said finally.

"Oh really. I hadn't noticed."

"Sarcasm isn't your strong suit, Dave."

Dave felt his control slipping and tried to care, but lost the battle. "Whatever, man. I don't need you to tell me how to live my life, you dig? I'm doing just fine on my own, so you can just take your friendly concern and shove it, all right?"

"Look, Dave, I'm not trying to get under your skin. I'm your friend. I know things haven't been great between you and Clarice; you've told me so yourself. I just don't want to see you . . ."

Brock's voice was still low and controlled, and that just made Dave madder. "See me what? Mess up my life? Mess up Julie's life? Is that where this is going, Brock, because if it is, let me save you some trouble, awright? Nothing's going on between Julie and me. I like her kid, you know? I think he's great, and his dad doesn't seem to notice he's alive, and I think that's a shame. But that's it, you got it? Nothing else."

Brock held up his hands. "Okay, man, okay. Whatever you say. Sorry I brought it up."

"Yeah, well, me too."

Dave drove on, all the while wishing he could shake the feeling that was clinging to him like the smell of dirty socks: the feeling that he'd just told a lie to his best friend. But he wasn't sleeping with Julie, and it aggravated him to think Brock imagined things with her were headed that way. Julie was a friend. She was someone who appreciated Dave for who he was, and that felt pretty good, for reasons Brock would probably never understand. And Dave wasn't so sure Brock didn't have his eye on Julie, anyway.

Him sitting over there all high and mighty, talking about me doing something I shouldn't be doing, all the time he just wants to move in on her . . .

. . . But he is single, isn't he, bro? And you aren't. Right?

The voice turned up the heat on his anger. The whole universe was on his case today. What did a man have to do to get some slack?

"Whoa, dude. How fast you going?" Brock said.

Dave looked at the speedometer. The needle quivered just above the eighty-five mark. He pulled his foot off the pedal. He thought about apologizing for not paying attention, but then Dave decided he didn't feel like saying anything at all right then.

He dropped Brock off at his house. Brock got out of the pickup and put his hand on the door to shut it. He looked in at Dave with an expression that signaled he had something else he wanted to say.

"All right, I'll holla atcha later," Dave said, staring straight ahead through his windshield.

"Yeah. I'll . . . I'll talk to you later," Brock said. His door swung shut and Dave pulled away.

∞

Clarice's mind tumbled like a cement mixer as she drove home; she was going over and over her conversation with Michelle, her own mixed emotions, her observations of David, Mama's anger. All of it was going around and around, and so far, there wasn't a single part of the mix that she could get a hold on. Everything just kept moving and eluding her grasp.

David's pickup wasn't in the driveway when she got home, but today was a baseball practice day, so that was nothing unusual. She went into the house, managing the cane pretty easily. She was hoping the doctor would even clear her to walk without it after her next appointment.

She changed clothes and went to look in the fridge to see what would be easy to fix for dinner when she heard David's vehicle pull into the drive. His door clunked shut and in a few seconds the door leading from the garage into the kitchen opened. He looked at her, then away, before walking toward the bedroom.

"I'm going out of town on Saturday," he said over his shoulder.

"Bryson's got a swim meet I want to go see. Just so you know." He walked on into the bedroom, peeling his T-shirt up over his head as he went through the doorway.

Clarice stood there for a moment wearing a puzzled expression. Something was trying to come through to her, trying to pierce the swirling fog that had passed for her thoughts for the last several hours. And then, just like that, Mama's face was in her mind. It was as if she'd been standing in front of Clarice instead of talking to her on the phone. "Why can't you see what's going on in front of your face?"

The sudden intuition was so sharp and strong, Clarice almost had to grab the kitchen counter to keep her balance. Of course! Why hadn't she seen it before? Julie's strangeness, David's unchar-acteristic aloofness . . . it made so much sense that she would've laughed at herself if the implications weren't so painful.

David and Julie were involved. That explained so many things. And suddenly, Clarice knew what she had to do. With the clarity that comes only through a sudden crisis, Clarice realized she didn't want to lose her marriage. Not to Julie, not to anybody.

She went into the bedroom. David was in the bathroom, so she stood and waited for him to come out. The door opened and he saw her standing there, and she could tell by his face that he knew every-thing was different now.

"David, I'm going to ask you a question, maybe the most impor-tant question I'll ever ask." Clarice surprised herself by how calm she sounded. "And I need for you to understand that if you lie to me, I'll know. David, are you having an affair with Julie Sawyer?"

She watched his face. His eyes flickered back and forth like a cornered animal looking for an escape route that wasn't there; his jaw clenched, then opened, but no words came out. The longer he looked at her without saying anything, the more certain she was that this whole thing wasn't just in her imagination.

In her sales courses, they'd taught that once you asked the prospect a closing question, the next person to speak is the loser. A sale could be killed by an agent who couldn't stand the silence that inevitably followed the closing question. She'd just asked David the closing question and she had no intention of losing.

"What made you ask me that?" he said finally. His voice wasn't loud or angry, just curious more than anything. Clarice nearly lost it; she'd have felt so much better if he'd blustered or yelled. But he didn't. He sounded like a criminal who thought he'd pulled off the perfect crime and was honestly surprised at getting caught.

"That doesn't really matter, does it?" she said, still able to control her voice. "The point is, I asked you a question. What is your answer?"

Chapter Fourteen

∞

"*C*an I sit down?"

She shrugged. She had no intention of moving from her spot.

He crossed to the corner of the bed and sat. He looked away from her into a dark corner of the bedroom. He scratched his face and ran a hand across his hair.

"Nothing's happened," he said finally. Clarice was surprised at how much it hurt her that he didn't even bother with the pretense of a denial. "We've talked on the phone. We've had lunch. Once." He looked at her. "I swear to you, Reesie. That's all."

She knew the next question she had to ask, but it was slicing her throat like a thousand tiny knives. She closed her eyes for a few seconds, then looked at him again. She felt like Mama was looking over her shoulder and judging her daughter as harshly as her son-in-law.

"Does that mean nothing's happened because nothing's ever going to, or nothing's happened—yet?" Clarice said.

He took a deep breath and let it puff out his cheeks as he released it. He shook his head.

"I don't know, Reesie. I honestly don't."

"Can you please try—" her voice started to tremble and she stopped talking, swallowed, and went on "—try to tell me what you were thinking?"

"Clarice, you got to understand. She appreciates me. She likes me for who I am. That's a nice thing to feel. It's . . . it's been a long time."

He still wouldn't look at her. Clarice felt his words jabbing her like thumbtacks, hurting her with the sting of truth. Again, his quietness had more impact than if he'd ranted and raved. David was telling her what was on his heart, and it was ripping her apart.

"Reesie, come and sit down. We got to talk this out."

Clarice wavered for a moment, then moved toward a chair.

∞

As Dave looked at his wife, he thought about the words he'd exchanged with Brock and realized he still felt soiled by what he'd said. Granny used to say she thought maybe lying was the worst sin a person could commit. "Even worse than killing," she'd say. "Sometimes you can't help killing. But the truth ain't never done nothing to nobody that didn't deserve it."

Or maybe . . . maybe he really had wanted Clarice to know, in some strange, roundabout way. Maybe he wished she'd care enough to do something about it.

"I'm not going to even try to pretend we can settle this between us right now," Dave said. "But we got to get started. If we don't, then it's all over."

"Maybe it's all over anyway," she said, looking at him with shimmering, pain-filled eyes.

"Maybe so. Can you look me in the face and tell me with no doubt in your mind that's what you want?"

He watched her and waited.

Dave tried to figure out what was happening. When she asked him point-blank and out of the blue, he knew he couldn't just deny it as he had with Brock. If he looked deep, deep down within himself, Dave knew he still loved his wife. The way things had been for a while now, it would have been easy for him to say otherwise, but he knew it wasn't true. Things weren't all bad with Clarice; if they were, he'd have already been gone. No, the misery of marriage problems was that you had something that was worth saving—you just didn't know how to do it.

It didn't make any difference one way or the other now; the beans were spilled, and they weren't going back in the bag. He wondered what she was going to say. He thought about saying a little prayer, but he couldn't quite bring himself to do it right this moment.

"David, right now I honestly don't know what I'm feeling. When I walked in here, I had every intention of telling you I'd do whatever I had to do to keep our marriage alive. I think part of me was hoping my guess was wrong, that I was making it all up in my head, that we'd be okay like we've always been. But now . . ."

"Clarice, I'm going to say this as easy as I can: we haven't been okay for quite a while now."

The tears spilled over her eyelids; they followed each other in quick tracks down her smooth brown cheeks. "I know," she said, in little more than a whisper. "But I couldn't ever figure out what to do about it."

After a while, he said, "What we're doing now seems like a start."

She nodded.

"I'm not saying I was right to let myself get in this far with Julie. But, Reesie, it didn't happen in a vacuum. You understand what I'm saying?"

She nodded again.

"I know I'm not everything you want in a man. But I'm a man who wants to be with you. I haven't known how to ask for that, but that's what I've always wanted. I've wanted to take care of you and protect you. But sometimes, baby girl, you . . ."

She wiped her face with the back of her hand.

"Here, let me get you a tissue or something," he said, getting up and going into the bathroom. When he came back and handed it to her, she said, "Do you know what I was looking at on the computer, those times you came home?"

He shook his head.

"I was on the Internet, looking for information on depression."

He started to say something like, "Julie told me that might be a problem," but thought better of it. Instead, he just waited.

"I couldn't understand what was happening to me, David. All my life I've prided myself on being independent, on taking care of myself. Even after we got married, I was determined to be an equal partner, not some little woman you kept in the kitchen and the bedroom."

"Aw, Reesie, I never—"

"I know, I know. You backed me all the way. I guess some part of me kept expecting it to wind up being a trick to get on my good side so you could get something you wanted later. And when you started talking about having children, I . . . I guess I thought that was the sound of the other shoe dropping. I think I started pushing you away."

"I might have pushed back a little too hard sometimes," he said after a few seconds.

She shrugged. "I guess there's plenty of blame to go around."

For maybe as much as a couple of minutes, neither of them said anything.

"Well," Dave said finally, "what's the next step, do you think?"

She looked at him. "I know you wish we could just kiss and make up, David, but I think this is too complicated for that."

He shrugged and nodded.

"I think we might need to talk to somebody. A counselor, maybe, or somebody from church."

"I'll do whatever you say, Reesie."

"And I think neither one of us needs to see Julie again."

Dave sat for a minute and let this soak in. Of course he knew Clarice was right. What chance did they have to put their marriage back together if Julie was always in the background, literally or figuratively looking over their shoulders?

But . . . never see her again? Never again be able to see the look on Bryson's face when somebody put a gold medal around his neck?

Dave felt as if he were staring down a long dark tunnel and some-body had just taken the flashlight out of his hand. They might come out of the tunnel together, he and Clarice, or they might not. But once he walked in, it was for sure he was going to be in the dark for a while.

He took a deep breath. Without looking at her, he said, "You're right. But I think it needs to come from me."

"You handle that however you need to," she said. "But just make sure you handle it. This is nonnegotiable, David."

"I know, I know."

He knew, all right. What he didn't know was how.

❦

A low-hanging cloud had been following her around all morning, but Julie couldn't figure out what it was. Sitting at her desk, she was staring blindly at her day planner and wondering why none of the marks in her own handwriting made any sense to her. Her cell phone rang.

She looked at the screen; it was Dave. Feeling a ray of sunshine break through her personal overcast, she answered. "Hey there!"

"Hi, Julie. I've, uh, got something to tell you, and it's not going to be easy."

A cold place started in the pit of her stomach and began spread-ing up toward her heart. She knew where this was going. "Yeah, sure, Dave. What's up?"

"Julie, what we're doing is wrong. At least, what I'm doing is wrong. I've got a responsibility to my wife, and when I'm with you, that responsibility goes way on the back burner. I'm sorry, and really, this is my fault, but I've got to tell you I can't see you anymore."

Julie suddenly felt divided in half. One part of her was holding her phone, trying to get her mind around what Dave had just said—words that, though she knew they had to be spoken, were still bang-ing in on her like an emotional pile driver. The other part of her was watching like a director watches a play, waiting to see what the character named Julie would say next.

So this is what breaking up feels like. It's a little better than being abandoned, but not much . . .

"You can hate me, cuss me out, whatever you need to do," he was saying. "I deserve whatever you can dish out, most likely."

"Oh, Dave, don't be ridiculous. Of course I'm not going to cuss you out, you sorry son of a—" she broke off and gave her best attempt at a chuckle.

"That was a joke, by the way."

"Yeah. Nice." She could feel his sad smile coming through the line.

"The fact is, you're exactly right. And we both know it. And no, it's not your fault alone. I was skating along on the same thin ice, in case you didn't know it. And starting to wonder when it was going to crack."

"For real?"

"For real."

"Well . . . I guess I won't be watching Bryson's meet this weekend, after all. Actually, I almost feel worse about that than anything else."

"I'm going to take that as a compliment to my son," she said. "Although some less charitable women would actually start swearing right about here."

This time she actually heard him chuckle.

"Don't worry, I'll take care of it with Bryson," she said. "He's a pretty tough kid, in his own way. He'll deal."

"He's an awesome kid," Dave said. "I'm really going to miss him . . . and you."

"Now, let's not start back down that trail," she said around the growing constriction in her throat. "That way lies madness."

"Okay, well . . ."

"I take it this also means I'm now one physical therapy patient short?"

"Yeah. 'Fraid so."

"Well, no problem. I'll just have to go out and hustle up some more business. For what it's worth, I owe Clarice a thank-you. I kind of like this idea of working in the patient's home. I may start doing some more of that."

"Cool. Well, you'll be great at it, because you're great."

"Yeah, well . . . you're not so bad, yourself, Mr. Johnson."

"There comes that path again."

"Yep. Sorry. Okay, well . . . I guess that's it, then?"

"Yeah, I guess so. You, uh . . . you take care, awright?"

"You can count on it."

"Okay, then. Well . . . bye."

"Bye, Dave."

She pushed the end button before either of them could say anything else. She got up from her desk and walked at a brisk pace through the double doors into the main hallway, out through the front reception area, and onto the sidewalk outside. She crossed the tightly clipped lawn to a bench that sat in a secluded corner of the hospital grounds, partly shielded by hedges of red-tipped forsythia. And there, she sat down and held her face in her hands and wept like a little lost girl.

∞

Dave hung up feeling as if someone had just reached down his throat and yanked one of his lungs out through his teeth. But there was one more call he had to make. He started dialing.

"Bryan, Wilkes, and Houseman; how may I direct your call?"

"Brock Houseman, please."

"And who may I say is calling?"

"Dave Johnson."

The music on hold was some kind of white folks' elevator music. That was bad enough. What made it unbearable was that it was some syrupy arrangement of "Three Times a Lady." Dave was pretty sure Lionel Ritchie would get indigestion from listening to it, no matter how big the royalty check was.

"Yeah, Dave?"

"Hey, Brock. I, uh . . . I owe you an apology, man."

"For what?"

"For being out of line last night, coming back from practice."

"Hey, forget about it. So was I, probably."

"No, that's the trouble. You were right."

"I was? About what?"

"About me and Julie. Or at least, you used to be right."

"No kidding."

Silence.

"But I just wanted to tell you, first of all, that I'm sorry I acted like a jerk," Dave said, "and second, that Julie and I won't be seeing each other anymore."

"I see."

"She's a classy lady, and she deserves a lot better than being somebody's squeeze on the side. Not that that ever happened; I mean, we never—"

"Yeah, I get it."

"Anyway . . . that's all. I just wanted to tell you that, and that I'm sorry. And thanks for having the guts to say something about it. That's what a friend would do."

"You got it, bro. Anytime, day or night."

"Yeah. Well . . . thanks again."

Dave hung up, suddenly realizing that through the haze of pain and sadness, he was also feeling cleaner and more honest than he had in a while. That had to be a good thing, didn't it?

His phone rang. "All-Pro, this is Dave."

"Hey, Dave, it's Brock again. You and Clarice . . . you guys are going to try and work things out, right?"

"Right. That's what started all this, actually."

"Okay, cool. Well, glad to hear it. Do whatever it takes, you know?"

"Yeah, I intend to. Thanks, man."

"You got it."

Dave hung up again. He realized then that neither Julie nor Brock had asked him, in so many words, if Clarice knew what was going on. Dave guessed they assumed she did. He wondered briefly if he ought to call Julie, at least, and let her know, in case she should ever run into Clarice in the store or something. Yeah, maybe he should . . .

No. That was just a goofy way of talking to her one more time, he decided. No point in it; the sting wasn't going to go away any quicker if he kept putting her back in his mind.

When he got home, Clarice was on the computer. But this time she didn't close the Web browser when he walked in the room.

"I'm looking for marriage counselors," she said. "I called the church today, and Pastor Wilkes recommended some people. I'm checking out their Web sites."

Dave had to hand it to her. When Clarice got started on a project, she went full bore. She'd attacked her physical therapy that way, and now she was attacking marriage rehab.

"What else did the pastor say?"

Clarice swiveled her chair to look at him. "He said he was sorry to hear we were having trouble, but that he appreciated the courage it took to admit it and then seek help. He said no marriage was past saving until somebody gave up trying, and he would pray that we'd both have the strength not to do that."

Dave nodded. "Sounds like good advice. Anybody on here look good to you?"

Clarice turned back to the screen. "I'm kind of interested in this one, here." She tapped the monitor with a red-lacquered fingernail. "Carmen McAtee. She's got a PhD. I guess that's good."

"Beats me," Dave said. "But I'll go wherever you say, baby girl. You hungry?"

"Not really."

Dave warmed up a helping of whatever casserole they'd cooked most recently. He poured himself a glass of tea and sat down at the kitchen counter to eat. He hoped Clarice came up with somebody good; he really wanted things to work out. But he was worried, because the only thing on his mind all day had been Julie.

He felt bad about it, he really did. And it wasn't as if he had sat at his desk mooning over her all day, writing her name on his blotter. He'd worked. He'd completed his quarterly spreadsheets; he'd gone out and called on some prospective accounts; he'd even interviewed several applicants for crew positions, a task he usually left to his office manager. He'd done his best to keep himself busy all day, because he knew if he didn't, he'd probably do something stupid.

And still, at least four times during the day, he'd dialed all but the last digit of Julie's cell phone number before making himself clear the screen and put the phone back in his pocket.

What was wrong with him? In his head, there was no question about the best course of action. Clarice was his wife, the woman he'd promised in front of God and everybody else to love, honor, and cherish until death. That wasn't something you just walked away from. Keeping his marriage together was the hundred-percent right thing to do.

And then he thought about the last few months and years, about his growing sense that nothing he did ever quite measured up to whatever standard Clarice was using. The success of his business, his desire to have children, his ability and wish to care for her. None of it registered with her, it seemed.

He shook his head. That kind of thinking wasn't going to get him anywhere except in trouble. He shoveled a bite of casserole into his mouth and chased it with a gulp of tea. To Dave, the food tasted about like yesterday's oatmeal, but he knew if he didn't eat, he'd get sick or something. And he was going to need his strength to keep it together while he and Clarice figured out if they could keep it together.

∽

Clarice rolled over and looked at the alarm clock: seven o'clock. What she wanted to do was become unconscious again so she could elude the burden of getting through another day of dragging around all the uncertainties of her life. But she'd gleaned enough information from the Internet to know what she had to do instead was keep moving. "Depression is like a fungus," one of the Web sites had said. "It grows best in dark, unused places. Get out there and force yourself back into life. Exercise. Go to work as much as you can. Taking just a few proactive steps can build a foundation for coping and recovering."

All right, all right. Enough with the morning sermon. I'm getting up, so lay off me . . .

David was already gone. He'd slept next to her, but he might as well have been in the next county for all the good they did each other. It was as if there were an invisible divider in the center of their king-size bed, one that neither of them had apparently tried to cross. The middle third of the bed looked like nobody had touched it. The covers and sheets were disturbed only on the edges where she and David had been. That was for the best, Clarice told herself. Any attempt at lovemaking, based on how they both felt right now, was likely to be a disaster, and liable to do more harm than good.

Clarice sat up and reached for her cane leaning against the nightstand. She pushed herself upright and trudged to the bathroom. Then she went to her closet and changed into some fairly ratty-looking shorts and a tank top to do her morning PT.

She stretched on her back and extended her right leg, then did several reps of the lifting exercises Julie had showed her. As she did, she thought about Julie. She wondered what it had been like for David to tell her what he told her. She wondered if Julie really had designs on David's affections, or if she'd just gotten caught up in something that got away from her. She considered what she knew of Julie's personality and tried to work out in her mind what the experience with Julie had been like for her husband. And she tried to shove away the guilt that came when she faced the realization that David had needs his own wife wasn't meeting . . . needs Julie was evidently prepared to fulfill.

She stood up and walked to the kitchen counter to do her kicks and bends, gingerly putting a little more weight on her right leg as she went. She still used the cane at work and around the house, but since the orthopedist had rated her "weight-bearing as tolerated," Clarice reasoned it was a good idea to see if she couldn't tolerate a little more. So far, there was no pain or swelling. Her biggest trouble was with her toes, as Julie had rightly predicted. They were still a little too weak from disuse to give her secure balance when she walked. She meant to keep working on that, though.

The picture came to her then, as it did multiple times each day—the picture she tried to keep out of her mind but at the same time felt perversely drawn to, like a rat hypnotized by a snake: the picture of what David and Julie were like together. She imagined them in a restaurant, talking and laughing. She thought about them strolling along a shaded street, holding hands. She imagined them in bed together, David's fingers twined in her hair, David's mouth on hers, David's dark hand gliding along the curves of her white body.

She shook her head, trying to physically fling the hated image away from her. *It didn't happen! David was telling the truth about that, and you know it. Quit making things worse than they already are.*

She almost wished David had gone out and had a one-night stand somewhere. Clarice thought that would be easier to deal with, in some ways, than the knowledge that another woman had touched her husband's heart. She finished her exercises and got into the shower. She had some clients coming in this morning, and she wanted to get to work a little early to do some prep. Michelle had laid out their files on her desk yesterday afternoon.

She also wanted to call one or two of the counselors Pastor Wilkes had recommended. Clarice knew that any credible counseling was likely to be a two-edged sword. As she'd said to David, there was plenty of blame on both sides. She wasn't looking forward to seeing herself in the mirror the counselor would probably hold up. *But it's the only way.* If they didn't get started, things would just get worse.

Chapter Fifteen

*C*larice waited on hold, going over the list of questions she'd jotted down. She felt a little nervous, but she kept telling herself that was a good sign; she'd be more alert that way.

"This is Carmen."

The voice was quiet and well-modulated, musical almost. Carmen McAtee could've had a career in radio. Or with one of those 900-number phone places. Clarice immediately wished she hadn't had that thought.

"Yes, I'm Clarice Johnson, Dr. McAtee, and—"

"Please. Call me Carmen."

"Well, all right then, Carmen. I was referred to you by my minister, G. A. Wilkes."

"Oh, Gary! Yes, we've known each other since seminary."

So that's what the "G" stands for.

"How can I help you, Clarice?"

"Well, I think—that is, my husband and I—we're in need of some . . ."

"Marriage counseling?"

"Yes. Something like that." Clarice felt as if she'd just admitted to being a shoplifter.

"Clarice, I am a family practitioner, you know. Just about a hundred percent of the people who call me are wanting help in some personal area of life. There's no need to be embarrassed."

"Thank you. Do you mind if I ask you a few questions?"

"Of course not. I've still got about ten minutes before my next client comes in, so fire away."

Clarice ran down her list, asking about insurance, confidentiality, privacy, length of sessions, scheduling, and everything else on her list. And then she took a deep breath and asked a question that wasn't on her list, but the only thing she'd been able to think about.

"Carmen, what sort of chance do we have? I mean, I know you haven't met David or me, but we're both pretty decent people. I know I want to save our marriage, and I think he wants the same thing. Do people work these things out?"

After a few seconds of silence that gave Clarice ample opportunity to regret allowing such childish vulnerability to show to a perfect stranger, Carmen said, "Well, of course, as you say, I don't know either of you, nor do I know anything about your situation. But to answer your last question, I can say absolutely yes, people do work these things out . . . when there is a commitment on both sides to keep doing the hard work of making the needed changes."

Of course, Clarice. What else did you think she was going to say?

"As far as what kind of chance you and—David, is that your husband's name?"

"Yes, David."

"You've got the same chance as anybody who walks into my office or any other counselor's. You pretty much get out of counseling what you put into it, Clarice. And that part's not up to me. I can guide you, I can make suggestions, I can offer some fairly informed opinions, and I can referee if I need to, but I can't fix your marriage. Whatever may be wrong with it, the fixing is up to you and David. And frankly, you should find that comforting."

"Yes. I see. Well, uh . . . do you have any openings?"

"Actually, I don't know. I'll have to pass you back to Karen for that information. Would you like me to do that?"

"Yes, if you don't mind." Clarice had a good feeling about Carmen McAtee.

∞

Dave opened the door for Clarice, then followed her inside. The counselor's offices were at the end of a carpeted hallway on the fifth floor of one of the older downtown buildings. Walking up to the door, Dave felt the same way he used to feel when he'd been sent to the principal's office in elementary school. Clarice was a woman and the counselor was a woman. The way he figured it, that pretty much meant he was in trouble.

But this was the place Clarice had picked, and he'd told her he'd go wherever she said. Well, here he was. The reception area was decorated in soft blues, greens, and tans, with a little white tossed in for accent. The chairs were all big and overstuffed, and Dave was pretty sure he was catching whiffs of one of the aroma-therapy air fresheners that were always being advertised in his supplier catalogs. Dave was instantly suspicious of any place that worked so hard to get you relaxed. Clarice went to the desk and the receptionist handed her a clipboard with about a quarter-inch of paper on it. She said they'd need to fill out all the forms and hand them back in. No wonder she'd told them to get here a half hour early.

They sat in a couple of the chairs and Clarice started working on the forms. Every now and then she'd ask a question that made Dave have to dig in his wallet: Social Security numbers, insurance plan carrier, that sort of stuff.

While Clarice wrote, Dave looked around. Some of the art on the walls was vaguely African, in a kind of homogenized, politically correct way. There were lots of stylized scenes of families. All done in tasteful, low-stress colors, of course; that was the politically correct part. Clear plastic racks on the counter held pamphlets with titles like "Family Stress: Some Practical Solutions" and "Depression: How to Recognize It and What to Do About It." A framed certificate proclaimed Alicia Carmen McAtee, PhD, a member in good standing of the American Association for Marriage and Family Therapy. Dave figured that had to be a good thing.

Clarice handed him the clipboard, pointing to a question that read, "I'm here today because I'm concerned about . . ." Following this lead phrase were several responses with empty check boxes. Clarice had already marked the ones labeled "My marriage" and "Depression." There was a tiny dot inside the one that said, "Having thoughts of suicide," but no check. He looked questioningly at her, and she motioned with her eyes toward the clipboard. He scanned the list, trying to find something he was worried about besides being here in the first place that Clarice hadn't already marked. There were a few other choices: "My job," "My children," "Aging parents," "Paying bills"—Dave thought about marking that one and writing beside it, "How much does this place cost, anyway?" but thought better of it—"Alcohol or drug use," "Communication with significant others," "Sexual issues," and "Loneliness." He stabbed quick checks into the boxes for "Sexual issues" and "Communication with significant others" and handed the clipboard back to Clarice without looking at her.

It occurred to him that the simple fact of completing this intake form in each other's presence was about as much actual communication as they'd done in the last several months combined, other than the recent confrontation that had led them to this counseling session. The level of his discomfort also gave him the vague sense that something was wrong when a man and his wife had to come to a pastel-painted, spa-smelling office to talk about things that really mattered.

There was another sheet with a whole battery of questions about marital matters; two copies of this sheet were included, and Clarice told him he was supposed to complete one and she was to do the other one. Dave went to the desk and asked for a pen, then sat back down to start on his form. He hadn't gotten far into it when he started getting the urge to go someplace behind a closed door to fill it out. It asked things like, "List five attributes that attracted you to your partner initially," followed by, "Does your partner still possess these attributes?"

Another question wanted him to write down five dreams or expectations he'd had at the beginning of the relationship, and to indicate whether or to what degree those dreams or expectations had come about. There was a lengthy statement at the bottom of the form letting him know that "Marriage therapy, though geared toward bringing about a higher level of enjoyment and general satisfaction with life, can sometimes have unintended consequences. What is viewed as a positive outcome by one partner may not be viewed in the same way by the other." The form also warned him that if, in the judgment of the therapist, he was ever considered a danger to himself or others, the therapist had a duty to inform the authorities, as well as any other person who could potentially be involved. There was a line for Dave's signature at the end of this paragraph.

He finished the form as quickly as he could, but then he couldn't decide what to do with it. If he handed it to Clarice, she'd see all his answers. And he didn't think he wanted to see hers, either. Luckily for him, about the time Clarice finished marking her sheets, the receptionist called their names and asked for the clipboard. Clarice handed her the board and Dave gave her his paperwork at the same time. The receptionist told them Dr. McAtee would see them now. She pointed toward a door around the corner from the desk.

They walked into an office with walls covered in a dark green, with small splashes and daubs of lighter greens and a purple so subdued it was almost brown. The African art was in here, too. On the wall facing the door hung a watercolor of a black Jesus with little nappy-headed children seated about his knees, smiling up at him. There was up-lighting in the corners, and the mini-blinds—dark green to match the walls—were open just enough to reflect some sunlight toward the ceiling.

"Hello, folks. Come in and sit down."

Carmen McAtee stood in the center of the office on a rug that had been fashioned from some kind of quilt. As Dave might have guessed from the art, she wore a tie-dyed kitenge with the neck embroidered in an ornate design executed in white silk. She was short—maybe five feet six—and pretty round, judging from her face and what he could see of her arms. She had skin the color of well-creamed coffee and the tight cornrows on her head were white, sprinkled with gray. She held out a hand jingling with hoop bracelets, first to Clarice, then to Dave. She motioned them toward chairs. Dave sat on one side of an upholstered love seat, and Clarice took the armchair beside it. Carmen settled herself in another armchair, facing them both. She sat back and smiled, bridging her fingertips in front of her. She started with some small talk, asking about Clarice's cane and finding out about the wreck, learning the name of Dave's business and Clarice's real estate firm, asking how long they'd known Gary Wilkes, as she called the pastor. She let this go on for about five minutes.

"Well, I want to congratulate you two for showing up together today," she said. "That tells me there's some level of commitment on both your parts to work together toward some solutions to the things that are troubling you. That in itself puts you quite a bit ahead of the game." She then turned to Dave, still wearing a smile like someone who'd just won a lifetime supply of peace and quiet.

"All right. Dave, why don't you tell me your view of what's going on with you two?"

Dave had the brief thought that she could've just read what they'd written on the clipboard, but decided not to mention that. "Well, uh . . . we've been married for fifteen years. I've got a good business and Clarice is a successful real estate professional. But the last few years have been . . ." He could see Clarice's shoulders stiffening. "They've been kind of hard, I guess. I think we've kind of, you know, lost touch with each other," he said, looking to Clarice for something—confirmation? Rebuttal? He wasn't sure.

"What about children?" Carmen said.

"None," Dave said, and something in his tone must have alerted the counselor; in the silence that followed, she appeared to be studying him. After a few seconds, she started nodding. She turned to Clarice.

"All right. Clarice, how about you? What would you like to tell me about how things are going with you and Dave?"

Clarice's eyes were moving back and forth between Dave and Carmen. "Well, I suppose I'd like to say first that the reason we're here is because David has been seeing someone else."

If this surprised Carmen, she masked it extremely well. Dave guessed counselors were trained to be pretty shockproof, but to him, Clarice's words sounded so big in the room, he was surprised to see Carmen react as if Clarice had made a passing remark about the weather.

"And how do you feel about that?" she said to Clarice.

Clarice was fidgeting with her hands in her lap. She was sitting on the edge of the armchair, her back ramrod-straight. "I'm . . . embarrassed, I guess. And a little betrayed."

"Only a little?"

Clarice was staring at the center of the quilt-carpet. "A lot."

"May I ask the first name of this woman you've been seeing?" Carmen said.

"Do we really need to do that?" Dave asked. "I mean, isn't that a violation of privacy or something?"

"I didn't ask for any last names," Carmen said. "Besides, she's already here in the room, whether we talk about her or not. We might as well give her a name."

"Well . . ."

"Julie," Clarice said. "She's—she was my physical therapist."

At this, Carmen's eyes actually widened ever so slightly. "I see. Mmm-hmm. Dave, can you tell me what it was about Julie you found attractive enough to have an affair with her?"

Man, she gon' pull my file somethin' proper, ain't she?

"Well, we didn't have an affair, not really. I mean, we—"

"You didn't have sexual intercourse with her?"

"No."

Dave realized that he, a former coach who'd been in countless locker rooms with adolescent boys, had just been completely embarrassed by this grandmotherly counselor.

"But you wanted to?"

"Well, see, I don't know, you know? I mean, Julie was nice and all—"

"Nice how?"

"She liked me, you know? She valued me without wanting to change everything about me."

"I see." Carmen seemed to ponder this for a few seconds, then she turned back to Clarice. Dave breathed a silent sigh of relief.

"Clarice, I wonder how you're reacting to what Dave is saying. I hear him saying that Julie was attractive to him because she sort of took him where he was. I wonder if that sounds like anything you and Dave have dealt with before."

Clarice's eyes were still pinned on the carpet. "David has mentioned something like that lately," she said.

"And do you expect Dave to change?"

Clarice crossed her arms in front of her; she looked like she was hugging herself. Dave watched Carmen's eyes flicker over Clarice's pose and mannerisms. He had the feeling she was catching everything that went on, both what was spoken and what was remaining unsaid.

"I don't know . . . I guess so, in some ways," Clarice said. "Is that so bad?"

"I'm not sure," Carmen said. "All of us need to change something at some point in our lives. The problem is what's motivating the change. Can you give me an example of something about Dave that you want changed?"

After a few seconds, Clarice said, "I've been encouraging David to think about other career options."

Looking at Clarice squirming under Carmen's scrutiny, Dave

almost felt sorry for his wife. It was intimidating having your private thoughts and assumptions dragged out into the light by someone who was a relative stranger. Somehow, when Carmen repeated your feelings back to you, you felt kind of guilty just for having had them. It didn't matter how accurately she restated them; just hearing them voiced so dispassionately was a lot like looking at yourself naked while standing in front of a full-length mirror under bright fluorescent lights.

Things went back and forth like this for most of the hour, with Carmen putting first one, then the other under her magnifying glass. Dave had to hand it to her; she didn't miss much. When you were the object of Carmen McAtee's scrutiny, you knew she wasn't going to lay off until she'd heard all she wanted.

With a few minutes left, she said, "Well, I think we've done some good work here today. I want to thank you both for being honest and forthcoming. As you know, I can't really do much unless you two are willing to work with me as cooperatively as possible.

"I think I've got a pretty good grasp of what's at issue between you. But next time we get together, I'd like to take a look at how you're presently negotiating or failing to negotiate these differences. And I'd like to give you some homework, all right?"

Dave and Clarice waited.

"I want both of you to keep a journal this week. Doesn't have to be anything fancy, just a written record of your thoughts and feelings. I'm especially interested in having you write down how you feel after any significant interactions between you, whether they're positive or negative. Make sense?"

"You want us to record our fights?" Clarice said.

"I wouldn't have put it quite like that," Carmen said, "but yes, among other things, I want to see how you handle conflict as a couple. Conflict is pretty inevitable between human beings living in close quarters; what matters is how it's handled and resolved—or not resolved. Okay?" Dave nodded, but he wasn't looking forward to the prospect. He'd never been much of a note-taker or writer in school; trying to untangle his thoughts about disagreements with Clarice enough to put them on paper didn't exactly sound like his plate of cornbread.

"Just see Karen when you go out, and she'll handle all the particulars." She stood and escorted them to the door. She shook their hands, giving them both that quiet, Buddha-like smile. "Good luck, you two. Hang in there, all right?"

Chapter Sixteen

*J*ulie considered talking to Bryson about Dave not coming to the out-of-town meet, but then she decided not to bring it up unless her son did. First, she'd never told him Dave was coming, so Bryson wouldn't be expecting to see him. Second, she couldn't think of a way to explain Dave's absence—which, Bryson would eventually realize, was a permanent situation—that sounded plausible without being an outright lie. Finally, every time she started thinking about it, she got so down in the dumps that she could barely function, so she mostly just shuffled the entire matter into a little-used wing of her mind and did her best to leave it there.

This, of course, was only partially successful. She'd catch herself, even during sessions with patients, remembering the way he'd looked at her, say, after Bryson won a race. Now and then, she'd say something that sounded to her like something Dave might say. She had dreams about him at night; when she woke, she could remember brief impressions of him, but she was always disappointed she never remembered the whole dream. In a way, this seemed a bit symbolic of the entire history of their relationship—"friendship," she corrected herself.

She went through whole cycles of guilt and self-justification—often several times an hour. Of course Dave was married; of course his first obligation was to his wife; of course it was the right thing for them to stop seeing each other; of course the things she was thinking about him, if followed to their logical conclusion, constituted a violation of Julie's standards for herself . . . and Dave's too, apparently.

And then she tried to figure out exactly what she'd say to Bryson when the day came, as she knew it would, that he asked why Coach never came to his meets anymore. At these moments, she'd ask herself a different series of questions: Why can't my son have the company of a man who genuinely cares about him, since his own father doesn't seem to? Why should my weakness and poor judgment deprive Bryson of something he desperately needs to grow up and become a well-adjusted man? Wasn't there some way to salvage the parts of their relationship that were positive—and Julie could think of many such parts—and insulate themselves from the more doubtful aspects? Why couldn't Clarice go with Dave to some of Bryson's meets, for example? Or why couldn't Dave bring Brock with him? If she and Dave had chaperones, nobody could think they were up to something inappropriate . . . could they?

Then again, the thought of seeing him and knowing, beyond all doubt, that he could never be to her what she longed for him to be was almost worse than the prospect of never seeing him again. A clean break, she told herself finally, was the best thing for everybody. And then she'd start back at the beginning and run the whole mental obstacle course again.

Julie had just such a game of emotional ping-pong with herself while driving back from the out-of-town meet. Bryson sat on the other side of the front seat, hardwired into his portable CD player via the headphones she'd gotten him for his last birthday. The Sunday afternoon sun was coming through her windshield for the whole drive. By the time they got home, Julie's face was locked in a perpetual squinting scowl. She was wishing she hadn't missed church that morning, which reminded her of Dave. Almost everything reminded her of Dave these days. They'd barely walked into the house when her wall phone started chirping at her.

She picked it up and glanced at the caller ID on the screen, holding the faint, unreasonable hope that it might be Dave. But it was a number she didn't recognize. She thumbed the talk button.

"Hello?"

"Julie? This is Brock Houseman."

"Oh . . . hi, Brock." She was pretty sure her disappointment was audible only to herself.

"Hi. I just wanted to call and see how you're doing."

This caught Julie slightly off guard. "Fine, I guess," she said. She groped around for some sort of follow-up and finally came up with "How are you?" Not too original, but good enough in a pinch.

"Oh . . . I'm good. Doing good—yeah. Uh, how's Bryson?"

"He's fine. Actually, we just got back from out of town; he had a swim meet."

"Oh yeah? How'd he do?"

"Really well. He won both his individual events and his relay team won, too. His team placed first overall."

"Wow! That's really great. Impressive."

"Yeah, I'm pretty proud of him."

"Well . . . I guess you must be pretty tired from the drive. I ought to let you go, huh?"

"Sure, I guess. Nice to hear from you, Brock."

"Yeah, well . . . take care, okay?"

"I sure will."

She hung up. *Take care.* That was the last thing Dave had said to her.

"Who was that?" Bryson said, strolling into the kitchen. His headphones were still around his neck.

"Brock. Coach Brock, remember him?"

"Sure I do. What'd he want?"

"Wanted to know how you did at the meet. I told him."

"Oh yeah? What'd he say?"

"The only thing a reasonable person could say: you're an awesome dude."

"Whatever, Mom. Was that the only reason he called?"

Good question, Bryson. Julie wondered how much, if anything, Brock knew about her and Dave. It felt weird even thinking of it that way: her and Dave. It made them sound like an item. But if they were, or had been, what would Brock know about it? And if he did know something, what might he have said to Dave about it? And if he said something to Dave, what might Dave have said in reply? Did Brock know, for example, that they weren't seeing each other anymore? Did he know why? The thought embarrassed her, then began to intrigue her . . . just a little.

"No, he pretty much just wanted to know how the meet went."

"Oh. Cool." Bryson donned his headphones again and went back toward his room.

∞

Clarice sat at her desk at home, fiddling with her rather expensive pen, her chin propped in her hand. Her elbow rested on a sheet of creamy vellum from the box holding more of the same, which she'd purchased earlier that week, along with the pen, as an incentive to making and keeping a journal, per the instructions of Carmen McAtee, PhD. She stared at nothing in particular and tried to harness her disorganized, indistinct thoughts.

She'd never guessed she might actually feel worse after a counseling session than she did before. But somehow, after they left Carmen's office that first time, the reality of actually being in marriage counseling bore down on her in a way she was entirely unprepared for. *Marriage counseling*—the phrase hung in her mind like a sign crafted of black neon, if there could be such a thing, floating like an accusation above everything she did, said, or thought about.

True, she'd made the suggestion that put them there in the first place. But her uneasy mind wouldn't let it go at that. She worried and teased at it, turning the whole history of the problem over and over until it was as ratty and soiled and creased as a Sunday crossword puzzle that you couldn't finish but couldn't throw away.

The thing that especially stung her was Carmen's accusation—maybe it was a suggestion, but in Clarice's memory it rankled like an accusation—that maybe, just maybe, part of the problem with David was really a problem with her. At her best moments, Clarice knew, of course, that what she'd said herself was true: there was enough blame to go around. But then she started pondering the implications, especially the hard things she might have to admit or agree to. She began to feel the roots of resentment creeping under the foundation of her resolve.

She'd tried to put something down in her journal about that. She wanted to write about how she'd been raised to be completely self-reliant and self-confident; that in the world she was trained to know, no greater value existed than the ability to identify a worthy goal and dedicate yourself to achieving it, no matter the cost. She wanted to say something about how David's soft, self-effacing manner frustrated her. She wanted to put on paper some words that could explain how disappointed she was that the dashing, handsome, idealistic young man she'd married had allowed himself to settle for running a small company that wasn't growing or expanding, and he seemed fine with that. She wanted to talk about the ways she thought her husband was ignoring his potential as a leader for the community. She wished she could find some way to express her suspicions that for all David's talk about supporting her and admiring her and loving her, what he was really doing was creating a subtle pressure to cause her to finally give in, get pregnant, and settle into a life that was less than the uncompromising adventure she'd always dreamed of.

But when she tried to put ideas like these on paper, the picture that emerged was not one she was happy contemplating. She imagined Carmen reading her journal and then peering at her in that calm, saintly way, like somebody's great-aunt, and repeating the content back to her in a manner that made Clarice sound like a cross between Leona Helmsley and Evilene from *The Wiz*.

She wasn't that bad, was she? She was willing to listen to David.

She at least wanted to want him, even if she hadn't actually made the mind-to-body migration with the whole physical aspect of their relationship. Surely Carmen would understand that, wouldn't she?

What Clarice needed was to write herself a letter explaining all this. Maybe that was it. Maybe if she just spoke to herself, without thinking so much about how all this was going to sound to somebody else, she could break the deadlock within her own mind and get things moving.

Moving toward what?

She put this question out of her mind; that was an answer that would have to come later. For now, it was enough that she was picking up the pen and starting to write.

∽

Dave drove up to the office. He went inside and grabbed the handful of pink "While You Were Out" notes the office manager held toward him.

"Anything good in here, Alma?"

The office manager shrugged and kept making keystrokes on her computer.

Dave went back to his desk. He slid his chair out and put his feet up on the desk before sorting the message slips like a hand of cards. And then his eyes fell on the name of the top slip: Mrs. Clark. No. It couldn't be. He looked at the number the caller had left and groaned. *Clarice's mother.* He sorted through the rest of the slips and found that three of the five were from his mother-in-law.

I don't need this today.

But Dave knew she'd keep calling until she talked to him. She'd call him at home at three in the morning if she had to. That woman was about as hardheaded as anybody Dave had ever met. Even Clarice didn't come close.

He took a deep breath and reached for the phone on his desk. He punched in the number, praying she'd be out getting her hair done—or maybe having major surgery.

"Hello?"

"Mrs. Clark, this is—"

"I know who it is, and I know what you're doing, even if my daughter's too blind to see it. I'm telling you, boy, you better leave that little white heifer alone if you know anything about what's good for you."

Dave had expected her to be talking smack; this was even worse. "Now, Mrs. Clark, nothing's—"

"Don't even start with me, boy. I haven't lived as long as I have to believe every honey-mouth story some man thinks up. I'm telling you, I know what you fixing to do, and I'll make sure Clarice takes care of it the right way if I have to come down there myself."

"All right then, thanks. Glad you called." He hung up the phone with Mrs. Clark still talking.

"I gotta go, Alma. Making some sales calls." He scooted back from his desk and started for the door. Alma gave him a distracted wave.

He needed some time to just . . . be. Maybe he'd drive to a few of the buildings where All-Pro had contracts, just to drop in on the building managers and see how things were going.

Dave let the pickup coast through the morning traffic and tried to clear his thoughts. Clarice's mother couldn't have picked a worse time to start in on him. Tomorrow was their next appointment with Carmen McAtee, and Dave wished he wasn't dreading it so much. A few times this week, he'd tried to start a conversation with Clarice about some of the things that were on his mind, but somehow he couldn't summon the energy. Then, he thought about trying to write down some stuff in the journal he was supposed to be keeping. But when he sat down with a pen, he couldn't get beyond the opening sentences: "Thought about talking to Clarice about stuff. Couldn't think what to say." And that was it. And now, on top of being discouraged, he was mad.

He wondered how Bryson was doing. He kept thinking Julie might call, just to update him, you know? Nothing serious, no talk about either of them, just telling him about Bryson's latest meet, how he was doing in school, that kind of thing. That would be enough, wouldn't it? He told himself he didn't need anything beyond that and tried to ignore the voice that kept suggesting he was kidding himself about that, too.

Bryson . . . Dave really wanted to know how he did at the meet. His phone was lying on the front seat, right beside his hand.

Why shouldn't I call? Everybody else in the world seems to know what I ought to be doing; why shouldn't I decide one or two things for myself?

Before the voice could talk him out of it, he pulled into a parking lot and hit the speed dial button that he knew would still take him directly to Julie's cell phone. She answered on the second ring.

"Hey, Julie, it's Dave."

The two or three seconds of silence that followed were just enough to make him think this was a terrible mistake.

"Hi," she said.

"Listen, uh, I was just wondering . . . how'd Bryson do at that meet ya'll went to a couple of weekends ago? I never found out about that, and I was just wondering."

Dave sounded pathetic, even to himself. He almost ended the call, but decided to hang on, just to see what she'd say.

"He did really well."

She sounded like she was having to concentrate really hard just to remember how to form words. Dave closed his eyes. Why had he called? He knew better.

"He won both his events and his relay team won, too."

"Is that right? Now that's what I'm talking about!" He tried to dredge up some enthusiasm. He was trying to think of some way to end the call without embarrassing both of them.

"Yeah," she said, "he was really happy with the way it all turned out. And his team placed first overall."

"Fantastic. That's really fantastic."

There was another pause and he was just about to make some lame attempt at disengagement when she said, "I miss you, Dave."

Dave felt like a very small, precise bomb had gone off in his chest—a laser-guided missile that honed in on cell phone signals.

"I know," he said. "Me too."

Damn! Why'd I say that?

After another few seconds, she said, "How are things at home?"

The pause before his answer was just long enough for Dave to have an internal shouting match with the voice, which he won. "Not great. We had our first counseling session last week, but you know . . . I guess we need to hang with it a while."

"Back in therapy, huh?"

He gave a sound that was trying to be a laugh. "Yeah. Turns out there are things harder to heal than a busted leg."

"Yeah. Wish I could help you there, but I can't."

"Oh, I don't know, Julie. There's help, and then there's help."

More silence.

"Yeah, well . . . I'd better get back to work, I guess."

"Yeah . . . me too. Take care, awright?"

He heard a tiny chuckle but couldn't figure out what he'd said that was funny.

"That's your patented parting line, is it?" she said.

"What you talking about?"

"'Take care.' You said that the last time we talked. It was the last thing I heard you say."

"Well . . . maybe it won't be. The last thing, I mean."

"Okay, I've really got to go," she said after another pause.

"Yeah. Catch you later."

"Bye."

Dave disconnected. He sat for several seconds and stared at the phone in his palm. What had he just done? What had happened?

∞

The bell clattered against the door as Julie came into the salon. She glanced at her watch to see it was a quarter past noon. There were women in two of the chairs but nobody in the small waiting area, so maybe she could get her trim and be on her way in time to grab a quick lunch before rushing back to work.

"Hi, welcome to Talk of the Town," said the girl behind the cash register. She looked like she should be in school at this time of day, Julie thought.

"Hi. I'm here to see Kathy? Julie Sawyer?"

The girl studied the appointment book. "Oh, yeah . . . here you are. Kathy went to grab something to eat. She ought to be back any time now, though. You want to wait?"

Julie looked at her watch again, chewing her lip. "Yeah . . . I guess so." She went to the table in the corner of the waiting area and sifted through the stacks of dog-eared magazines piled haphazardly there. She found a copy of *Us* that was less than a year out-of-date and sat down to flip through the pictures of beautiful people in expensive clothing.

After a few minutes, the bell clattered again. Julie looked up hoping to see Kathy, her favorite stylist, but instead she saw two African American women—one older and one younger. She went back to her magazine for an instant, then had a sudden sinking feeling. She stole another careful glance at the two women and confirmed her worst fear: it was Clarice and her mother.

"I'm here for Jacqueline," Clarice was telling the young receptionist. "She assured me she'd work me in during the lunch hour."

The girl was scanning the appointment book, slowly shaking her head. "I'm sorry, ma'am. I don't see your name here anywhere."

"She called yesterday," Clarice's mother said, leaning past Clarice. "I heard her."

"Yes, ma'am, but I can't find—"

Clarice made an impatient sound. "I've got a business appointment in forty-five minutes. I really need to get this done."

"Well, I guess I can call Jacqueline," the girl said. "She's at lunch by now, but . . ."

"Doesn't look to me like they take care of business around here,"

Clarice's mother said. "I heard you tell her specifically that you wouldn't have much time."

"Umm . . . would you ladies like to wait for a few minutes?" the receptionist said. Julie wanted to choke her.

"I guess we don't have much choice," Clarice said. "Call her, and please ask her to hurry."

"Yes, ma'am." The girl picked up the phone and Clarice and her mother sat down across from Julie.

Julie was doing her best to disappear. She held the magazine as close to eye level as possible, hoping desperately to avoid notice. But in the sudden quiet, she could practically feel Clarice's mother staring at her.

Maybe she doesn't know about me. Or maybe she's forgotten who I am—

And then she heard a stage whisper from Clarice's mother: "Well, would you take a look who's here?"

Chapter Seventeen

❧

Clarice leaned over and said something to her mother that sounded like a warning against making a scene.

"I'm just sitting here, Clarice," her mother said, looking at her daughter as if she'd been insulted. "I don't know what you mean by that."

There was a period of quiet, punctuated by the flipping of pages on both sides of the waiting area. The receptionist was talking into her phone, and Julie hoped she was telling Jacqueline that if she hurried up and got here, she could prevent an ugly situation from getting uglier. Julie realized she was staring at the last page of her magazine. There was no way she was walking over to Clarice's corner to pick up another one; she flipped back to the first page and started over.

"I'm glad you're taking care of your appearance, Clarice," her mother said in a voice that could probably be heard in the restrooms at the rear of the salon—with the doors closed. "You know, a woman can't be too careful. She lets herself get lazy, stops worrying about the image she presents, pretty soon her man starts looking around."

"Mama, stop it," Clarice said in a low voice.

"Stop what? I'm just saying . . . you owe it to yourself to keep yourself looking nice, do things for yourself, that's all."

Julie felt her face getting hot. She stared at the center of her magazine, but the words on the page might as well have been in Sanskrit. *Just sit still . . . don't look up . . . pretend you're not here . . .*

"Of course, there are women out there who'll do whatever they have to do, too. You can't forget that."

"Mama, this is not—"

"They just looking for someone to butter their bread, and don't care about whose kitchen the knife came from."

"Mama!"

"Don't you look at me like that, Clarice! I can say whatever I've got a mind to say."

Julie realized her teeth were grinding together; her jaw muscles ached from being clenched. The edges of the magazine were crumpled in her fists. *Just breathe, Julie . . . in and out . . . in and out . . .*

"And besides, if you're not going to look out for yourself, you need somebody to do it for you."

That was it. Julie wasn't going to make it, and she knew it. Moving as slowly and carefully as she could, she stood and put the crinkled copy of *Us* in her chair. She looked at the receptionist and said, "You know what, um, I'm . . . going to have to go."

"I know that's right," Clarice's mother spoke just loud enough for Julie to hear.

"Just tell Kathy I'll reschedule, okay?"

"Well, um . . . sure." The poor girl was looking back and forth from Julie to the two other women as if she was afraid a riot was about to break loose.

Blinking rapidly against tears of embarrassment and anger, Julie made for the door. Just as she was going out, she heard Clarice's mother mutter something that sounded quite a bit like "Good riddance."

She was almost to her car when she stopped in her tracks.

No!

She didn't deserve this kind of abuse. That old biddy back there was talking about her like she was some kind of slut, and it just wasn't true. Julie turned and walked back to Talk of the Town. She flung open the door and faced Clarice and her mother, who looked as if they'd just been going at it themselves.

"Mrs. Clark, I deeply resent the insinuation in your words. You make me sound like something I'm not, and I think you ought to apologize."

The look on the older woman's face slid from surprise to something close to murderous rage. But before she could say anything, Julie turned to Clarice.

"And speaking of apologies, Clarice, I owe you one. I'm sorry I did anything to let things get started the wrong way between Dave and me. But you need to know that absolutely nothing happened between us. We talked, and that's it."

"Oh, it is?" Clarice's mother said, pushing herself up out of her chair. She leaned over in Julie's face. "You think that's all it takes to fix everything, missy? Just 'I'm sorry' and it's all done, is that it? Well, let me tell you something, white bread—"

"Ma'am . . ." The girl behind the register was pale as a ghost.

"You don't get off the hook that easy with me. My daughter may not have enough backbone to stand up to you, but if you think I'm just going to let you talk trash in my face, you can kiss my—"

"Mama, sit down," Clarice said, grabbing at her mother's elbow. "You're not helping anything."

"Oh, is that right?" she said, wheeling on her daughter. "And what are you doing to help? Just letting this little piece of angel food cake bat her big blue eyes at your husband when she comes to your house to work on that leg? I think something's wrong with you, Clarice, and it's not your leg."

"I did not have sex with Dave!"

The girl behind the register was staring at Julie, openmouthed.

"Okay, I'll admit I was vulnerable, and he probably picked up on that, but Dave is a good man. He'd never—"

"My daughter doesn't need you to tell her what kind of man she's married to, you little—"

Clarice stood up. "Mama, stop it right now! I'm a grown woman; I can speak for myself."

"Well you better start doing some speaking, girl, 'cause this little tramp here doin' all the talking right now."

"Excuse me?" Julie said. "Did I just hear you call me a tramp?"

"Mama, that's enough," Clarice said.

"Enough what? Enough of me trying to defend my daughter? Well, all right then. I guess I can go somewhere else since you got things under control here and all." And Clarice's mother stomped to the door, flung it open, and left. The bell clanged against the glass so hard it was a wonder the pane didn't crack.

Julie was staring at Clarice, trying to get her breathing under control. "Clarice, you've got to believe me—"

Clarice closed her eyes and turned her head away, holding up a hand in a stopping motion. "Don't. I can't listen to this right now, Julie."

"What do you mean? You'd better listen, because I'm telling you the truth. Dave loves you. He's devoted to you, whether you realize it or not."

"I don't think I need to hear from you—"

"You need to hear it from somebody, Clarice. You need to wake up and realize you've got a good husband who thinks you don't care what's important to him."

"Julie, don't start this with me. Not right now. I can't handle it."

"You'd better figure out a way to handle it, Clarice. You'd better get your head out of the real estate office long enough to pay some attention to—"

The door clanged open behind her and Julie spun around, half expecting Clarice's mother to be coming at her with a hatchet. But it was Kathy, her stylist, along with another woman wearing the same smock as the receptionist and a name tag that said "Jacqueline."

The two hairdressers stared at the two women standing like boxers in the middle of the reception area. Kathy found her voice first. "Hi, Julie. Um . . . you been waiting long?"

Julie shook her head and looked away.

"Clarice, you ready?" Jacqueline asked. Clarice gave her a tight nod and went back to the styling area.

Julie was about to walk out again, when she suddenly decided she had as much right to be here as this stubborn woman and her mother. "Kathy, I just need a quick trim. Can you take me now?"

Kathy looked from Julie to the catatonic receptionist. "Yeah . . . sure. Come on back."

From her chair, Julie could look in the mirror and see Clarice and Jacqueline across the way. She was pretty sure Clarice was looking at her.

∞

Clarice caught Julie looking at her in the mirror again. Jacqueline was chattering like she usually did, but today her voice was like static on the radio.

Mama might have been a little out of line, but what right does Julie have to tell me something about my marriage?

Clarice stared into the mirror, watching Julie and her stylist and fuming about the scene in the reception area. She needed to do something, needed to take control somehow.

She had a sudden idea and told Jacqueline to wait a minute. She got up out of the chair and walked back to the reception area. She batted the plastic drape out of her way and dug through a handful of magazines until she found the one she was looking for, the issue of *Vogue* with the picture of Naomi Campbell on the front. She carried it back to Jacqueline. She pointed to the picture.

"There. That. Give me that look."

Jacqueline made a confused face. "Well . . . okay, but you usually go for something a little more conservative—"

"Not today. Just give me that."

Jacqueline shrugged. "Whatever you say, Clarice. Have a seat."

∞

Julie watched as Clarice ordered her stylist around.

"Hang on a second, Kathy," she said. "I just got an idea."

She went to the reception area and found an issue of *People* with Meg Ryan on the cover. Meg was sporting a bushy down-in-front do that made her look like she'd just crawled out of bed. She showed the picture to Kathy. "Let's go for that, okay?"

Kathy's brow wrinkled. "But I thought you were just in for a trim."

"I changed my mind. I want to shake things up a little."

Kathy shrugged. "Okay . . . I guess."

∞

Jacqueline stood back from her work. "Well, what do you think?"

Clarice pulled her eyes away from what Julie's stylist was doing and gave her hair a critical appraisal. "Can't you do something a little more dramatic? Right in here, and right there?"

Jacqueline frowned. "I thought you had an appointment."

"It'll wait."

Jacqueline blew out her cheeks. "I can try. More dramatic, you said?"

Clarice nodded. She settled back in her chair with her arms crossed.

∞

Kathy spun Julie around to face the mirror. "How's that?"

Julie saw Jacqueline crossing the floor toward Clarice with a handful of various products. She looked at her own reflection in the mirror. "I don't know. Can we make it a little dressier?"

"You want Meg Ryan and dressy?"

Julie glanced at Clarice again and nodded decisively. Kathy sighed and picked up her comb.

∞

After an hour, Clarice had to admit to herself that it was time to go. But she didn't have to admit defeat. "I think that's what I'm looking for," she said, looking into the mirror. She made sure her voice was loud enough to carry to where Julie was sitting, still fussing with her hair and giving her poor stylist impossible instructions. "Yeah, I like it."

"You sure?" Jacqueline said. "It seems a little . . ."

"What?"

"Nothing. It's just a different look for you. You'll grow into it."

"Yes, I think so." Clarice gave herself one more leisurely inspection, then got up out of the chair and followed Jacqueline to the front. She paid her bill and gave a final hard stare back toward where Julie was sitting. She smiled sweetly at Jacqueline and handed the receptionist a five-dollar tip. "Sorry about all the fuss earlier," she whispered, and patted the astonished girl's hand.

She went out to the car. Mama was sitting in the front seat, waiting for her. Clarice braced herself for a tirade, but when she got in, all Mama did was stare at her for about ten seconds.

"Girl, what the hell happened to your hair?" she said.

⋙

Dave watched his team come in from the field to take their fourth at bat. Tonight they were playing the Boyd's Pharmacy Bears, and everything was working. By the third inning, Jaylen had struck out half of the twelve batters he'd faced, and four of the others either grounded or popped out. George, James, and Marcus teamed up for one of the prettiest 6-4-3 double plays Dave had ever seen to end the inning. Dave was standing at the dugout, getting some skin from the boys as they ran in to get ready for their plate rotation, when he glanced up in the stands and saw Julie. There was something different about her; was it her hair? But it was Julie, no doubt about that—even if she did look like Meg Ryan on a bad day.

She and Bryson were sitting up high, in the corner behind third base. She was waving, but not, Dave realized, at him. Brock, hurrying over to his coaching position by third, was returning the greeting. Dave felt something go sour inside. He called up the leadoff batter and the on-deck man, then took his spot by first base, trying to forget he'd spotted her.

For the rest of the game, he tried to pretend the horizon ended just past the third baseline. Every now and then, he'd catch Brock glancing up toward where they were sitting. Once or twice, when the boys did something good on the field, he thought he heard Bryson's voice hollering with the rest of the crowd. But as much as he wanted to, he didn't allow himself to look. He didn't need this . . . especially if she was here to see Brock.

By the top of the fifth inning, they were up by six runs. Dave took Jaylen off the mound to save his arm and give some of the other boys a little experience. It wouldn't hurt anything if the Bears got a few hits; they could use the boost, and his fielders were kind of rocking back on their heels. It worked out pretty well. The other team got six at bats and Dave's less-experienced pitchers walked in two runs before the Bears' first baseman flied out to end the game. The score was a little more respectable and Dave's boys still got the win by a handy margin. Something for everybody.

The boys were bunched around Brock's trunk for the post-game treat when Dave felt somebody pulling on his sleeve. He turned around.

It was Bryson, and his mom was standing right behind him.

"Good game, Coach," Bryson said, holding up his hand, palm out.

"Thanks, my man." Dave slapped Bryson's hand and they completed the handshake Dave had taught him, ending with the ever-popular palm-slide-snap-point combo. "Glad you could make it. Hey, I hear you've been tearing it up as usual in the pool."

Bryson shrugged. "I've been doing okay, I guess."

"Good enough to earn a Milky Way and a Coke?" Dave said, looking at Julie. Bryson spun to give his mom a hopeful look.

She smiled and shrugged. Bryson took off toward the mob gathered at Brock's car.

Dave watched Bryson go for a second, then returned to sacking up the bats and other equipment. "Nice that Brock told you about the game," he said. "I hope Bryson enjoyed it." He didn't look at her.

"Yeah, he's called once or twice," she said. "Just to check up on me."

Dave looked at her. "I had nothing to do with—"

"It's okay, Dave, really. He's nice."

Dave gave her a little smile and a nod, then leaned over to grab a handful of the catcher's gear.

"But he's not you."

Dave's hands paused, then resumed their work.

"It was good to see you, Dave," she said. "And Bryson could hardly wait to get to you after the game was over."

"He's a great kid."

"Thanks. Well, you take care, awright?"

He shot her a look. She smiled over her shoulder at him as she strolled toward Brock's car to retrieve her son.

∽

"So how have things been this week?" Carmen asked. She was sitting in her chair with her hands folded in front of her and wearing that half-smile of hers that made Clarice think of either the Mona Lisa or Whoopi Goldberg, depending on her mood.

She stared hard at David for a few seconds, trying to get him to step up, but he wouldn't look at her.

"Carmen, I've tried and tried to get David to open up to me, but he just won't. We hardly exchange a dozen words, on the average, during the time we're both at home."

Carmen looked at him, and he shifted this way and that before meeting her eyes. "It's just hard, you know what I'm saying? I'm tired when I come in at night, and I don't always feel up to getting lectured about everything I ought to be doing."

"Don't *always* feel? How about don't *ever* feel?" Clarice said. "And I don't appreciate your use of the word *lecture*. Especially when I don't get any feeling that you're hearing a word I'm saying."

"What do you do, Clarice, when you're talking and you don't think Dave is listening?" Carmen said.

Clarice stared into the empty air above Carmen's head. She returned her eyes to Carmen's. "Try to get some response from him, I guess. Or . . . maybe sometimes I just give up and go do something else."

Carmen nodded. "Dave, how does it make you feel when Clarice is talking to you, say it's about something you'd rather not hear or talk about?"

He thought for a few seconds. "Beaten, mainly. I just feel like there's no point in answering, because anything I say is probably going to be wrong."

Clarice looked at David. "I don't understand. How can you say I always think you're wrong?"

"She asked me how I feel," he said, nodding his head toward Carmen. "I just gave the most honest answer I could."

"Dave, if you could pick out a theme for the things Clarice says to you, what would it be? What's the one topic that comes to mind?"

"She wants me to be in a different business and have different priorities than the ones I have." He said it almost instantly.

Clarice was starting to feel like she was playing on somebody else's home court. "I've always had high goals for myself," she said. "I thought David had high goals, too. At least, I used to."

"Why do my goals have to involve a bigger and better career and a higher profile in the community? What if I don't think those are the most important things in life?"

"It's not about bigger and better," Clarice said. "It's about potential, David. What's wrong with wanting to live up to all you're capable of being?"

"Maybe I am," he said, his voice rising, "but it's just not on your scorecard."

"Clarice, you look a little surprised," Carmen said. "May I ask why?"

"He . . . doesn't usually raise his voice."

"What does he usually do?"

"Just sits there. Or walks away, or something."

"What did you think, just now, when he answered you the way he did?"

"I guess I thought he was saying something he felt strongly about."

Carmen turned to Dave. "How do you feel right now, Dave?"

"I don't know. Okay, I guess. A little angry."

"Good! That's honest. Do you think you could do what you just did in here today the next time you and Clarice are in a—let's call it a discussion, all right?—and you have something you need to say? Could you put your cards on the table with Clarice? Could you trust her enough to do that?"

Dave shrugged. "I could try, I guess."

"So I've been wrong all this time, is that what you're saying?" Clarice said.

"Not exactly," Carmen said. "But because of your strong opinions, and because of Dave's reluctance to upset the apple cart with you, honest communication between you two has just about stopped."

Dave was nodding.

Clarice and David looked at each other for the first time in maybe two months. She looked at her husband, and he looked at her, and the moment stretched into a crystalline silence that narrowed the whole world into the space between their eyes. At some point, Clarice realized, they were both nodding.

On the drive home, Clarice started to wonder what, exactly, she risked by allowing herself to be more vulnerable to David. Part of her wanted to be, desperately longed to be, nurtured and looked after. But it was hard to go against her raising. And, Clarice supposed, if she was honest, she had to admit that a part of her feared being abandoned as Mama had been.

Why, then, did she continue in the very behaviors that made her less appealing to the man who'd promised to stay with her forever?

David pulled into the driveway and triggered the garage door opener. He stopped just outside the garage and shut off the engine. Clarice opened her door and got out. She was barely using her cane these days, and her walking pace and balance were getting better and better. She felt sure that the orthopedist would okay her for full weight-bearing at her next follow-up. It would be a while before she'd be ready to boogaloo, but it felt so good to be almost fully mobile.

David held the door for her as she went into the house.

"Reesie, I've got some stuff to take back over to Brock. I'll just run that over there and come right back, all right?"

He went out. She heard the pickup door open and shut, then heard the engine start. She went into the bedroom, got her writing box out of the drawer in her bedside table, arranged some pillows against the headboard to lean her back against, and sat down to begin writing in her journal.

∞

Dave felt good, he really did. He'd seen some things in a different light today at Carmen's office, and his spirits were lighter than they'd been in a while.

And he wanted to tell Julie about it.

He knew it made no sense, but he decided he was going with it. He pressed the speed dial button and put the phone to his ear, waiting to hear her voice on the line. But after six rings, he heard her voice mail. He disconnected and dialed her home phone. Voice mail again. He looked at his watch. Where would she be this time of the day, if she wasn't home? Maybe in the shower or out in the yard or something, he guessed. He might try again later.

He drove to Brock's house and knocked on the door; Brock's doorbell had been messed up for about a year now and he was still "getting around" to fixing it. Dave waited a minute, then knocked again, louder.

About the time he'd decided that God didn't want him talking to anybody this evening, he heard the sound of bare feet slapping across hardwood toward the door. Brock opened the door, wearing a T-shirt advertising some obscure microbrewery and a pair of ratty gym shorts. He was sweating and breathing hard.

"Hey, Dave, what's up? Sorry if you've been standing out here awhile; I was working out on the Bowflex."

"Hey, no problem, dawg. Here's the scorecard from the last game."

"Oh, yeah. I wanted to make sure we had all the stats up-to-date before we head into these last couple of games." He took the sheets from Dave. "You wanna come in for a minute?"

"Yeah, maybe so. Why you hitting the machine so hard all of a sudden?" Brock had a roomful of exercise paraphernalia, most of which he'd bought off the Internet or some 800 number on his TV screen. The best Dave could figure, Brock averaged using his latest gadget, whatever it was, for about two weeks before getting bored with it. Dave had told Brock he could set up a medium-sized health club with all the stuff he had gathering dust in his garage.

"Oh, I don't know . . . just got the urge to get back in shape, you know? Want a Coke? Or a beer?"

"No thanks, man. I got to head back pretty soon." He tossed several days' worth of newspapers out of Brock's low-slung black leather armchair and sat down. "I told Clarice I wouldn't be gone long." He looked around Brock's apartment. "So . . . what? You got a new lady you trying to impress?"

Brock rolled his eyes. "Can't a guy get in shape just for his own benefit?"

"Some guys can, but I never suspected you of having the instinct for it. Well, babe, I got to hit the road." Dave pushed himself out of the chair. "Holla atcha later."

"See ya."

Dave was about half a block away from Brock's house when he dialed Julie's cell number again, and again he got voice mail. Ditto for her house phone.

Oh, well . . . probably for the best, anyway.

He drove home thinking about Brock and Julie—especially what Julie had said to him at the game: *He's not you.* Dave wasn't exactly sure what she'd meant by that, but it didn't sound like the door was closed to him in her mind. Dave wasn't sure that was a good thing; he really did mean to do everything he could to make it work with Clarice. You didn't just toss out a fifteen-year marriage because you were in a tough spot.

But was that all this was? Was there really any chance Clarice would be able to give some weight to the things that were important to Dave? He just didn't see it happening. The farther she went in her career, the farther she was from being able to consider ever having children, for example. The desire to be a father was a deep ache in Dave's soul; could Clarice ever understand that? And even if she did, would she be willing or able to do anything about it?

Dave pulled into his garage and went in the house. He tossed his keys on the kitchen counter and started to dig around in the freezer until he found the carton of premium ice cream he'd bought earlier in the week.

"Reesie? I'm getting some ice cream. You want some?"

No answer. Dave looked out into the living room. She was on the couch; hadn't she heard him?

"Reesie? You want some ice cream?"

She was acting like he wasn't even talking. What was going on? Dave straightened up for a better look. The news had started and Clarice appeared to be fixated on the screen. Dave looked at the screen to see what could be so gripping.

There, behind the attractive blonde anchorwoman, was a backdrop: a school picture of Bryson Sawyer. The headline across the top of the backdrop read "Pool Tragedy."

Chapter Eighteen

*D*ave walked toward the TV like a zombie, his heart freezing in his chest.

". . . struck his head on a diving board, according to witnesses. By the time EMT personnel arrived at the scene, Sawyer, age eleven, hadn't been breathing for several minutes, despite resuscitation efforts attempted by others poolside. The boy was pronounced dead upon arrival at St. Joseph's trauma center just after eight o'clock this evening. Funeral arrangements are pending."

The TV stayed on, but Dave didn't hear anything else; the newscast droned on and the sound was as meaningless to him as the buzzing of insects. He felt as if all the air had been sucked out of his chest, as if he had just been shot with some kind of paralyzing radiation. He could hear the blood pounding in his ears, but that was the only way he knew he was still breathing.

Bryson—dead? How was that possible? How could a kid drown when he could swim fifty meters in thirty seconds? There had to be some mistake, a wrong identity, something. There was no way Julie's son could have been jostling the boys around Brock's car at the game last week and be lying dead on some steel table right now. The world could not turn upside down this quickly without his noticing. Could it?

"Oh, David. I'm sorry. I'm so sorry, baby."

He looked at Clarice. She was still sitting on the couch, looking back at him, her hand over her mouth. He could feel the confusion on his face, saw it reflected in the way she looked back at him. So she'd heard it too? It wasn't some cruel hoax meant for his ears only?

"Bryson?"

"Yes, honey. That's what they just said."

"I can't . . . it's not possible, Clarice. That boy can't drown. He swims like a fish."

"Baby, I don't know, but that's what they said. He hit his head or something." She looked like she wanted to come to him, but didn't know how. Dave wished he could tell her, give her some opening, but right now he was trying to figure out how to keep his feet in a landscape tilting madly out of control.

A thought began to coalesce slowly from the swirling fog in his brain: Julie. He had to go to Julie. She needed him, and he had to go to her.

"She's . . . I've got to go," he said, when he was finally able to make his voice respond.

"David, are you sure that's a good idea?"

He looked at Clarice as if she'd just sprouted another head. "What?"

"I said, are you sure you should go? Go to her?"

"Clarice, the woman has just lost her son! Yes, I'm sure."

She got up and came to him, reaching for him with both her hands. "Then let me go too, David. I'll go with you. We'll do this together."

He pulled his hand out of her grasp. "You don't trust me, do you? You think I'm going to hit on her, right there in the emergency room. Good Lord, Clarice. How sick do you think I am?"

"David, I don't think you should go to her by yourself. If you won't let me go, then take Brock. He cared about that boy, too."

"That boy? Is that all you can come up with? You didn't even know this kid, Clarice; he was special. He needed me. I was good for him and—"

"And his mother?"

"Don't even say that, damn it! Do not say that to me, do you hear?"

"David, listen to me—"

"No, Clarice! Forget that mess you thinking! I been listening to you for the last fifteen years. All I been doing all day, every day, is listening to you. And you know what, Clarice? It's all one way. You talk, and I listen. I'm tired of listening, can you hear what I'm saying? Tired! And I'm not standing around here arguing with you about it anymore. I'm going to the hospital and I'll be back whenever, and you can just deal."

He whirled away from her, striding toward the kitchen counter and his keys. He'd just swiped them up when he heard her speak.

"David."

Clenching his jaw, he turned to face her.

"You need to know something, David." Her voice was low and calm—almost scary. She was holding her elbows, as if trying to keep herself in control. "If you go see Julie and refuse to take anybody with you, I won't be here when you come back."

He stared hard at her for several seconds. Was she actually threatening him at a time like this?

"You do what you got to do, Clarice," he said. "And I'll do the same." And then he was out the door.

Dave drove through three red lights on the way to the hospital. He screeched to a stop in the parking lot and ran toward the doorway into the trauma center; the automatic doors barely swished back in time.

Inside, he went quickly toward the first desk he saw. "Julie Sawyer, Bryson Sawyer—the boy that came in from the YMCA pool. Where are they?"

"Sir, she's in Meeting Room A, down the—"

The attendant pointed and Dave dashed off before he could finish his sentence. He found the room and pulled the door open.

Julie was inside, sitting on a couch. An older man with a chaplain's badge was with her. When she looked up and saw Dave, she gave a low, keening moan and stood, holding out her arms. Dave grabbed her and held her close, feeling her sobs against his neck.

"Oh, Dave, he's gone, he's gone. Oh, God, my baby's gone."

"Shh now, easy, baby. Easy now, just take it easy."

In the face of her overwhelming grief, Dave felt his own throat closing with the urge to weep. The fog was back in his brain, obscuring his vision, tangling his thoughts around each other. All he could do was hold her and pat her gently on the back and keep saying the words that already sounded all but meaningless: "Easy, baby. It's all right. I'm here. Easy, now . . ."

The chaplain stepped close. "I'll leave for a bit. I'll be right outside if you need me, though."

Dave nodded and the chaplain went out.

"He was at a practice with the relay team," she said. "They were finished, just goofing around before going to change. The older boys started doing stupid dives off the one-meter board, seeing who could do the worst belly flop, make the biggest splash. They said Bryson was trying to run backwards off the end of the board. He slipped . . ." Her words drowned in another surge of deep sobs.

Dave held her in his arms and felt her body shuddering against his. At that moment, he would have stepped in front of an oncoming train if he thought it would ease her pain. He would have picked her up and carried her until she felt strong enough to walk again— if that was what she wanted. He tried to add up the sum of what she was feeling, tried to measure the depth of the pit that had swallowed her up, but his mind reeled back, completely overthrown by the magnitude of her suffering. He was defenseless against it, helpless as he contemplated it. There was absolutely nothing else he could do right now except hold Julie, stay with her, and promise to help her any way he could. He hoped that would be enough.

"They had him on a respirator when they first brought him in," she said a few minutes later. "They kept him on it until I got here. But I could tell he was already gone." She looked up at Dave, her eyes silently screaming for understanding, for a hint of why. "His chest was moving up and down with the respirator, but Bryson wasn't there. He just . . . he wasn't there."

By now, her voice was a ragged, breathy rasp. She sounded drained. Maybe she'd wept herself dry for a while.

"You want to sit down, or maybe walk somewhere?" Dave said.

"They came and asked me about donating his organs," Julie said, as if she hadn't heard him. "It's funny—I never even gave it a second thought. My son's dead. If somebody else's son can live, why not help?" For the first time since he'd walked in the door, she looked up at him with something like recognition in her eyes. "You think I did right, Dave?"

"No doubt about it. Bryson would've wanted it that way. That's the kind of person he was."

"I wonder when his dad'll get here," Julie said.

"Has anybody called him?"

She nodded. "The hospital called his cell and his home phone. No answer either place. I don't think I want to see him. I don't think I even care if he shows up or not."

"Don't try to take that on right now, okay? You got enough on your plate. Think you could drink some coffee or something?"

She thought about it a few seconds, then nodded. Dave put an arm around her shoulders to guide her, then pushed open the door.

The chaplain was there and he was holding some papers on a clipboard.

"Mrs. Sawyer, the medical examiner's office needs you to sign these. For the autopsy."

Julie took the pen and clipboard and scratched her signature wherever the chaplain pointed. She handed him back the forms.

"Anything I can get for you?" he asked.

She shook her head.

"We'll be down in the cafeteria if they need her for anything," Dave said. The chaplain nodded. He gripped Julie's shoulder for a couple of seconds, then walked away to deliver the forms.

Dave kept his arm around her as they walked; the way she was moving blindly forward, he thought maybe she'd faint any second. But they made it to the cafeteria and into a booth. She waited there while he got two paper cups full of coffee from the self-serve bar and paid the cashier.

"You want anything in yours?" he said when he got back to the booth.

She shook her head. "Doesn't matter. Doubt I can taste anything, anyway."

He slid into the booth across from her and cupped his hands around his paper cup. He looked at her; she was staring at the tabletop and her eyes were as dull as burned-out bulbs. Dave guessed you couldn't come any closer to seeing the face of death and still be looking at somebody who had a pulse.

"What do you need?" he said, after maybe two minutes of silence.

After a few seconds, she shook her head. "I don't know," she said, after another few seconds passed. She looked up at him. "I really don't know. How do I keep on from here? Bryson was everything I lived for. What's left?"

He covered one of her hands with his. "Listen, Julie. I'm not going to try to tell you I understand, because I don't. Nobody does. My grandmother used to say that pain can't be shared, it can only have company. I'll be company for you, Julie. I'll stay with you, or I'll get somebody else to stay. Whatever. I'll make sure you don't have to be alone unless you want to be. But I'm telling you, even if it's too early for you to hear it, that the world needs Julie Sawyer. You hear me? The world needs you. Bryson doesn't, not anymore. You still need him, but he's taken care of now. I believe that, Julie, and I think you do, too. He's taken care of, so now we got to figure out how to take care of you. And I'm going to help. You don't have to get through this alone, you hear what I'm saying? Not alone. You gon' have help. That's a straight-up promise."

She looked at him and when she tried to smile, Dave thought it was maybe the most heroic thing he'd ever seen anybody do.

"Thanks, Dave. I believe you."

They sat some more. Nobody spoke for a long time. Dave figured there wasn't a whole lot that needed saying. But he kept his hand on hers, and she didn't pull away.

"Julie? Oh my God, our son, Julie, what's happened?"

They looked up, and a man was coming toward them, followed by one of the trauma center nurses. The man was holding onto a woman who looked maybe ten years younger than he. He was of medium height and had a narrow, rangy build. Dave took one look at him and recognized where Bryson had gotten many of his features. It had to be Ted.

He was weeping uncontrollably; the young woman with him seemed to be almost carrying him at times. Julie watched him coming with an unchanged expression. As he neared the table, Dave got up and scooted a chair over from a nearby table. Ted collapsed into it, holding his face in his hands.

"His cell phone was turned off," the young woman said. "We came here as soon as he got the message."

"Ted, get ahold of yourself," Julie said. As Dave watched, she seemed to stiffen, almost to grow. "He's gone, Ted. I'm sorry. But we've got to deal with it." She was becoming more collected as her ex-husband continued falling to pieces.

"I just can't believe it," Ted sobbed, shaking his head. "I just can't. Bryson . . . Bryson . . ."

Julie looked up at the young woman. "Have they taken you to see him, Kate?"

She shook her head. "When we got here, Ted asked for you. He said he had to see you."

Julie closed her eyes with an expression that suggested she was trying to find some previously overlooked stash of patience. She turned to the trauma nurse. "Can you take him down to the morgue? I think that's where the body is. He should see Bryson at least once more."

The nurse nodded. She and Kate gathered Ted up by the arms and led him off, still sobbing and moaning.

Julie watched them go for a few seconds, then turned back to Dave. "He hasn't seen Bryson or talked to him on the phone for over a week."

Dave shook his head. "I'm sorry, Julie."

"I think I'm ready to get out of here," she said. "I'm pretty sure I've signed everything there is to sign. I want to go home."

"You want me to call somebody to come over?"

She looked at him, and her eyes were as steady as if she were taking an oath. "Not really. But I guess you should, for your sake."

They called one of the women in Julie's Sunday school class and by the time Dave had driven her home, the other woman's car was parked alongside the curb near Julie's driveway. She got out and met them by the car, enfolding Julie in a hug that lasted quite a while. Dave could hear soft sobs and sniffs as the two women held each other and patted each other on the back. The other woman had a daughter Bryson's age and a couple of older kids, Julie had told him.

Dave promised Julie he'd bring her car back from the hospital parking lot. He saw the two women inside and was turning to leave when Julie called his name. He turned around and she came to him, gathering him close. He could feel her tears moistening his neck.

"Thank you so much," she said in a near-whisper. "I don't know what I'd have done if you hadn't come."

"Ain't no thing, sister," he said, trying to smile. "Anytime, day or night."

She nodded and released him.

Driving home, Dave felt the loss crashing in on him again. He kept replaying scenes of Bryson in his head: swimming, sending wild pitches in from right field, taking his cuts at the plate and connecting with the ball, sitting across from Dave at Gino's, the day of the meet. It made no sense; it was so random it made Dave angry at

God. He tried to pray away the bad feelings, but they wouldn't go. About the best he could do was a half-hearted apology to the Almighty for his ambivalence, followed by a weak promise to get back in touch later.

He got to his street and pressed the garage remote. The door ratcheted up and Dave realized the garage was empty. Clarice's Accord was gone.

Clarice. Dave hadn't given her a thought since pulling into the hospital parking lot. Was she really gone, or was she just out somewhere, driving around until she cooled off? Right now, he was too emotionally drained to care. He drove the pickup in on his side of the garage, switched off the engine, and pushed the button to close the garage door.

He walked into the house, half expecting to see a handwritten note on the counter explaining Clarice's absence, but there was nothing. The TV was off and the house was dark.

He walked through the living room and entered the bedroom, which was also dark. Dave reached for the wall switch and when the light came on, it revealed signs of recent frantic activity on Clarice's side of the room: some of her dresser drawers were open, while others, though closed, had clothing hanging out of them; her closet door was open and Dave could see the empty spaces where dresses, skirts, and blouses had once hung. He went into the bathroom and saw that her vanity area was almost devoid of cosmetics.

So she really was gone.

Dave searched around inside himself for feelings of remorse. He came up mostly dry. He replayed their confrontation just before his leaving and remembered his unbelieving anger; how could she be so callous toward Julie's grief as to put her own anxieties at the front of the line?

He looked at his watch. It was nearly one in the morning; he'd been gone nearly three hours. Plenty of time for her to pack her suitcases and go . . . where? Dave didn't know, and right at that moment, he didn't care.

He thought about Brock. Should he call and inform him about Bryson? Dave decided to let Brock sleep. And besides, Julie could tell him, in her own way and her own time. Dave just didn't have the strength right now to talk about it with anyone.

He undressed and fell into bed. Dave closed his eyes and tried to empty his mind. He hoped he could get at least a little sleep. Maybe then, in the morning, he'd start figuring out what to do about . . . everything.

Chapter Nineteen

∞

When David walked out, Clarice stood in the same spot without moving for probably five minutes. Her mind was a blur. Everything was shouting at her at once: Bryson's shocking death, the agony Julie must be feeling, David's anger, the searing pain he was experiencing, her own fear, and closely allied to it, her indignation. She felt like someone standing in a room with a hundred leaks in the roof; which one do you tend to first?

None of them, she decided finally. You just walk out of the room.

She made herself move toward the bedroom, made herself start packing. She watched her hands and arms getting down her suitcase and overnight bag. They seemed like the arms of a stranger—or maybe a puppet. It was almost as if she'd lost all feeling, all sensation. But somewhere down in the well of her mind, she was determined to do what she'd decided to do. She grabbed clothes out of the drawers, not paying much attention to what she was packing. A part of her mind hoped that somewhere in the tangled heap she had shoved into her suitcase were enough necessary articles to clothe herself for work. Where was she going? She wasn't sure. Just out of here. For tonight, she could get a hotel room somewhere. Tomorrow she might see about something more permanent.

She scooped an armload of underwear into her suitcase, then carried her overnight bag into the bathroom and raked most of her makeup, creams, and perfumes off the counter. She went to the closet and started grabbing hangers.

Clarice carried everything to her car and dumped it in the back-seat. She thumbed her remote to open the garage door and started the engine as she waited for the door to open.

As it rose, she realized she was holding on to the faint hope that David's pickup would still be there, maybe idling in the driveway as he pondered his decision. But it wasn't there. He had gone to be with Julie, and that was that, and it was up to Clarice to decide what she was going to do in response. Well, she'd told him. She'd given him every chance to reconsider, and he'd still gone out the door, and she was going ahead with what she'd settled in her mind.

Clarice backed out of the driveway and closed the garage door behind her. She pulled into the street, took a last long look at her house, and drove away.

For a while, she wasn't really conscious of where she was going. It was sometime between ten thirty and eleven, so the traffic in the neighborhood was somewhere between light and nonexistent. She coasted along, stopping at the stop signs and red lights, thinking of everything at once and nothing in particular, just trying to sort out what to do next, whom to call, what to say.

Should she call Carmen? Pastor Wilkes? She even thought about trying to reach Michelle, but she quickly shied away from that. Most likely, Michelle would sense something was wrong the minute Clarice walked into her office; she seemed to have some kind of radar. And once that happened, Clarice would wind up telling her pretty much whatever she wanted to know. It was strange. Michelle was younger and actually worked for Clarice, but there were times when Clarice felt as if Michelle was senior to her, as if she were some kind of older sister. Michelle was a more experienced guide, helping her navigate in places where the currents were shifting and uncertain.

Uncertain was definitely the word right now. Though Clarice had been able to keep her cool when she was presenting her ultimatum to David, she felt anything but calm and in control at this moment.

Though she tried to resist the impulse, Clarice found herself remembering Mama's advice: "You got to take care of yourself in this life, 'cause nobody else gonna do it for you. The more you depend on you, the better off you gonna be." She hated to admit it, but Mama might be right after all. She probably ought to call Mama and let her know what was going on. But not tonight.

Clarice realized she was getting close to the freeway. She saw the sign for a hotel that had interior doors and was reasonably priced. She pulled in beneath the covered parking and went into the lobby.

The clerk on duty was a bored-looking girl with multiple facial piercings. "Help you, ma'am?" she said in a flat voice.

They had a single nonsmoking room left, the girl told Clarice, but it was a king-size bed in a room with a whirlpool tub. "The rate's a hundred and ten dollars, plus tax," she said.

Clarice thought about objecting, but she really didn't have the strength. She slid her credit card across the faux marble counter.

She parked and wrangled her luggage out of the car, through the glass doors, and into the lobby, then found the elevators. She pressed the up button and waited.

For a few seconds she permitted herself to wonder where David was and what he might be doing. A small part of her mind made the timid suggestion that she'd perhaps been a bit hasty about her decision to leave the house, that maybe David really was the person whom Julie most needed in her hour of crisis. Shouldn't she at least consider going back home and trying to talk through the situation as Carmen had outlined at their last counseling session?

Then the elevator dinged and the door slid open. She'd already paid for the room, after all, and maybe a night away was what she needed to clear her mind and decide what to do next. She stepped inside, hauling her suitcase in behind her, and the silver brushed-aluminum doors slid shut.

She found her third-floor room and finally managed to get the card key to work. The LED on the latch switched from red to green and the lock snicked back. Clarice turned the handle, leaned against the door, and half stumbled into her room.

She ran the tub full of the hottest water she could stand and slipped out of her clothes, dropping them in a heap on the tile floor of the bathroom. She submerged herself gingerly in the steaming bath until her face was the only part of her above the surface. She was hoping the heat and steam would iron out the kinks and tangles in her mind and body, allowing her to sleep. Clarice longed deeply for the sanctuary of unconsciousness—just for a few hours. In the morning she'd resume the obstacle course of her life. But tonight all she wanted was to switch off her mind and sink into oblivion.

She realized she'd left her cell phone in her purse, which was lying on the bed in her room. She wondered what she'd do if it rang. The only person likely to call her right now was David. Would he call? Would she answer if he did? Clarice honestly didn't know.

When she could feel the perspiration beading on her face, Clarice pulled herself out of the bath. She toweled off and dug through her suitcase for something to sleep in. She brushed her teeth, cleaned her face, and dragged the suitcase to one edge of the bed, then pulled back the cover on the other side. She lay down, switched off the light, and closed her eyes.

In the dark and quiet, the last words she'd exchanged with David ran on a continuous loop in her head. The movie screen behind her eyelids showed the same clip over and over: David standing in the living room, staring in horror at the TV, followed by a jump-cut to David telling her that he was going to go to the hospital whether she liked it or not.

Do you honestly think I'm that sick?

Clarice tried taking deep breaths, counting to seven on each inhalation and each exhalation. She tried reciting poetry she'd learned in school. She tried spelling words backwards, then whole sentences. Nothing worked. Her exhausted mind was like a trapped bird hurling itself repeatedly against the hard glass pane of reality, apparently preferring injury to surrender.

When she'd stared at the red numbers on the nightstand clock for maybe the fiftieth time, Clarice gave up. She switched on the bedside lamp and sat up. The TV remote was on the table, and Clarice peered at it for a few seconds. No, she decided, not TV.

For some reason she couldn't quite understand, she pulled open the drawers of the dresser and nightstand until she found it. In the bottom drawer, all by itself, was the inevitable red-bound, hardback copy of the Bible. "Placed by the Gideons," the gold foil stamp on the front read.

Clarice hefted the Bible. She riffled the pages with her thumb; the tissue-thin paper made a sound like a hundred restless moths. Choosing a spot somewhere near the center, she let the Bible fall open.

There is one alone, and there is not a second; yea, he hath neither child nor brother: yet is there no end of all his labour; neither is his eye satisfied with riches; neither saith he, For whom do I labour, and bereave my soul of good? This is also vanity, yea, it is a sore travail.

Two are better than one; because they have a good reward for their labour. For if they fall, the one will lift up his fellow: but woe to him that is alone when he falleth; for he hath not another to help him up.

Again, if two lie together, then they have heat: but how can one be warm alone? And if one prevail against him, two shall withstand him; and a threefold cord is not [easily] broken.[1]

Where had she heard these words before? Clarice looked at the top of the page to see "Ecclesiastes." This didn't sound like the Bible she remembered. Had she ever heard Pastor Wilkes preach out of this part of the Bible? She wasn't sure. But somewhere . . .

She and David were standing in the front of the church, and the minister was draping a cord around their shoulders. "This cord I've just draped across you represents the cord in this passage I've just read. . . .

As long as you both put God first, your marriage will be a threefold cord that nothing can break . . ."

Clarice felt her eyes getting wider and wider as the memory bloomed in her head. That was where she'd heard this before. A feeling started at the base of her neck and crept across her scalp, a feeling that she was no longer alone in this room.

She held the Bible in her lap and stared at the strange words until they began to blur. She closed her eyes and leaned her head against the headboard.

A threefold cord is not easily broken . . .

Her life certainly seemed to be unraveling, Clarice thought. She felt like both the frayed rope and the person hanging at the end of it. If the cord was David, Julie, and her, Clarice didn't see much chance for any of it to hold together.

. . . not easily broken . . .

The words ran through her mind. The first part of what she'd read seemed to be describing her life—or maybe her life as David might view it. She was somebody always scrambling for more, and doing it alone, with no child, no friend to help; pushing ahead, never pausing to ask why. *A sore travail . . .*

Is that what her life was becoming? A sore travail? She'd never thought so. Right up until the moment her smashed leg tumbled her over the edge of the ditch into depression, Clarice had never seriously considered the ultimate outcome of all her work, her hustling, her relentless self-improvement, her single-minded focus on becoming a mover and a shaker. It had never occurred to her to wonder if the goals she had so clearly in mind were worth the effort she was putting into them. Clarice had never actually thought too much about where she'd be when she got where she was going.

She switched off the light and sat in the dark, still thinking about the words she'd read. Some time later, with the room's air conditioner sighing a lullaby in white noise, she drifted off to sleep.

*   *   *

She woke up the next morning and the first thing she saw was the thin yellow line of sunlight tracing the place in the middle of her window where the two halves of the heavy tan drape met. She looked at the clock; it was twenty minutes before eight.

For several seconds, she was completely disoriented. This wasn't her room and the windows weren't supposed to be over there, were they? Gradually, memory returned, along with a tide of deep sadness. Clarice felt pressed down, flattened beneath the burden of everything she had to face. She considered the advantages of staying right here, in this bed, and hoping for some miraculous change that would make everything better. But she remembered enough from her Internet research to know that wasn't going to work.

She sat up and rubbed her face. She had apparently pulled the sheets up over herself during the night; her last conscious memory was of staring into the dark, her body still leaning against the headboard. Good, maybe that meant she'd slept some. Her mind still felt as tired as if she'd been on guard duty all night.

She swung her legs out and slowly leaned her weight onto her feet. For the first time, she realized she'd left her cane at the house. Aside from a slightly fatigued feeling in her right calf, though, she didn't notice any problems. Another good thing. In her present state of mind, she should probably start writing these thoughts down.

She allowed her body to go on autopilot, taking her through the motions of showering, dressing, and getting made up for the day. She was going to be a bit later than usual this morning, but Clarice reasoned that was acceptable for someone who'd just left her husband. Graded on the curve, she was probably an A-plus—item number three for her "small victories" list.

She was ready to go. She studied her suitcase, which was still lying open on the unused side of the king-size bed. Should she take it with her, or was this room—or another one like it—her home for the foreseeable future? Clarice decided to bet on faith; she zipped and latched the suitcase and wrestled it to the door. After she gathered up all her cosmetics, she gave herself a final inspection in the mirror. She decided she looked reasonably together, all things considered.

Clarice walked into the office and went to her desk. According to her calendar, she had no appointments for the day. On a usual day, this would mean she spent her time making follow-up calls to prospective buyers or sellers, checking the new listings bulletins, writing congratulatory notes to current or former clients who'd been in the newspaper, or doing one of the score of other things she'd trained herself to do during downtime. That's what winners did, she told herself, and she was a winner.

But today, she could no more focus than she could fly. She kept something in front of her so the casual passerby wouldn't know she was struggling to keep from losing it, but inwardly she felt barely able to function. As in the days when she'd first struggled with depression, it seemed to take all her concentration to keep from having an emotional meltdown.

Clarice picked up her cell phone and dialed Mama's number, then stared doubtfully at it for a long time. Finally, she entered the call and put the phone to her ear.

"Hello?"

"Mama? This is Clarice."

"Oh."

"Mama, I . . . I've left David."

"What?"

"I said I've left David."

Michelle was coming down the hall. Clarice pasted on the best smile she could find and nodded as if she were having the most agreeable conversation imaginable. She even gave Michelle a little wave as she passed by.

"Clarice, what's happened? Did he hurt you? Did he leave you for that white girl?"

Clarice kept on smiling and nodding without saying anything. When Michelle turned the corner, she said, "Not exactly Mama, he . . . well, never mind. I just wanted to let you know. I'll talk to you later—"

"I'll be there this afternoon," Mama said. "I'll call Freddy right now."

Clarice closed her eyes. She really didn't have the strength to fight her mother over this. "Mama, I—"

But the line went dead. Clarice ended the call and looked up. Michelle was just crossing back in front of her office on the way to her own desk. Clarice hoped fervently Michelle hadn't heard anything.

She needn't have worried; just before noon, Michelle came in and, without stopping at the door of the office, came right around to where Clarice was sitting. She put a hand under Clarice's arm, as if to help her stand.

"Come on, sister girl. It's lunchtime and you're going with me. We got to talk."

Clarice knew there was no point in objecting. As they were going outside, she started digging in her purse for her keys.

"Never mind that. I'm driving today. You don't look like you're in any shape to concentrate on traffic." When they got outside, Michelle held the door open and Clarice collapsed into the passenger seat of Michelle's clean, but slightly road-worn, Chevy.

"Okay, talk to me," Michelle said as they drove down the street. "I could tell you were struggling from the time you hit the door this morning. I left you alone because I thought you might need some time to just be, you know?"

"Oh, Michelle, I don't know where to start." Clarice's voice sounded strained and hopeless, even to her.

"Just pick a place," Michelle said. "I'll catch on as you go."

"I've left David."

"Oh my sweet Lord, honey. What happened?"

Clarice told her about Julie and her suspicions about David's feelings toward that woman. She explained about Bryson, then related his shocking death and David's reaction to it. She told Michelle about the ultimatum, and about how David left anyway.

"So, I packed up some clothes and went to a hotel. Then I came here. I don't know what to do next, Michelle, I really don't. I slept some last night, but my mind's just going around in circles."

"Well, I tell you one thing, my sister, and that is that you're not sleeping in a hotel anymore. Todd and I have an extra room, and if you need a place to stay, you're staying with us."

Clarice caught the delicate emphasis Michelle had placed on the word *if*.

"You think I ought to go back home?"

Michelle kept her eyes straight ahead. "I'm not ready to say that yet, Clarice, but I do know something about walking out on somebody when I shouldn't have. Todd is a good man and I left him for all the wrong reasons. I'm not saying that's what you've done, but one thing's for sure: if you want to have any chance of putting things back together with Dave, you got to get face-to-face with him sometime or another."

"But what if he doesn't want to put things back together with me? You should have seen his face, Michelle. He was angry, really angry. It was like he never heard anything I said to him."

Michelle drove for a long time before saying anything else.

"Ya'll were seeing a counselor, weren't you?"

Clarice nodded.

"Maybe you ought to talk to her. See if she's got any advice. But Clarice—" She reached over and grabbed one of Clarice's hands. "I know enough about Dave to know he's got a good heart. I just can't believe he's going to throw his marriage away this quickly. I've got to believe that sometime, after the hurt isn't quite so bad anymore, he's going to come to himself. And when he does, you want to be there."

A threefold cord . . . not easily broken . . .

"It took me a long time, honey," Michelle said. "I had to sow all kinds of wild oats before I realized what I was missing with Todd.

But all the time, he was there, waiting for me. I didn't deserve it, but he never stopped believing in me. Todd and Miz Ida, they never lost faith in me. I'm a big believer in second chances, Clarice. When you've been given as many of them as I have, you can't help it. Now . . . where we gonna eat lunch?"

True to her word, Mama got to town that afternoon. Clarice's cell phone buzzed, and when she answered Mama said, "Where are you? I'm at your house, but there's nobody home."

"Mama, I'm at work."

"At work? How come you're not at a lawyer's office?"

"Mama, I don't know—"

"I know that's right. You don't know anything."

Clarice heard her mother ordering Freddy to take her to Clarice's office. She sighed and thumbed the off button on her phone. Then she buzzed Michelle on the intercom.

"This is Michelle."

"Michelle, I've got to go for a while."

"Whatever you need. You still got the key I gave you?"

"Sure. And . . . Michelle? My mother's on her way over here."

"Uh-oh."

"Really. Just tell her I went back to your place to rest. You can tell my brother how to get there, right?"

"You sure about that? Maybe you don't need that kind of company."

"Michelle, it's my mother."

"Well . . . okay. *Mi casa, su mama's casa,* I guess."

"You're awesome, sister."

"You know it."

Clarice drove to Michelle's house and pulled up in the driveway. She carried her suitcases up the sidewalk and managed to unlock the door with a minimum amount of fumbling. She went inside and the first thing she saw was a large leather couch. She let the suitcases slip out of her hands to the middle of the living room floor, walked to the couch, and laid down.

The next thing she knew, her mother's hand was on her shoulder, shaking her.

"What you doing here, Clarice? You got a house. You need to take a nap, that's where you ought to be—in your own house."

"Mama, I'm trying to sort out some things . . ."

"What is there to sort out? What? Your husband is cheating on you. How long does it take for you to figure out what any self-respecting woman would need to do?"

Clarice's head was pounding. "It's not that simple, Mama."

"Oh, really? Is that right? 'Cause it looks pretty simple to me. I tried to tell you, Clarice, but you wouldn't listen."

In the slight pause that followed, Freddy, standing in the doorway, said, "Where you want your stuff, Mama?"

"Just put it in that room over there," Clarice said. "I think that's the guest room."

"Yeah, we in the guest room because your sister doesn't have the backbone to stand up for herself."

Clarice flung herself up from the couch. "You know what? I've really got to go back to work. I'm sorry, Mama, but you can just . . . just wait until I get back."

She left her mother standing openmouthed beside the couch, stalked past Freddy, and crossed the yard to her car. Clarice managed to shut the door, back out of the driveway, and get about half a block away before the first cry of despair ripped from her throat.

Chapter Twenty

The casket at the front of the church was small, way too small. Dave watched as people came in and found their seats for the funeral. Bryson's school had given permission for any of his classmates to attend who chose to. There were probably thirty students seated close to the front on the right. The swim team was here, of course, all members wore black armbands. Bryson's coach sat close to the front; it appeared to Dave he was struggling to hold his emotions in check.

Dave heard a minor commotion coming from the back of the sanctuary. He turned around and saw Jaylen and Darius coming in the back doors, followed by the rest of the baseball team. As he watched, Brock held open the door for them and directed them toward seats close to the back. Dave felt his eyes stinging with tears as these kids, many of whom had probably never darkened the doors of a church, filed in wearing their baggy jeans, their extra-long shirts, their wide-laced tennis shoes—their best and favorite clothes. They sat quietly and stared at the unfamiliar surroundings, but they were here.

Dave got up and went back to where they sat. He moved down the line, shaking each boy's hand in turn. He had to keep swallowing and blinking as he tried to tell them how much he appreciated their coming to pay their last respects to a kid they didn't really know. When he got to the end of the line where Brock sat, he leaned over and whispered, "Thanks. I don't know how you did it, but thanks for getting these guys here."

206 ∞ *T. D. Jakes*

"When you called and cancelled the last practice, they all wanted to know why. When I told them, they wanted to come. They know how much he meant to you."

Dave waited for Brock to ask him why he hadn't called from the hospital or something, but Brock didn't. Dave didn't know why, but he was grateful just the same. The lump in his throat made it impossible to talk right this second anyway. He mouthed the words "thank you."

"Anytime, day or night," Brock said. He squeezed Dave's shoulder. "You doing okay?"

Dave shrugged. "It comes and goes. I better get back over there."

Brock gave him a measuring, evaluating look for a few seconds. He nodded and gave Dave's shoulder another squeeze.

Julie had asked Dave to sit immediately behind the pew where she and her mother, father, and brother would be sitting.

Dave wondered if Clarice would come. He hadn't spoken to her in two days, since the night he went to the hospital. A few times he'd thought about dialing her cell number, but he kept talking himself out of it. He couldn't quite decide if it was because he was still angry, or because he felt guilty. Maybe some of both.

But Julie needed his help; there was no mistaking that. She'd asked him to be with her when her family arrived. They all lived out of state and were staying at her house. Dave shook the hands of her parents and her brother as Julie introduced him as her friend and Bryson's coach. Dave had told them what a wonderful kid Bryson was, so gifted and polite. He told them "shame" didn't begin to describe the waste of such a promising young life. They looked back at him with faces so blank with questions and grief that they would have seemed mentally impaired if Dave had met them under any other circumstances.

Dave had tried to excuse himself from the midst of Julie's family as soon as he could, but she called him the next day and asked him to go with her to the funeral home to pick out the casket. "I can't ask my dad to do it," she'd told him. "He's just barely functioning as it is. Bryson was their first grandchild. And I don't think I could stand being there with Ted."

Dave said sure, he'd come, but within minutes of walking with Julie into the casket showroom, he was regretting his decision. The reality of Bryson's death smacked him in the face all over again. It hadn't ever really hit Dave that caskets came in kid sizes.

The service was starting. Pastor Wilkes came out, along with the music minister and the youth pastor. Wilkes raised his hands and the audience stood. Julie and her family came from the side room: Julie, her father, her mother, and her brother. Ted and the young woman who'd come to the hospital with him were next. They walked a little apart from the others. Ted looked like he'd found some strength from somewhere; he was walking without anybody's help. The family group made its way to the front of the sanctuary and sat down, then the rest of the audience took their seats.

The music minister came to the podium and asked them all to turn to a song in the hymnal that was, he said, one of Bryson's favorites. The organist played the intro and they all sang. Dave's voice kept shutting off on him; he had to stop frequently and regroup before singing the next few words, after which he'd have to stop again. At one point, he realized Julie's hand was reaching back, over the pew, toward him. He grabbed her hand and squeezed.

They finished the hymn. Pastor Wilkes came to the podium. He gripped the edges of the lectern for a few seconds and closed his eyes. Then he opened his eyes and looked intently at Julie.

"Julie, Ted, I don't know if you'll remember anything we say or do here today. At times like these, when the whole world consists of the single, unanswerable question—Why?—words and ceremonial actions seem somewhat irrelevant. But try and take this message with you: This church loves you. Bryson was our friend, our classmate, our child in the faith. No one can carry your grief for you, but to the extent possible for fallible, selfish humans, each one of us here feels at least some small corner of the burden on your heart.

Remember that, if you can. And in the dark days and weeks ahead, call on us. We're here, and we're not going anywhere."

In his resonant, velvety voice, the pastor read Bryson's eulogy. He named Julie and Ted, along with her parents and brother and Ted's father, as survivors. He looked out over the crowd for a few seconds and Dave thought he was going to say something else, but instead he just sat down.

The music minister sang a solo after that, a song about hope and resting in the arms of God. Then the youth pastor stood up.

"I've had a few years' experience as a pastor," she said, "but nothing I've ever learned or heard has prepared me to do the funeral for a child. Not because I have any questions about Bryson's fate—of all of us, he is most to be envied right now, because of where he is— but because of how keenly we feel the loss of an innocent one such as he. There are only a few Scriptures I've found that speak to my heart in times like these: the Psalms, of course, especially those sad ones that frame the words I find myself wanting, but unable, to utter; the story of the Resurrection, perhaps, since that hope is the anchor that people of faith have clung to for centuries upon centuries, especially in times of trouble. But oddly, I also find myself turning to that book in the Bible that is perhaps noted more for its strangeness than any other, the book of Ecclesiastes.

"The writer of this book, like us today, found himself at a loss for adequate explanations. He looked around at everything and found it all meaningless. He didn't try to understand life, he just described it. And he used words like these: 'For everything there is a season, and a time for every purpose under heaven . . .'"[1] She read the entire passage. When she got to the end, she looked out over the crowd.

"There could be lots of reasons why we chose to be here today. Maybe we wanted to show our appreciation for Bryson's life. Maybe we knew him as a teammate," she said, looking to the side where the swim team sat. "Maybe we wanted to show our support and sympathy for his mom or some other member of Bryson's family.

"But I hope nobody came here today looking for answers—or at least, not from me, because I don't have any. At times like these, I have lots of questions, maybe similar ones to those asked by the writer of Ecclesiastes. But like he did, about all I can do in the end is say, 'Here it is; now what do I do with it?'

"The good thing is, the writer does suggest an answer. At least, I think it's an answer, or part of one. The answer comes in two places: the first is about a third of the way into this book and the other is near the end, in chapter twelve.

"In the first part, the writer talks about how bad it is if you're all alone. He talks about how much better it is to have friends around during the hard times. Then he says, 'a threefold cord is not [easily] broken.'[2] I'm not sure, but maybe he's saying that two people who hang in there with each other, along with God, make a rope you can hang onto when you're at the end of all your other ropes. At least, that's how I read it—especially on days like today.

"Then, close to the end of his book, after he's pretty much spent a lot of words telling us how meaningless everything seems, he says this: 'Fear God, and keep his commandments; for this is the whole duty of man.'[3] That's it. That's his answer—or as much of one as he's willing to give.

"And the more I think about it, the more it starts to make a little bit of sense, even in times like today. When we don't know what else to do or where else to turn, maybe we need to pay attention to God and stick close to each other. Because maybe, in the final analysis, that's about all there is for us to do.

"I think Bryson did that. That's why so many of you are here today. And if he were here, I've got a feeling he'd give us the same advice: Hang onto God and stick close to the people you love."

She sat down and the music minister sang another song. Then the people from the funeral home started dismissing the crowd, one row at a time, starting from the back. When the usher got to Dave's row, Dave started to stand, but Julie grabbed his hand.

"Stay. Come to the cemetery with us. Please?"

❧

Clarice drove away from the funeral service shaking like a leaf. When the youth pastor said "Ecclesiastes," she could hardly hear anything that happened afterward.

Of course she'd seen Dave sitting up front, right behind Julie and her family. She'd felt the anger and resentment she'd expected to feel, even though she tried to remind herself that she was here to show sympathy for a mother who'd lost her son, not to spy on an errant husband.

She'd tried to concentrate on Pastor Wilkes's words of compassion and done her best to listen to the words of the song, but when the youth pastor announced the name of the one biblical book that had been gnawing away at a corner of her mind for the past two days, Clarice lost all pretense of focus. Why did this rather obscure biblical text keep showing up in her life? Maybe she ought to ask Michelle about it.

Michelle and Todd had been more than gracious. They'd taken her in without judgment. It was clear they were concerned for her, and just as clear they'd walk with her as far as she wanted them to. They didn't even complain when her mama showed up with her suitcase and installed herself in the guest room. Her mama was missing no opportunity to announce her disgust that the wife of a cheating husband would leave her own home instead of making him pack up and get his own sorry self out.

She drove back to the office and returned to her desk. Within seconds, Michelle was closing her door and sitting down in her armchair.

"How was the funeral?"

"Heartbreaking."

"Was he there?"

Clarice nodded.

"Sitting with her?"

"Right behind her."

"How are you?"

Clarice shook her head. "I don't know, Michelle. I really don't."

"Well, I hate to tell you this, but your mother's here."

Clarice groaned. "Michelle, I can't—"

"I know. I tried to tell her to just wait, that you'd be home later and she could talk to you then, but when she heard you went to the funeral, she made Todd leave work and bring her down here. She's in the restroom."

"No, she isn't," Clarice said, staring out the door. Mama was bearing down on them, and her face said she was taking no prisoners.

Michelle stepped aside as Mama entered and quickly closed the door. Michelle made a praying hands sign through the glass wall at Clarice as she walked toward her desk.

"What in the name of conscience do you think you're doing, having anything to do with that woman?" Mama said, plopping herself into the chair across Clarice's desk. "I thought I raised you to be able to stand up for yourself and not take any nonsense. And here you are feeling sorry for the woman who's stealing your husband."

"Mama, it's her child."

"Mmm-hmm. And where was he sitting?"

Clarice closed her eyes. "Close to her."

"Close? How close? In her lap?"

"Mama, don't be ridiculous."

"Ridiculous? Me ridiculous? I tell you what's ridiculous, Clarice. It's ridiculous that you left your own house instead of telling that man to get himself the hell out. It's ridiculous that you can't stand up to him and tell him that if he wants his little white hoochie-mama so bad, he should just take her and go on with himself."

"Mama, maybe it's not like that. Maybe he really is just trying to help her get through this awful place in her life, and maybe there really is something left for us to work on together."

"Only thing you need to work on, girl, is getting those blinders off your eyes. You can't trust a man like that. They all the same. Sometime or other, they going see something that looks better to them and that's all of that. You better wake up, girl, and listen to me."

Clarice felt her chest burning with anger. With a trembling hand, she picked up her phone and started dialing.

"What you doing?" Mama said.

"I'm calling you a cab," Clarice said through clenched teeth.

"What do I need a cab for? I'm not finished talking to you."

"No, ma'am. But I'm done listening. Hello, City Cab? Can you please come to 1457 Westchester and pick up a passenger? Yes. Mrs. Mary Clark. Yes, thank you. She'll be waiting out front." She hung up and stared at her mother, panic and rage twisted up under her breastbone like a tangle of fighting cats.

"I had a thought the other day, Mama. Do you know what it was? I finally realized that maybe my daddy and the other men who left you weren't the only ones to blame."

Mama jumped to her feet and started to wag her finger in Clarice's face.

"Sit down, Mama!"

Clarice had leaped up out of her chair. She had screamed the words so loud that she could feel the eyes of everyone in the whole place staring through the glass walls into her office. She forced herself to take several deep breaths before saying anything else. Her voice, when it came, was low and dangerous.

"I . . . said . . . sit . . . down."

Mama subsided back into the chair.

"You taught me many things, Mama. Many wonderful and important things. But you left something out. Compassion. That I'm having to learn on my own."

Clarice walked around her desk and opened her door. "Good-bye, Mama. I'll have Michelle write down her address for the cab. And you can use their phone to call Freddy. I think you're done here."

Michelle was in the hall, standing beside her; Clarice felt Michelle's hand rubbing up and down her back, up and down. "Come on, Mrs. Clark," Michelle said. "Let's get you home."

When Michelle came back to Clarice's office, Clarice was in her chair behind her desk; tears were streaming down her face. She put her head in her hands. "Michelle, I'm a mess. My life is a mess, and I'd like to blame David for all of it, but I know that's not the way it is. What can I do? I don't know what to do."

Michelle was kneeling beside her now, her arm around Clarice's shoulders. "Oh, honey, I'm so sorry. I'm so, so sorry, and I know you don't know which way to turn and it doesn't seem like there are any answers that make any sense right now."

Clarice gave a harsh laugh. "You sound just like the youth pastor at the service! She talked about feeling that way, when life is just one big question. Next thing you're going to do, I guess, is start quoting Ecclesiastes at me."

"What are you talking about?"

Clarice shook her head and sniffled. Michelle handed her a tissue.

"Oh, the other night in the hotel, I got out that Bible they put in all the rooms, you know? And I just let it fall open, and I read something in Ecclesiastes about a cord with three parts. I remembered it was a verse the minister used in our wedding, and it's been bothering me, like a song you get in your head and can't get out, and then today one of the ministers at the service started quoting from the same passage. It was just weird, that's all. For years I never heard the word *Ecclesiastes*, and now it's everywhere I turn, seems like."

Michelle's hand never stopped: rubbing across her shoulders, then down one arm, then the other arm, then the shoulders again. "Well, honey, I don't know for sure, but sometimes God can be funny like that when he wants to get somebody's attention."

"You honestly think God has something to do with this?"

"Sister girl, I think God's got something to do with just about everything."

"Now you sound like that Miz Ida you're always talking about."

"That might be the nicest thing you've said to me all week."

Clarice cut her eyes at Michelle, and from some unexpected source, a smile tried to gather up on her face. Michelle returned it.

"There you go. Sister found her grin, just a little bit, anyway. Guess things might not be as bad as we thought."

That day after work, Clarice decided to call Carmen McAtee. She was in way over her head, and the way she saw it, Carmen had more experience to work from than anybody else she knew of at the moment. The next morning, she called and made an appointment; it so happened Carmen had an open time that afternoon.

"Where's Dave?" Carmen said when Clarice walked into her office.

"That's why I'm here," Clarice said. She sat down and looked Carmen in the eye. "I left him. Or he left me; I can't figure out which."

"Talk to me."

Clarice related the whole chain of events, starting with the news of Bryson's death and David's reaction to it. She did her best to describe the conversation word-for-word. When she finished, Carmen sat for a few seconds without speaking.

"What should I do?" Clarice asked finally, just to break the silence.

"What do you want to do?" Carmen said.

"You know, I had a feeling you were going to answer my question with a question, and right now I feel like screaming. I need some advice and some answers, not more questions."

Carmen looked at her and nodded. "I can certainly understand your frustration. And if I had a pill to give you or a surefire way to put you back on the road to happiness, I'd give it to you. But my job isn't to decide what will help you; it's to help you discover for yourself what works and what doesn't. And the only way I can do that is to start by finding out where you are. Then we go from there. Make sense?"

Clarice took a deep breath and nodded.

"Okay. So what do you want to do about the situation?"

Clarice thought for a long time. She looked at Carmen and said, "What do you know about the book of Ecclesiastes?"

∞

Dave rode to the cemetery in the car with Julie and her parents. When the brief graveside service was over and it was time for the family to leave, Julie's legs wouldn't work. She was sobbing uncontrollably, trying to say Bryson's name but unable to control her voice well enough to get out much more than the first syllable.

Dave helped her up and practically carried her to the car. Her parents and brother walked behind them. He drove and she leaned against him the whole way back to the church.

By the time they got back, Julie had gained enough composure to ask him to come by the house for a while. Her Sunday school class had brought tons of food, she said, and he might as well have some of it. Dave tried to excuse himself by telling her that she probably needed time with her family.

She grabbed his arm. "Please, Dave. I need you there," she said in a low, desperate voice. "I'm losing it."

He put her in the car with her parents and brother and walked to his pickup. How could she know that what she'd just said was like food to his soul? She needed him. How could he keep himself from responding?

Some people from church came over; a few of the women from the Sunday school class were in the kitchen when Dave got there. They peeled back foil covers and found serving spoons and plates as they bustled around the kitchen and spoke to each other in low, efficient voices. Full plates were brought into the den, where Julie and her family sat, stared at the floor, and tried every now and then to make a little talk around what Dave knew had to be gaping holes in their hearts.

He sat with them and listened to their stories about Bryson. The funny things he'd said when he was a baby; how soon he learned to walk; the way Julie could hardly keep him out of the bathtub from the time he was old enough to crawl. She said the sound of water running in the tub was enough to make him drop whatever he was doing—watching *Barney,* playing with his favorite toy, whatever—and come scooting into the bathroom as fast as his hands and knees could take him. "The only time he ever bit me was when I was trying to get him out of the tub and dry him off," she said, chuckling a little. The smile on her face was barely a memory of what Dave remembered, but it was still good to see.

When the ladies from the church had served everyone and made a couple of unsuccessful attempts to bring seconds or dessert, they packed up the rest of the food and somehow managed to shuffle it all into the fridge or freezer. They came and hugged everyone, then left.

"I want to go look at his grave," Julie said during the next lapse in the conversation. "Dave, will you take me out there?"

"Honey, you sure about that?" her dad said.

"Yes, Daddy. You and Mom don't have to come. Dave'll take me." She looked at Dave again, and her expression didn't carry a question—it was more of a command. Dave looked in her eyes and saw he had no choice.

"Sure. We'll be right back, folks."

He held the door for her as they went out.

Chapter Twenty-one

"Turn here," Julie said when they'd gone to the end of her block.
"That way."

"But the cemetery's—"

"I know. I was just saying that to get out of there. I've got to have
some space; I was about to have a meltdown."

"Whatever you say. I'll just drive till you say whoa."

"Thanks."

Dave cruised aimlessly up and down the streets of Julie's neighborhood. It was one of the original "nice" neighborhoods in town,
with lots of established old trees and houses. The homes were set
well back from the street at the ends of curving sidewalks that might
have been edged using barbers' scissors. The sun was starting to set
and there was a nice, calming orange glow settling down over everything. Dave let the pickup ease along at little more than an idle.
Now and then he'd cut his eyes toward Julie. She sat with her arms
lying limp in the seat on either side of her, like a life-size rag doll
somebody had propped up to look like a passenger. Her eyes stared
dead ahead.

"You want to talk?" he said after they'd been driving for maybe
ten minutes. She shook her head.

"How about something to drink?"

She was still for so long that Dave assumed the answer was no.
Then she said, "How about something from Billy Bean's?"

Billy Bean's was a place that served fresh-ground imported

coffees with enough syrups and special flavorings to justify charging as much for a cup of java as Dave usually paid for lunch. "Sure," he said.

They got to the place; for some reason, there weren't too many cars in the parking lot. When they got to the counter, Julie ordered a decaf mocha latté and told Dave she'd go get them a place to sit. Dave ordered a diet soft drink, paid when their order was ready, and turned around to look for Julie.

Billy Bean's was walled off into lots of nooks and crannies that were wonderful for promoting cozy, private discussions but lousy for finding somebody you were looking for, especially with the dim mood lighting they used in the evening. Dave finally located her, though, leaning into the corner of a nook that was completely filled by a round booth and table. She had her eyes closed. She reminded Dave of those pictures on the sports channel of people who've just finished a marathon. She had that same used-up, fragile appearance.

"Here you go," he said, sliding into the booth and scooting her drink toward her. She gingerly touched her lips to the surface of the steaming cup and took a quiet sip.

She looked at his cup. "You didn't get coffee?"

"Never acquired the taste. My grandmother used to tell me it'd turn my toes white. Scared me plumb off."

She gave him a tired little smile.

"Second smile today. Pretty good," he said.

"I'm scared, Dave."

He looked at her curiously.

"I'm scared of the way the house will sound when everybody's gone and it's just me there. I'm scared of what I'll do when I go to wake Bryson up for school and remember why he's not in his room. I feel like I'm about ready to fly apart into a million pieces, and there won't be any finding them all, much less putting them back together again."

She looked at him, and he could see the fear she was talking about. It was naked on her face, as open and unadorned as a child afraid of a thunderstorm.

"Hey," he said, scooting closer to her. He put an arm around her and she leaned into him, shuddering with dry sobs.

"I told you, you not gon' have to do this alone," he said. "Somebody gon' be there when you need them."

"Will you?" she said, her voice muffled by his shirt.

"Sure, sometimes. You know I will. And the ladies from your Sunday school class—"

"You're my connection with Bryson," she said. "You saw him closer to the way I do than anybody else on this earth. Even his own father. I need you, Dave. I really do."

She was saying it again, and the words were stirring up all kinds of feelings Dave didn't know how to name. He didn't trust himself to speak, so he didn't. He just held her and patted her arm and tried to think of a way to keep from going down a path he knew he'd probably regret. What he was having trouble figuring out was how to do that without causing further damage to this woman who was as close to the edge as anybody he'd ever seen.

They sat that way for a while, until Julie said, "Okay, I'm ready to go now."

She hadn't touched her mocha latté other than that first tentative sip. "You want to bring this?" Dave said, pointing to it. She shook her head.

They scooted out of the booth and walked to his pickup. He opened the door for her and walked around. When he got in, he realized she had scooted over on the seat so that she was sitting close to him. Very close.

She watched him start the engine and studied the side of his face as he backed out of the parking space. He pulled into the street. Dave wouldn't look at her; he didn't trust himself that much.

"Do you think Bryson can see us right now?" she asked him.

"I don't know. I guess so. I think my grandmother's up there somewhere, too, watching out for me. So, sure, I guess he is."

"I think so, too. When he was a baby and he'd get croup, I'd always take him outside. The doctor told me the best thing for croup was moist air, so I'd walk outside with him and he'd look up at the stars and point."

She turned toward him; she was so close Dave could smell the hint of mocha on her breath. "Drive out to the hills above the airport, okay? The lights from town aren't very bright out there; I want to look up at the stars."

They drove out past the edge of town, then Dave turned aside from the highway onto one of the narrow blacktop roads that wound up into the foothills just south of the city. There was a place he knew on this road where you could pull up close to a spot where part of the slope had broken away, leaving an unobstructed view of the skyline. He tried to ignore the stab of guilt he felt; he used to bring Clarice up here when they were dating.

He parked the pickup and Julie got out. She walked around to the back and climbed up into the bed of the pickup. "Oh, good, you've got one of those rubber bed liners," she said. "Much more comfortable than metal." She slid the baseball practice bag over and used it as a kind of lumpy pillow. She settled herself and stared up at the night sky.

Dave stood beside the pickup and looked out over the city, trying to figure out how he was going to bring this episode to a graceful close.

"Hey, turn on some music, okay?" Julie said.

There was something about her voice that was worrying Dave—but in a good way. She sounded like she was talking further back in her throat, somehow . . . deeper, maybe. It was doing things to him he had to try not to think about.

He punched the power on the radio and soon they could hear the sounds of the Motown oldies station he usually listened to. Gladys Knight and The Pips were shuffling their way through "Midnight Train to Georgia." When that one faded, the Temptations started singing about Papa being a rolling stone.

"Come back here with me, okay?" she said.

"What's the matter, can't you find any stars?" Dave said. He tried to make it sound like a joke.

"Yeah. Not the ones I'm looking for. Come on, Dave. Just this once, all right?"

Boy, you know better than this, you know better, you know better . . .

This was what ran through his mind as he climbed into the pickup bed and sat on the driver's side wheel well.

"No, come down here," she said. "You can't see what I'm talking about from up there."

"What do you mean? I can see just as much from here as you—"

He'd turned around to look at the starry panorama, so the first hint he had she was coming was when he felt her hands on the front of his shirt. She dug in for a good grip so she could pull his face around and cover his mouth with hers. She pulled him down into the truck bed and Dave knew he could and should have resisted, but . . . her mouth was there and her tongue was soft and somehow, whatever the reasons had been that had made him so nervous earlier, they were fading away, blown by the warm night air along with the chorus from the Temptations.

"I just want to feel something besides hurt, just for a few minutes," she whispered into his ear. "Just give me that, Dave. Please, just for a few minutes."

Their hands were slipping effortlessly under each other's clothing. Dave's heart was pounding so hard his lungs could barely keep up. Julie's breath was hot and sweet on his face, his neck, his chest.

The Temptations dissolved into an instrumental lead-in that sounded vaguely familiar to Dave, even though his pulse was just about drowning out every other sound except Julie's breathing. And then, Lionel Richie started singing about the times his lady had given him, about the memories and coming to the end of a rainbow.

Dave pulled away from her and sat up.

"What? What's wrong?"

He turned away and rubbed his face.

What are you doing, man? To her, to Clarice, to yourself?

He hauled himself over the side of the pickup. "I got to take you home, Julie. I'm sorry. I just can't do this."

She sat up and held her face in her hands. "I'm sorry, Dave. I—"

"No. It wasn't just you. I knew better, too. This isn't what you want, Julie. Not really. It's not what either of us wants. And if Bryson was looking down on us right now, I can't believe he'd be happy with seeing two people he loves and used to respect doing something they both know will end up hurting other people."

He heard her weeping softly into her hands. He kept his feet on the ground and reached over to grip her shoulder. "There'll be a time, Julie. Believe it. There will be a time. But not here. Not like this. And . . . not with me."

She wiped her face with the palms of her hands. She looked at him. "You're a good man, Dave. I hope Clarice figures out what she's got."

"Well, I don't know about any of that," he said. "But I just learned I've got to find out."

He drove her back to the house, sticking to the main streets. He walked her to the door. "This still doesn't mean you have to go through this alone," he said. "We can make sure of that."

"Thanks," she said, giving him a blurred smile. "I know. And I'll call . . . somebody. I will. I'm going to make it, somehow."

"There you go. Sister talkin' some sense now." He smiled at her. "You better go on. Your mama and daddy might be getting worried about you."

She nodded. She gave him a little wave and went into the house, closing the door firmly behind her.

Dave got in his pickup. For a few seconds, he leaned his head against the headrest and closed his eyes. He pulled in a deep breath and let it go. Then he backed out of the driveway and headed his pickup for home.

He pulled into the driveway. He started to reach for the garage door opener, but picked up his cell phone instead. He punched a number on the speed dial and waited.

"Hello?"

"Reesie. It's me."

"David?"

"Yeah. We gotta talk. When can we get together?"

"Well, why don't you come on in the house? I've been waiting for you."

They sat on the couch and talked until well after midnight. Some of it wasn't easy. Clarice told Dave she still wasn't ready to talk about having children, and that if he wanted to keep her trust, he had to be accountable—not only to her, but to a male friend like Brock—for keeping his heart safe from longing for another woman. And Dave told Clarice that he felt just as strongly about his values of helping others, mentoring kids, and providing jobs for people with low skills as she did about becoming a top real estate agent and agency manager.

They talked until they were both too tired to organize their thoughts in straight lines. And they still weren't anywhere near a place where Dave felt affectionate toward Clarice; judging by her body language, the same was true for her. But for once, Dave came away from a conversation with his wife without feeling he had a bunch of old, sour-smelling cloth stuffed under his shirt. He'd been able to say everything he had on his mind without shouting or making demands, and he really had the sense Clarice was listening to him. A couple of times he thought she was going to jump in, but somehow, she managed to keep her cool and hear him out. And that felt good.

"When can we see Carmen again?" he said as they were getting ready for bed.

"I've already—that is, I hope you don't mind, but I've already set up an appointment for next Tuesday at five."

"Ought to work," he said. He climbed in on his side of the bed, and she climbed in on hers, and they both switched off their lights.

∞

Lying in the dark of their bedroom, Clarice thought about everything that had happened that day. Carmen had given her a surprised look when Clarice asked about Ecclesiastes. In some small part of herself, Clarice felt glad she'd finally said something her counselor could be surprised about. When Carmen asked for an explanation, Clarice told her about her experience in the hotel room and its strange coincidental repetition at the funeral.

Carmen laughed out loud—actually laughed out loud!—and mumbled something under her breath that sounded suspiciously like "Praise the Lord." She asked Clarice if she really wanted to try and keep her marriage together, despite what seemed to be highly inappropriate behavior demonstrated by her husband. Clarice said yes, the conviction was growing in her that she did.

"Then you're going to have to begin practicing a skill at home that you've obviously honed to a high level at work."

"What's that?"

"Listening. Think about it. What sets you apart from the other agents, I'd be willing to bet, is that you pick up on buying cues from your prospects that others miss. Is that about right?"

Clarice nodded.

"Well, why is it that when you get home and your husband tries to tell you something, you turn off those same receivers that are obviously working so well for you at the office?"

Clarice hadn't ever thought about it that way.

"I see it all the time," Carmen said. "My word, I even see it with my fellow counselors. I had one of them in here the other day because his wife told him if he didn't get some help in learning to communicate with her, his next communication from her was going to be on an attorney's letterhead.

"What you've got to remember, Clarice, is that what's obvious to you is far from obvious to Dave. And vice versa. It doesn't make either one of you smarter than the other, it just means you're two different people. And the hardest thing for two people to do—especially two people who live together—is shut up their internal voices long enough to really hear what the other person is saying."

Carmen had a lot of other things to say to her, some of which Clarice didn't want to hear. She couldn't assume, for example, that what was important to her was just as important to Dave. And nothing shut down communication quicker than one of the partners becoming reactive or defensive. And if you really want someone to love you, you have to give them the choice. "Slaves make lousy lovers," was how Carmen put it. "Even God doesn't force you to love him."

Clarice's head was spinning when she drove away from Carmen's office. She went back to Michelle's house, but nobody was home when she got there. For a few minutes, she sat on the bed in the guest room she was using, just trying to figure out what to do next. She realized she wanted to go back to her own house. Dave would have to come home sooner or later, and when he did, she wanted to be there.

Michelle came home as Clarice was putting the last few things in her suitcase; Clarice heard the front door shut and smiled.

"What's going on up in here?" Michelle said a few seconds later.

Clarice turned around and saw Michelle standing there in the doorway with plastic grocery bags hanging from either hand.

"I'm going home," she said.

Michelle's smile started slow, but it kept growing until it covered her whole face. She dropped the groceries in the doorway and grabbed Clarice.

"Oh, my sister, my sister! I been praying so hard for this, and now look if it ain't happening!"

"Easy," Clarice said, smiling as she pulled away. "I don't know what David's going to be like, or if he even wants to see me."

"Oh, he will, Clarice, I just know it. And anyway, you're taking the first step, and that's what counts right now. Oh, thank you Jesus, thank you Jesus!"

Michelle, singing hallelujahs the whole way, had helped Clarice carry her stuff to the car.

"Now, tomorrow, at the office, you tell me everything," she said, leaning breathlessly through Clarice's window. "But, no . . . wait. Maybe you'll need to come in a little late tomorrow, if the reconciliation gets a little hot and heavy?"

"Oh please, Michelle. It's baby steps right now, remember?"

"That's right, that's right. Ohhhh!" She leaned in through the window for one more hug before Clarice could back away. As Clarice pulled into the street, she saw Michelle dialing her cell phone. She was probably calling Todd, Clarice guessed.

When she came home to an empty house, Clarice started to feel the tendrils of fear creeping between her ribs. What if David didn't come home? What if things were already too far gone? What if she'd already waited too long and their last chance at putting things back together was gone?

Somehow she held herself together as she waited. And then, while she was sitting on the couch, her cell phone rang. He was home.

It was a start, Clarice thought as her eyes closed. Just a start, but so much more than nothing. She didn't know what tomorrow would bring, but whatever it was, this was a better beginning place than they'd had before.

Chapter Twenty-two

∞

Julie carefully pressed the gray-haired woman's foot while supporting her calf with the other hand. The woman winced.

"Sorry, Mrs. Clancy, but we've got to stretch those thigh muscles a little bit more."

"I know, dear," the thin little woman said. "I'm trying not to be a whiner."

Julie laughed. "Oh, no, Mrs. Clancy. I've seen whiners, and you're not one." She leaned close. "They're mostly men," she said, giving Mrs. Clancy a conspiratorial wink.

"Okay, I think that's enough for today, don't you?"

"I certainly do," Mrs. Clancy said. Julie helped her sit up on the table, then carefully eased her down the stepped footstool to the floor. She waved as Mrs. Clancy walked away toward the front foyer, then grabbed the treatment folder and headed for her desk to fill out the session report.

She made it to her cubicle before the tears came; at least that was getting better. The first few times she'd had to explain to patients why she was suddenly weeping. They were very sympathetic, of course—one lady even gave Julie the name of her counselor and offered to pray with her. But it was better if she could hold it in until she had a little privacy.

The hardest thing was when she first woke up in the morning—it meant she had actually slept. But as soon as consciousness returned, so did the weight. Julie had figured out, though, that it didn't get any easier if she just laid there. She'd pry herself out of bed and get about the business of pretending to have a real life.

And once in a while, she surprised herself by saying or doing something she might have done before, ages long past it seemed, when Bryson's death wasn't riding on her shoulders like a backpack full of sand. Like just now, with Mrs. Clancy. It was nice when Julie could catch herself doing something a normal person might do.

She'd never realized how much she thought of Bryson in a typical day. But now, when every thought of him was like a tiny dagger in her throat, she realized he had never been far from the surface of her mind.

She dabbed at her eyes with a tissue and signed the session report for Mrs. Clancy. She was about to go file it when her desk phone rang.

"Hello?"

"Julie?"

"Yes."

"Hi, uh, it's Brock."

"Oh, hi, Brock. What's up?"

"Nothing, really, uh . . ."

This man actually earned his livelihood by speaking?

"I was just wondering how you were, that's all."

"Oh, you know, Brock. Ups and downs."

"Yeah, I guess. I don't suppose you'd be interested in lunch?"

These days, Julie's appetite was as sparse and unpredictable as the annual rainfall in Sudan.

"I'm really not very hungry, Brock."

"Yeah, I can understand that, I guess. But maybe you'd like to just sort of . . . get away for a while? Out of the office? Or gym? Or wherever it is physical therapists do their thing?"

"Well . . ."

"I mean, it's fine if you don't want to, really. I'll just, you know, go home and open up a can of cold chicken noodle soup, maybe watch a couple of *Jeopardy* reruns . . ."

"Hate to tell you, sport, but *Jeopardy*'s still prime time."

Now where did that flash of native wit come from?

"Oh. Well, maybe just the cold chicken noodle then."

"Now that I think about it, I could probably use some time away from here. You want to meet somewhere?"

"Oh, I can just pick you up at work."

"Don't be a doofus, Brock. I'm all the way across town from your office, remember?"

"Well, I had a client meeting over this way. I'm in the front lobby of your building, actually."

They went to a burger place a couple of blocks away from the hospital. Brock took bites from his double-decker with the works and Julie nibbled around the edges of her kid's burger with cheese, a very plain and dry selection. They chatted for a couple of minutes about various harmless topics. Then Brock said, without looking at her, "Um, what do you miss most about him?"

Julie was surprised. Most of the people she came in contact with on a daily basis treated the topic of her dead son as if it were contaminated. Her desk was covered with cards on the day she came back to work, of course, and her supervisor made sure she knew she could take a very relaxed approach to regular hours and the leave policy, but other than that, it was as if they were afraid of her somehow, afraid she might dissolve into weeping if they said the wrong thing. So mostly, they said nothing.

But here was somebody actually inviting her to talk about Bryson, about how flat and empty her world felt without him, about how she'd trade every single thing she owned or would ever own for five more minutes to talk to him and hear him talk back.

"Weekends are kind of hard," she said finally. "That's when his meets were, and we had some really good talks sometimes, in the car on the way there and back."

Brock nodded, wiping a spot of ketchup from the corner of his mouth. "Yeah. My biggest regret is that I never got to see him swim. Dave said it was an amazing thing to watch."

Julie studied her interior landscape, watching for any fugitive signs of emotional weirdness that might have been flushed out by the mention of Dave's name. But . . . nope. That was a good thing, probably.

"Yeah, it was amazing. Bryson always said he was never nervous before a meet . . ."

She talked on and on, about Bryson's sloppy penmanship, about how he always wrote "to" when he meant "too," about all the gold-painted crumbs of elbow macaroni she had in the bottom of the Christmas decoration carton from the year his elementary school made their own ornaments. She just kept talking, and it occurred to her that it might not even matter to her if Brock was really listening; just having someone else there as an excuse to say out loud the million things circling in her mind and heart, whether important or mundane, that added up to "Bryson"—it was freeing. It felt like taking off shoes that were too tight, or finally getting out of a traffic jam. At one point, she realized tears were running down her cheeks, but she just kept talking.

And Brock really was listening—or so it seemed to Julie. His eyes were locked on hers, as if he were trying to understand her words before she even said them.

"I remember that time he came to baseball practice," Brock said, once Julie finally stopped long enough to take a breath. "I couldn't believe he had the guts to stand at the plate and take batting practice in front of all these mean little kids from the hood he'd never even seen before. But he did. And he kept with it until he started getting the bat on the ball. I'll bet if he'd gotten interested in baseball instead of swimming, he'd have been amazing at that, too."

Julie smiled. "That's a nice thing to hear. And you might be right." She looked at him. "I really appreciate you letting me talk about him."

Brock shrugged. "Why not? I just wish I could've known him better, you know? You gonna eat those fries?"

Brock took her back to work, and as Julie got out of his car, she suddenly realized she'd had a nice time. The notion was so surprising and unexpected that she stood there for a few seconds on the sidewalk and turned it over in her mind. Brock started to pull away from the curb, then stopped. The window on her side rolled down.

"You forget something?" he said, leaning toward her.

She shook her head and waved him off. "No, that's okay. See you around, okay?"

He nodded and drove off.

It was true though, she thought, as she walked back toward the clinic. She hadn't forgotten anything—actually, she'd remembered something. A thing called life.

⁕

Dave got out of the Accord and went around to open Clarice's door. He looked at his watch; they were about to be late. He didn't like to think what Clarice might say to him if they were late. She got out and he closed her door, then took her elbow and walked her as quickly as he could, without pulling her, toward the glass doors of the office building.

Inside, he punched the up button on the elevator and waited. The main floor of the building was a bank. The building was one of the older ones downtown, and the bank had remodeled in a classic style: marble floors and counters, lots of brass everywhere, lots of oriental rugs on the floors. Dave wondered who had the janitorial contract on this place.

The elevator doors opened and they went inside. Clarice pressed the five and the doors closed. Dave felt the pressure on his feet as the compartment started to rise.

Clarice looked at him. "What's wrong with you?"

"What do you mean?"

"You've been fidgeting since we got out of the car. You're jingling the change in your pockets and even moving your feet around. Are you nervous?"

"Maybe a little," he said.

It was their first appointment with Carmen since Clarice came back to the house. Ever since he'd gotten up this morning, he'd had a growing sense of apprehension. He was trying not to think about all the ways the session could go wrong, but he wasn't having too much luck.

"Just be honest. That's all Carmen will ask you to do."

He nodded his head and stared at the floor indicator. When it got to five, the bell rang and the doors slid open. They started "the long walk," as Dave was coming to think of it.

The receptionist waved them right in. "Dr. McAtee's ready for you," she said.

How come my MD always makes me wait?

Carmen was wearing her trademark smile and clothing from the African import boutique. The three of them made a little chitchat for a few minutes.

"I can't tell you how pleased I am to see the two of you here together today," Carmen said.

"Yeah, well . . . it didn't look too good there for a day or two," Dave said.

"But we're here," Clarice said, looking at Dave, "and we've both got things to say."

"Why don't we get started, then?" Carmen said. "Dave, how about you tell me what's going on with you?"

Does she always start with me?

"Well, I, uh . . . I've just had a chance to do some thinking, you know, and . . . it seems to me like Reesie and I have a lot going for us. It'd be a shame to waste it."

"That's interesting," Carmen said. "I'd be curious what you think you two have going for you."

Clarice looked at him like she was pretty interested, too. How did he always manage to get himself into these situations?

"Well, we've been through a lot together, first off. We've built a pretty comfortable life—good jobs, nice house, that kind of stuff—"

"Is that what makes life good?" Carmen said.

Dave gave her a surprised look. "Well . . . no, not entirely. I mean, we care for each other. We've got a lot of history."

The counselor nodded. Today she was wearing some major bling; the gold circlets hanging from her ears looked big enough to leave bruises. "So when you think about your shared history, is that what makes you want to make your marriage work?"

"Yeah, I think so." Dave stared at the black Jesus painting on the wall above Carmen's head. "I mean . . . Clarice is the only woman I ever really loved. The first time I saw her, I knew she was special."

"What about you?" Carmen said, turning toward Clarice. "What was it about Dave that first attracted you to him?"

Clarice thought for so long that Dave started to worry she might not come up with anything. "Dreams," she said finally.

"Can you flesh that out a little for me?"

"He had big dreams. He wanted to make a difference. I liked that."

Carmen nodded. "What often happens in a marriage is that somehow, in the midst of all the details we have to take care of just to do life from day to day, we lose focus on the things that brought us together in the first place. For example, Dave, how long has it been since you could look at Clarice and see those special qualities that made you fall in love with her?"

"A while," Dave said.

"And Clarice, when was the last time Dave was able to share a dream with you, straight from the heart, and not worry about how you might respond?"

"Too long," she said after a few seconds. "It's just—" She shook her head and fell silent.

"It's just what?" Carmen said.

It took Clarice a while to speak, and when she did, she kept her face directed at the floor. Her hands twined in her lap.

"I know David wants children. At first, I thought I did, too. But with my job and our ages, I'm just not so sure anymore."

"Do you feel Dave is pressuring you to have children?"

She nodded. "Sometimes, yes."

"Dave, how do you feel about that?" Carmen said, shining the spotlight back on him.

"I guess I always wanted to be a dad," he said. "I can't remember a time when I didn't."

"And did you ever want to be a mom, Clarice?" Carmen asked.

"Oh, I'm sure I had the thoughts every little girl has, playing dolls and house and so forth. But it was so hard for my mother when I was growing up. At some point, I remember putting my dolls up because I didn't seem to have time for them anymore."

Dave stared at Clarice. Her voice was subdued and sad, almost like that of a child who'd just received a deep disappointment or some really bad news.

"So your mom had to work pretty hard?" Carmen said.

Clarice nodded. "Two, sometimes three jobs. She didn't want help from anybody. I really admired her strength. I still do."

"What about her softness, her compassion? Did she ever read to you or tuck you in?"

Clarice swung her face around to look out a window. Dave saw the tears glistening on her lower eyelids. "There wasn't so much time for that," Clarice said.

Carmen pondered this for a while.

"Reesie, I never remember you telling me you had dolls," Dave said into the silence.

She looked at him, then away. "Didn't I? That's funny. Oh, well . . ."

"Dave, I wonder what you're thinking right now about your wife," Carmen said softly.

"I'm wishing I knew more about her," Dave said. "I thought I knew her, but just now, I heard something I've never heard before. That kind of makes me feel bad. It makes me wonder what else I might not know."

Carmen nodded. "Those are good thoughts. I'd recommend pursuing them sometime." She looked at Clarice. "That is, if you'd be comfortable with that."

Clarice was wiping at her eyes with her fingertips. "I've probably forgotten a lot of things."

"But you remembered something just now, something that connects with the deeper parts of you," Carmen said. "Do you trust your husband enough to let him see more? Are you willing to take the risk of that kind of intimacy?"

She looked at her husband. "I think so."

"It's an awesome responsibility for two people to accept that they must be truthful with each other about what's deep inside. Sometimes we don't even know what's in there ourselves," Carmen said. "Sometimes there are hidden clues, keys that open locks we didn't even know existed. I happen to believe that when the timing's right—some folks might even say when it's God's will—the keys go in the locks and things open up. And when that starts happening, understanding can grow. And when there's understanding, well, lots of good things can happen."

Dave was still looking at Clarice, seeing her through different eyes, like they hadn't been used in quite a while. He realized there was a little girl, once, named Clarice. And she had the same need for affection and feeling special that all little girls have. But something happened somewhere along the way. He wondered if that little girl could be coaxed out into the open again with patience and understanding. He wondered if she'd like to be held, cuddled, protected. He sensed, though, that she wouldn't trust just anybody. No, it had to be somebody she could count on, somebody who wouldn't try to rush her or put her in places she didn't want to be. Somebody who would just be for her, always and forever. Could he be that somebody?

Dave realized he sure wanted to give it a try.

"All right, Darius, be a hitter, baby, be a hitter." Dave clapped his hands and chomped his gum. Brock was giving the signal to George, standing on second, that meant "run on any hit ball."

They were on the short end of a 2–1 score with two away in the bottom of the fourth inning, which was too bad, since they were playing the only team in their league with an identical won-lost record. It was the boys' first chance at a league championship, and Dave could taste victory, but somehow they had to get George home without getting the third out. Dave didn't want to go into their final at bat still needing a run.

Dave rubbed his face and adjusted his cap. The opposing pitcher was having probably the best night he'd had all season, unfortunately, and his infield was backing him up like a vacuum cleaner. Both teams were having good defensive nights, for that matter; hits had been harder to come by than a mother-in-law's good graces.

"Look 'em over, Darius, you can do it!"

Dave turned his head to look at Clarice, sitting up behind home plate. He had to smile; whatever happened tonight, it was great to see her here. She kept hollering encouragement at Darius, who stepped into the batter's box and got ready to take the first pitch.

The pitcher went into his windup and came straight over the top with his fastball. Darius started to lean into it but let it go past. The umpire called a ball. Clarice and the handful of the kids' parents who came to the games cheered with relief.

"Good eye, Darius, good eye."

Dave looked up in the stands behind third base. Julie was there, clapping and cheering as hard as she could. Dave had to admit, it was a welcome sight. He was glad when Brock told him he'd talked her into coming out tonight.

Dave sent the "take" signal to Darius, who stepped back out of the box to give the pitcher some time to think about how many ways he could miss with the next pitch. It didn't matter, though; the next pitch came right down the pipe for a called strike. Dave winced inwardly. That was the kind of pitch Darius could've taken into left field if he hadn't been told to let it go by. Dave gave him the "swing away" sign and clapped his hands together. "That's all right, baby, you're fine. Be a hitter, now, be a hitter. Make him pitch to you."

The other team was well-coached; the infielders were waiting on the balls of their feet, their gloves at the ready. They kept up the chatter, gradually increasing it as their pitcher worked toward the delivery.

And then, as the ball was coming over the top, Darius squared around to bunt. Dave almost swallowed his tongue. What was the boy doing? He hadn't told him to bunt!

The ball came in and Darius laid down a textbook safety squeeze bunt, rolling the ball down toward first base, just inside the line. Dave suddenly realized that the infield was playing Darius deep, since he was one of the three batters who'd been hitting their pitcher all evening. By the time they got moving forward, Dave's fastest player was nearly halfway to first base. And George, who was running on any contact, was about two strides from third.

The first baseman got to the ball. He made a move toward third, protecting against the tying run, but Brock was doing everything except grabbing George's shirt to keep him on the bag. The boy turned to make the play to first, but the second baseman, who should have been covering, was caught off-balance by the bunt and was out of position. The first baseman flipped him the ball, but then it became a footrace between him and Darius, which was no contest. Darius's spikes hit the bag a good half-second before the second baseman's. The umpire flung his arms out to the sides. "Safe!"

Clarice was jumping up and down. Dave was jumping up and down. The kids on the bench were jumping up and down. And the tying run was at third.

Chapter Twenty-three

*D*ave went over and grabbed Darius. "Next time you shake off my signal, you better hope it works out this good. You hear what I'm sayin'?"

Darius grinned. "They were playing me back. I been working on that bunt every day after school with Jaylen."

Dave grabbed his shoulder and gave it a good shake. "Awright. Stay awake out here; there's still lots of game left."

Marcus was Dave's next batter. He was o for 3 tonight and Dave could see the agitation in his face as he approached the plate.

"Go get 'em, Marcus!" Julie hollered. Brock wheeled around to look at her, but she was concentrating on the game. Dave hoped his third base coach was doing the same, but he grinned anyway. She was good for Brock, and he was good for her. Somewhat to Dave's surprise, it was nice to see them together. They were both good people.

Marcus stepped into the leftie batter's box. He worked the toe of his front foot into the dirt next to the plate, looking like somebody slipping a foot into a bedroom slipper. He stepped in with his back foot and peered out at the pitcher as he made a couple of preparatory swings with his bat.

The pitcher rocked, wound up, and threw; the ball went right down the middle for a called strike. Marcus shook his head and backed out of the box.

"That's awright, Marcus, that's awright. You okay, just stay in there and have a good eye." Dave gave him the "swing away" sign and hoped for the best. The next pitch came and Marcus took a hitch with his bat, then turned his front shoulder in toward the plate. The ball thumped into him just below the shoulder blade and the umpire told him to take his base. Clarice, Julie, and the other fans went wild as Marcus loped toward first, rubbing his shoulder. Bases loaded.

"I crowded in on him a little, and he went for it," Marcus said when he got to first. "But that boy got some heat; my shoulder stings."

"Taking one for the team, my man," Dave said, clapping him on the shoulder. "That's using your head. And your shoulder."

Tim was up. The crowd was going crazy and if you couldn't feel the tension in the air, you were either dead or somewhere else. Dave trotted over to his right fielder before the boy got to the plate.

"Now, Tim, you just chill up there, awright? No matter what happens, we still got another inning of ball to play, so don't be thinking you got to be the man, you feel me?"

Tim nodded.

"That's what I'm talking about. Now you just go up there and see what happens. If he gives you a pitch to hit, you know what to do."

Tim gave him another tight nod and grabbed the crown of his batting helmet, pushing it down on his head. He went to the plate and got set for the pitch.

Dave cupped his hands around his mouth. "Running on anything, boys, running on anything." Everybody in the park already knew this, with two outs, but it didn't hurt to remind the infielders that they weren't going to have lots of extra time to make a play. The other coach was standing in the opening of the dugout and rubbing his hands on his hips and clapping and working his gum for all it was worth. Dave felt for him. But he was still going to try his best to beat him.

"You can do it, Tim!" Julie yelled.

Tim stepped back out of the box and turned to look up at her. He waved at her, then got back in the box.

Brock had told Dave that Tim was hardest hit by the news of Bryson's death. Maybe it had something to do with Bryson playing in right field at Tim's usual position on the day he came to practice with Dave—or maybe it had something to do with Tim never having known his own mother. Brock said Tim had asked about Bryson's mom every time he saw him.

The first time Brock brought Julie to practice, Dave noticed Tim sitting and talking with her for quite a while during a lull in the activity. He guessed it was probably healing for both of them. Maybe Brock and Julie ought to spend more time with Tim, he thought; he'd suggest it to Brock. But first they had a game to win.

The pitcher sent the first throw toward the plate: ball one. "Atta baby, Tim, atta baby," Dave called, clapping his hands. "Good eye, now. Watch it all the way." Dave sent him the "swing away" sign. *Come on, Tim. You're doing fine, my man.*

The pitcher wound up, and just as the ball started forward in his hand, Tim squared off as if to bunt, then quickly went back to his regular stance. But the pitcher must have still been stinging from Darius's squeeze, because he tried to adjust his pitch in mid-motion. He threw wild into the dirt on the left side of the plate. Dave saw the white blur of the ball as it headed toward the backstop.

By the time he could form the thought *run* in his mind, Brock had already sent George. The shortstop streaked toward the plate, his batting helmet flying off behind him and rattling along on the ground just outside the baseline. The pitcher sprinted toward the plate, ready to make the tag when the catcher flipped him the ball, but George slid across the plate while the catcher's toss was still in midair. The game was tied.

They were all jumping up and down again. Tim was hugging George while the disgusted pitcher trudged back to the mound. Clarice was dancing in the stands behind home plate, her hands in the air like a high school girl at a Snoop Dogg concert. George came running toward Dave, then jumped into his arms like Dave was Santa Claus.

"Yeah, baby! You all that, my man, you all that!" Dave yelled into George's ear before he set him back on the ground. George headed for the dugout, where the rest of the team was waiting to give and receive high fives, hugs, and slaps on the back.

"Okay, Tim, you still the man," Dave hollered, giving Tim the "take" signal. Dave was willing to bet the pitcher had to be at least a little rattled. Sure enough, the next pitch was high, for ball three. Everybody in the ballpark knew Tim was taking the next pitch, including the pitcher, who must have tried to steer it just a little too much. It was right in the fat part of the plate, and Tim took it just over the second baseman's outstretched glove.

Darius was rounding third by the time the center fielder got to the ball. There was no chance of the fastest kid on the team getting thrown out; the ball bounced into the catcher's mitt a full second after Dave's third baseman stepped on the plate. Marcus was holding at second and Tim was standing on first, grinning like he'd just won the lottery.

In just a few minutes, they were suddenly up a run with a runner still in scoring position. Dave hollered until his throat was raw. Darius skipped all the way to the dugout, pumping both fists in the air. The team was standing on the bench of the dugout, yelling and slapping each other and hopping up and down. Brock was doing some kind of white-boy jig over by third base, and Julie was up in the stands, laughing her head off.

The other coach was walking out to the mound, along with the catcher. He put his hand on his pitcher's shoulder and told him, Dave guessed, what he'd have told his own player in the same situation: stay within yourself, it's not all on you, trust your fielders, relax, you can do it. And the pitcher responded like any eleven- or twelve-year-old kid would have. He listened with his face downcast, nodding every so often.

Next up was Carlos, the center fielder. He was one of the others who had this pitcher's number. He was smiling when he came up; Dave guessed he was already thinking all about how he was going to put Marcus across the plate.

But it didn't work out that way this time. The pitcher got down to business, striking Carlos out on three consecutive pitches. Dave had to respect the kid for shrugging off the wild pitch and two runs and getting his team out of the inning.

"Awright, gentlemen, let's get out there and be some fielders!" Dave said, slapping the boys on the rear as they came trotting out of the dugout. "We just need three, awright? Just need three," he yelled.

Jaylen came out last, walking toward the mound. Dave stopped him.

"How's your arm, little bro? Doing all right?"

"I got your back, Coach," Jaylen said. "We fit'n to take this thing home."

"Awright, then, my man, get out there and show me something."

Brock came over to grab a mitt and warm up Jaylen while Malcolm was donning the catcher's gear.

"How's he feeling?" he asked Dave, nodding toward Jaylen.

"I think he's all right."

"I think we ought to let him throw the curve."

"Are you on crack? We're in a position to win the league—"

"Listen to me, Dave, just listen. He can throw it. I've caught him. And nobody'll be expecting it since he hasn't been showing it all season."

Dave stared out toward left field, wrestling with his skepticism.

"Come on, man. I'm telling you, he can do this. Give him a shot."

"He and Malcolm got the signals worked out?"

Brock nodded.

Dave took a deep breath. "All right. We'll see how it goes with the first couple of batters. But I'll be on that mound in two seconds if something starts looking funky."

Brock shrugged.

While Brock warmed up Jaylen, Dave hit grounders to the infield and easy flies to the outfield. All the time, he kept one eye on Jaylen. *I hope I don't hate myself tomorrow.*

"Play ball!" the umpire yelled, and the butterflies in Dave's stomach started doing a rhumba. They were three outs away from the league championship. It would be something these kids would never forget, a hundred-percent winning experience based on hard work and cooperation. Sure, Dave wanted it for himself, but he wanted it for them too. *Three outs!*

By the time Jaylen had thrown two pitches, Dave knew it was all over. His little two-under curve wasn't really breaking as much as it was hesitating, but that was enough to throw off the batters and get them watching a little too hard. And Malcolm was smart; he kept mixing the curve with Jaylen's bread-and-butter fastball and circle changeup. It was the best series Jaylen had pitched all season. He struck out the first batter on four pitches and got the second one to pop up to shallow right. The third hitter got on board, courtesy of a bad throw by an overanxious George, but the fourth batter fanned on three straight fastballs. The game was over; they'd won.

All the players rushed the mound. Dave was right there in the middle of them, laughing and grabbing them to swing them up. He was in the middle of a swirling mass of small sweaty bodies, and all he could feel was the steady, high-energy throb of success.

Somebody grabbed him from behind; arms went around his middle and squeezed. He turned around to see Clarice laughing and yelling. "You did it, Dave, you did it! Your boys did it!"

"Hey—did you just call me Dave?"

She grinned and shrugged. "That's all I've been hearing all night, all around me; the boys' folks saying Dave this and Dave that. I couldn't help it."

She gave him a good tight hug. "I'm proud of you," she said, her lips close to his ear. "And now I'm starting to see why this is so important to you."

"Thanks, Boo," he said. "That means a lot, it really does."

Brock was over on the third baseline, hugging Julie. The boys were jumping up and down, chanting "Hawks, Hawks, Hawks." The few parents and relatives that had made the game were grinning and high-fiving like youngsters.

And for some reason, in the middle of all this delirious, unself-conscious celebration, Dave started thinking about everything that had happened since the beginning of this baseball season. He'd met one of the most amazing young men he'd ever known, and witnessed his untimely death. He'd met a woman who, under slightly different circumstances, he could have loved, and it had nearly cost him his marriage and his self-respect. He'd learned things about himself he wished he didn't know, and a few things he was glad to find out. He'd witnessed—and been part of—a dark pilgrimage through guilt, grief, and death that had turned slowly, slowly back toward life, light, and the rediscovery of love and respect.

At this moment, it seemed to Dave that it was all tied together, all twisted like the strands of a rope that pulled you forward, even when you weren't sure where you were going. A cord with three strands, maybe. You couldn't have the joy without the pain, the salvation without experiencing what it meant to be lost, at least for a little while. It was life, and he'd lived it, was living it. In this moment, that realization held enough truth to keep the confusion and unanswered questions quiet for just a little while.

Dave thought of something his grandmother used to say: "The road may go down and it may go up, but long as you keep walking, you going to get there. Just don't sit down on the side."

Brock and Julie were coming out toward the mob, holding hands. Clarice saw them and went over to them, smiling and talking. Brock yelled something over the racket and the boys broke for the entrance to the field, still screaming like an Apache raiding party. Brock trotted off behind them and Julie followed at a slower pace.

Clarice turned around to look at him. She waited for him to get to where she was.

"I think the boys are ready for their soda and candy," she said. "How about you?"

"Sounds pretty good to me," Dave said, taking her hand. "Let's go."